LIGHT BLINK

BOOK ONE

RICHARD HELLEWELL

This is a work of fiction. Names, characters, businesses, places, events, locales, and incidents are either the products of the author's imagination or used in a fictitious manner. Any resemblance to actual persons, living or dead, or actual events is purely coincidental.

Story concepts, content and implementation; cover illustration and design; book design, editing and production; Copyright © 2018 by Richard Hellewell – All rights Reserved. No portion of this book may be reproduced in any form without permission from the author, except as permitted by U.S. copyright law.

Some images and/or clipart are from Pixabay.com which are released under Creative Commons CC0 into the public domain; see their Terms of Use.

Other clipart and graphics are from other public domain sources, and are not required to be attributed by the license used to release the graphics for public use of any kind

The Light Blink book web site is at https://www.LightBlink.com ; web site design, content, and implementation by Richard Hellewell and CellarWeb.com, Copyright © 2018 by Richard Hellewell, All Rights Reserved.

Contact the author at https://www.LightBlink.com .

~1~

It all started when the lights blinked.

I was at the office, toiling away in my cubicle located in a corner of the basement level. That corner had five cubes. The room was built with concrete walls to support the rest of the five story building, with one entrance door to the rest of the basement offices that was usually kept open. Although when the lights blinked, the door was closed for some reason. I may have closed it earlier that day to keep out the noise of the other basement cube dwellers.

It was a late Friday afternoon, which meant that most everyone else was gone in the office – a lot of people 'escaped' early on Fridays. My fellow cubists had already left for the day, but I needed to finish up a project before the four day weekend. I had planned out getting out early like everyone else, but you know how the last part of projects work – the last 10% of a project takes the most time. And I was a bit behind, but almost done. Just not done enough to sneak out early like everyone else.

I was working on my computer. Not a surprise; everyone has a computer. At least one, and probably a laptop or pad computer, too. I was no exception. I had a powerful laptop computer with a dock that connected it to three 24" flat screen monitors, plus the requisite mouse (wireless) and connection to the company network.

I had plans for the four day weekend. My SUV was out in the covered parking lot, all loaded up with supplies to take back to my house. Well, more of a cabin, really. The supplies were for a bit of solitary hiking in the back country, as well as a bit of relaxing in the mountain air. My house – the cabin – was about a hour drive from the office. A long commute, but worth it for being a bit remote and out of the way.

The cabin – my home– was a small one, about 50 years old, but in good condition since I had remodeled it a couple years ago. It was a modified A-frame design, with a small bedroom downstairs and a loft bedroom area taking up half of the top of the A-frame. A living room area with a couple of couches and recliners, a small dining table, and a small kitchen with the basic stove/oven, refrigerator, sink and cupboards. The living area had full windows on the side of the house that overlooked a smallish creek in a large meadow surrounded by the forest. In back of the cabin was the mountain back-country area where I planned to hike.

There was a porch that wrapped on three sides of the cabin. The porch area next to the river – well, maybe a large stream – on the living room window side, was a bit larger and had a couple of comfortable Adirondack-style chairs. Sitting out on the porch was quite relaxing.

Since the cabin was at about the 3200 foot level, there was a tall pine tree forest all around the meadow, which was about a half-mile in width. There was the usual forest underbrush, but I had cleared the area 100 feet away from the cabin of any underbrush for fire protection. The big pine trees helped keep the cabin in shade most of the day.

The cabin was isolated, but did have electricity that was fairly reliable. I had a wood stove for heating on cooler summer nights, and for the cold winters. The elevation kept the snows to a reasonable level, not high-country deep, although the mountains around the cabin usually got a good amount of winter snow.

The cabin – I call it a cabin, even though it is my house - was in a fairly isolated area. No other cabins within 20 miles. The road to the cabin was roughly paved, but wasn't in very bad shape. My 4-wheel-drive SUV could handle it just fine during summer (and late spring and early fall). The winter snows usually weren't deep enough to cause problems. I'd sometimes get snowed in for a day or two, but my employer let me work remotely during those times.

I got water from the well next to the house; a large stream next to the cabin that was fed from a spring was the backup water source. A large-capacity on-demand water heater took care of my hot water needs. Power to the cabin was pretty reliable; but sometimes the area thunderstorms would interrupt the power for several hours. The wood stove took care of backup heating, and since it was an old-style stove, there was room for a small pot for heating meals or hot water.

So I was looking forward to a bit of R&R at home this long weekend. A bit of hiking, a bit of relaxing, and some reading was on my agenda.

But not until I finished this project at work, which was taking me a bit longer than I had planned. Everyone else had snuck out early for the four-day weekend. I was the only one there. And I didn't plan on being there much longer.

It was getting towards the end of summer, so it didn't get dark until about 8 pm. Even though it was about 5:30 pm, I thought I could get out of the office by six. About an hour after leaving the office I would be enjoying the end of the day on my back porch.

But I had to finish the project first. I stopped thinking about the cabin, and got back to the project. I was getting into the groove of finishing things up.

And then the lights blinked.

~ 2 ~

It was quiet in the office; the only sound was my computer keyboard clacking away. The lights flickered once, then twice, and then went off for 60 seconds. Then they came back on and stayed on.

That was an unusual thing to happen. Lights don't just flicker at the office unless there is a major power outage. There was no storm forecast for the weekend. I was in a fairly new office park, so the electricity infrastructure was pretty new. It was like somebody had flicked the light switch a couple of times.

When the lights went full out, I yelled "Hey, turn on the lights!" But I was the only one there. Everyone else had gone home. Besides, the door to my cube area was still closed. And the light switch was on my side of the door.

But I figured it was no big deal. No answer to my yell, of course. But the lights came on after a minute, and the computer was still working, as far as I could tell, thanks to a uninterruptable power backup system I had. I did a quick save of my project, and then got up out of my chair to take a look around.

I made my way to the door. The door is made of metal, but has a small glass insert with those wire things that supposedly make the glass harder to break. I looked out the window as I reached for the door handle, and the office looked normal. Except nobody was there, of course; everyone else had escaped before I could get out of there.

I opened the door, and went out into the general office area. It was the typical warren of cubes that you would find in any office. Pathways to the front counter and lobby, plus the aisles between the cubes. There was a small lunchroom in the other corner of the office. The area by the entrance door had a small reception area, with one of those half-doors that is used to get into the back area.

The reception area had one door to the basement lobby area. That door was one of those electronically locked doors that required a pass card or the receptionist to buzz you in. The doorway has windows flanking each side, with the glass embedded with that wire stuff to retard breakage. And there is an elevator and stairs to the other floors; the office building has five stories plus my basement office area.

As I entered the general area, it was quiet and empty, as I expected. There did seem to be a slight 'off-ness' of the area. I wasn't sure what it was. It wasn't the lack of noise; it was a very slight, almost unnoticeable, background noise in a low frequency.

I stood there at my office doorway, looking around. The noise wasn't obnoxious or unpleasant, but it wasn't a noise that I had ever heard before. The office looked normal. All the lights were on. No noise, except that strange background hum.

Then I noticed that the light was a bit different. Not really different, just not what I would normally expect. The ceiling lights were the same brightness as usual, but the 'color' of the lights was slightly different. Just a little bit different, not a lot different.

I walked around the office to the front reception area. I was starting to get a slightly uneasy feeling about the whole thing. I got to the front half-door, and pushed to open it. It didn't budge, and I smacked my knee against the door. There is a small carpet pad right in front of the door that has a pressure sensor underneath that automatically unlocks the half-door when you are leaving. But that wasn't working.

Since the door didn't have a manual release, I climbed over it (it was only three feet high, so great security!). As I got on the other side, I reached over the counter to the access button for the small door, to see if that worked. I pressed the button a couple of times, but nothing happened; there was no buzz like there usually is.

I thought to myself that that was interesting, and continued towards the front exit door. As I reached for the door handle, I stopped. Not sure why, even now, but I didn't grab the handle. I decided to go back to the magic button that the receptionist used to buzz open the main door. It worked just as well as the button for the half door – not at all.

"That is interesting", I thought. And I stood there for a moment, thinking about what had happened.

The lights had blinked. There was that strange background humming sound. The office lights looked different. The half-door sensor didn't work. Neither did the access button for the half-door or the main door.

The half-door had an access card sensor that employees used to get through the door when there was nobody at the reception desk. Since I carried my access card on a lanyard around my neck, I walked over to the half-door's sensor and waved my access card in front of it. It was then that I noticed that the red LED, which indicated that it was locked, was not lit. And it wasn't green either (which indicated that the door was unlocked). And waving my access card in front of the sensor didn't change things. The half-door stayed locked.

I stood there for a moment contemplating that bit of news. Then I turned around and looked at the main door. It had one of those access card sensors on the outside to unlock the door. Without a good access card, or a receptionist using the magic button on her desk, there was no entry into the office.

And if the half-door sensor didn't work, there was a good chance that the main door sensor wouldn't work either. And that would mean that I wouldn't be able to get back into the office.

So the situation required a bit more thought. The strangeness of the last few minutes, starting with the lights blinking, was not normal. And that would mean that I might need to get into a 'not-normal' mode. I wasn't sure that it didn't mean that I needed to get into a 'survival' mode. Maybe not yet. But the 'not-normal' mode was a good mode to be in, I thought.

I hopped over the half-door and went back to my office. And I sat down in my chair. And I thought.

~ 3 ~

Here's the situation. I'm working late in the office, last one here, and the lights blink. Then there is the background humming sound. And the lights in the office seem to have a bit different 'color'.

The electronic locks at the office reception area don't work. And my access card doesn't work either. Everything appears to have power – the computers, lights, vending machines in the break room. But anything mechanical, like the door locks or access card readers, doesn't work.

So I turn to the computer, and click on the web browser program. Nothing happens. In fact, now that I look closer, the mouse cursor on the screen doesn't move.

I look at the report I was working on. It's on the screen, so I tap a few keys on the keyboard. Nothing changes. That's certainly different.

I stare at the screen for a minute, and then take a look at the desk phone. The display has the usual stuff on it. I press the speakerphone button, and hear a dial done. That brings me a bit of relief. I'll just call someone to see what is going on.

I dial a number with the speakerphone on, but there are no tones associated with pressing the number keys. I pick up the handset, and I can still hear the dial tone. I press some numbers; nothing. I hang up the phone, and lean back in my chair.

I try my cell phone; same thing: no tones when I press the keys. Texting doesn't work. Calling up a web site doesn't work.

Nothing electro-mechanical seems to work. But anything electrical seems to work – the lights, for instance.

I think I need to go from the 'not-normal' mode into 'survival mode'.

~ 4 ~

I gather up my backpack. I reach into my small office refrigerator, and grab the three water bottles that are in there. Into my desk for the energy bars that I keep there. All of that goes into my backpack. I put on my light-weight jacket that I keep in my office.

As I shrug on my coat, I realize that my survival mode supplies are not very extensive. I need to get a more complete 'bug-out' bag. And that make me think that I need some protection. More than the multi-tool that is on my belt, and the small LED flashlight in my bag. Better to have some protection and not need it, than to not have protection and need it.

I look at the digital clock on the wall, which shows 6:30 pm. It has changed, and has the same time as my watch. So not everything electromechanical is broken, I thought. Then I thought "Digital clock. Not mechanical. So of course it works."

I walk out the door of my office area into the general area, and glance at the clock there, which is an analog type. It shows a time of 5:51 pm, and the second hand is not moving.

I head for the break room. Our office is lucky enough to have a boss that supplies some basic snacks for us, without a vending machine. I look over the selection and grab all of the energy bars. There are a couple of bottles of cold water, so I grab those and put them in my backpack. II open one of them and drink all of the water, tossing the empty bottle in the recycle can out of habit.

There is a side door exit to the basement lobby area. I decide to use that as an exit. I grab a few pieces of paper from a nearby printer. I need to allow myself a way back into the office area just in case of – whatever. I put my backpack by the other exit door, and then go back to the main entrance, grabbing a nearby book. I look through the window next to the main door, and don't see anything – or anyone.

I open the door, and then place the book between the door and doorframe, letting the door close, but still not closed all the way. Then I go back to the other exit door, grab my backpack and the sheets of paper. I open the door – still nobody out there – then position some folded paper over the door latch and let it close, ensuring that the latch doesn't latch. The paper is positioned so that it is not visible. I can open the door there to get back in if I need to.

A final look at that exit door, then over to the main doorway, where I remove the book that is holding that door open. And I let the main door close.

Here I go.

~ 5 ~

I am standing in the lobby area of the basement level of the office building, I take a look around. There are two other offices down here. Both have the same types of doors as my office: the electronically locked door, the card access pad, and a window next to the door with the 'wire in glass' features.

Both offices have the lights on inside. Both have no movement that I could see. And both have locked doors. Nothing available short of destruction of the door will get me into those offices.

I reach for the call button on the elevator, catching myself as I realize that it probably won't work. And I am right; pressing the button anyway doesn't light up the indicator. So I walk over to the stairs area, which has unlocked double doors with the 'crash bar' type of door handle that you press to open.

I open up the door into the stairway, but before I go entirely through the door, I make sure that the other door from the stairway to the basement lobby area will open with its 'crash bar'. It does, so I continue through the door and start climbing the stairs.

My footsteps echo on the stairs; as I climb the stairs, I realize that the echo is not the usual sound. It's slightly different, just enough to notice. The lights in the stairwell have the same slightly off-color tinge, and there is still that background humming sound at a very slight sound level.

I climb to the top of the stairs, and walk to the doors that lead into the main level's lobby. The doors there, like the ones below in the basement, are glass with wire. I look through the door windows, and there is no movement or people that I can see. I press on the door's crash bar handle, pushing it open, making sure again that the other door leading back into the stairwell also works.

The main floor lobby is a standard office park lobby - a couple of chairs, and the security guard's information desk area. There are no guards to be seen, which is unusual. Although everything that has happened since the lights blinked has been unusual.

I walk over to the guard's desk, keeping a watchful eye all around for any movement, or any people.

The guard's desk is a typical configuration. Some monitors behind the desk show various areas around the inside and outside of the building. There is a phone and a couple of chairs. Behind the desk is the guard's office area, with the door fully open.

And with nobody in sight.

~ 6 ~

As I approach the front door, I notice that the lighting outside is different than normal. I stand at the front door, my hand on the push bar, ready to push the door open. The door latch here is always open, not electrically operated, or unlatched via the push bar. A push on the door itself will open the door.

And that's what I do. Push open the door, then reaching back to the other door and making sure that it will open; it does. I don't know that I will be back, but an escape route into the building through an unlatched door seems like a good idea.

I step through the door, walking to the outside, heading out from under the covered area in front of the door. The typical office park landscaping greeted me - concrete walkways, bordered by grass and some trees and bushes. A parking lot in front, plus the three story parking garage between the two buildings. The parking lot in front is for visitors; employees get to park in the parking garage.

As I head down the sidewalk towards the parking garage, I keep my eyes open for any movement. Then I stop and take another look around.

The air is still. No breeze whatsoever. And there are none of the normal sounds. No dogs barking, no birds singing, no traffic noises, not even any insect sounds.

The air is entirely quiet, which is a bit disconcerting. Then I realize that there is not a total absence of sound. There is that very low-frequency humming sound that I heard inside the building. It is just a touch louder than inside, though.

I turn my head one way and another, trying to figure out the source of the sound. But is has the same volume no matter which way I turn.

And it's not only the sounds – the lack of sounds plus the humming sound. The light outside is different.

I look up towards the sky, and see gray clouds. Only they aren't the gray that you would see with rain or thunder clouds, or fluffy white clouds. The cloud's gray color is tinged with a bit of yellow. Not sunlight yellow, but a sort of dull yellow. It is a color that I have never seen before.

Then I take a closer look at the clouds. They stretch all directions to the horizons. And they have this strange, bubble-like protrusions hanging from the clouds. I've seen pictures of that type of cloud formation. They are called 'Mammatus" clouds.

I remember seeing pictures of these types of clouds on some web page once. They were a bit spooky looking on those pages. I recall that they are often associated with thunderstorms or even tornados.

But the pictures I saw were nothing like the clouds above. In the pictures, there would be small patches of these Mammatus clouds. In the sky now, that cloud formation stretched to the horizon in all directions. And they had that strange yellow-grayish color, not the typical shades of gray that you see in clouds.

It was pretty strange to see those clouds stretching as far as I could see. With the total lack of sound (other than the humming sound), the strange color of the light, I found myself getting a bit deeper into survival mode.

And I decided I needed to get out of town. The cabin – my home – seemed like the best place to be.

If I can get there.

~ 7~

Still keeping a sharp eye out for any movement, I headed for the second floor of the parking garage. This was an open-air type garage, with exterior stairs plus the usual elevator (which doesn't work, of course), and no entry/exit barricades. I climbed up the stairs, ever-watchful for anything. I got to the second floor, and then turned left towards where I had parked my SUV.

As I approached the SUV, I reached into my pocket for the key fob, and pressed the button to unlock the vehicle. And there wasn't the usual chirp-chirp sound when I pressed the unlock button. And the SUV lights didn't flash either.

So I got to the driver's side door, and used the key to manually unlock the door. That worked, and I threw my backpack to the passenger seat, and sat down. I put the key into the ignition, and turned it to start the engine.

Nothing.

No click, no sound of engine turning over.

Nothing.

The interior lights worked, though, so I left them on while I turned the key again. The light stayed the same brightness when I turned the key. If the battery was dead, the lights would dim with the key press. But with each turn of the key – nothing.

This is not good.

I took the keys out of the ignition. I looked around for any movement.

Any my survival mode kicked into an even higher gear.

I took stock of my situation. And decided it wasn't good. I needed to get out of town. Not sure why I thought that, but the current environment didn't seem safe, even though I hadn't seen any threats.

Yet.

Wherever I needed to be, it wasn't here. And the only place I could think of getting to was home. That seemed like the safest place to get to for some reason. So I needed to get to the cabin.

All I have to do is figure out how to get there. It's usually a 60 minute drive. And my car doesn't work.

I need to make sure that I have the supplies I need to get there. I can't drive; the car doesn't work. Nothing electromechanical seems to work. Lights are OK. Doors open. Flashlights work. Guns work.

Wait. I am not sure about that last one.

You can't take weapons into my workplace. But I do have a EDC – Every Day Carry – weapon that I keep in my car.

I grabbed my backpack as I opened the car door and got back out of the car. I placed the backpack next to the car, and then took the gun out of the holster. I removed the clip, cleared the chamber, and then did one dry-fire. The action seemed good. So not everything that is mechanical is broken. At least the gun seems to work.

I considered firing a single shot just to make sure, but then thought that the noise might call attention to me. Even though I hadn't seen anyone or anything around since the lights blinked, firing off one shot did not seem like a good idea. The gun appeared to work OK, and I also had some pepper spray for defense.

I reloaded the clip, and racked the gun to get a bullet in the chamber. After double-checking that the safety was on, I put the gun back in the holster on my belt.

With the SUV dead, it was time to figure out alternative transportation. There were still a few cars in the parking garage, but my hot-wiring skills are non-existent, so that wasn't an option. I needed an alternative.

But before finding that alternative, I needed to build up my supplies.

~ 8 ~

I was planning to head directly home after work. The plans included some relaxation on the deck next to the river, plus a day hike or two. So I had some basic hiking supplies in the back of the SUV; I keep them there just in case I decide to go on a short hike somewhere else. It was also useful as a 'bug-out bag'. With the car unusable, it looked like it was time to change to an alternative transportation mode.

I went to the back of the SUV, and unlocked the back hatch with my key. I placed my small backpack inside, and then took a look at what was available.

The bug-out bag was a bigger backpack, so that would be the primary one. I emptied it out, then re-packed it with the things that I would need. A spare set of clothes (jeans, shirt, sweatshirt, socks, etc). The water purification kit. The emergency kit (space blanket, compass, whistle, topo maps, first aid supplies, hand sanitizer, LED flashlight and a headlamp plus a spare set of batteries, fire-starting magnesium stick). The fold-up hatchet/shovel; sunglasses, a small camp stove, and a mess kit. I didn't have a sleeping bag or a tent in there; although I had that at home, I had packed for just a day hike. There was a knit cap and gloves, along with my good pair of lightweight but tough hiking boots. Plus the hunting knife and sheath, and a bigger multi-tool.

And a roll of toilet paper. Of course.

I packed all of that into the larger backpack, and also transferred the stuff from the smaller backpack. I then changed my clothes, putting on jeans, t-shirt, a lightweight flannel shirt, hiking socks and boots. I strapped on the holster and gun, the multi-tool in its small pouch, the knife in its sheath, all on my belt. I put on my floppy hiking hat.

Everything in its place, mostly like I would be outfitted on other day hikes. Although this hike was apparently going to be longer than a day.

With the small backpack now empty, I used it for some of my food supplies: the water bottles, energy bars, etc. I would probably need the extra room of the small backpack for additional food supplies.

While I was doing all of this, I kept a peripheral eye out for any movement. After finishing the preparation of the two backpacks, I sat down on the SUV tailgate, grabbed a bottle of water, and took a long drink. As I sat there, looking around for movement (I saw none), listening for any sound (nothing, except that low humming), the outside light still had the yellow-grayish color. I took a look out of the parking garage, and still could see those strange clouds. No movement up there, either. No birds, no planes. No Superman either.

Just me.

I finished the water in the bottle, tossed it back into the car, and shut the back hatchback door. I locked the doors out of habit (manually, the electric door lock wasn't working). Then I put my keys back in my pocket. Also out of habit, I suppose. Not sure why I would need them, though.

With one last look around, I headed back to the parking lot stairs to the ground level.

~ 9 ~

As I exited the stairs, I looked around. My plan, for now, was to get home. Driving seemed to be out of the question, as my SUV was dead in the water. Walking was an option, but walking that distance would take quite a long time. The drive is about an hour, depending on traffic; the distance is about 60 miles. I could probably do 10 miles a day walking, so about six days to the cabin. And I was not sure what I would find between here and there.

I needed an alternative form of transportation. Anything with a motor wouldn't work, if my experience with my SUV was any indicator.

Which left me with the bicycle alternative. And that was a valid alternative. There was a bike rack out in front of the building. And, even though it was past the normal end of the work day, there was a bike in the bike rack.

Which also meant that there might be someone else left in the building.

I was still on the alert for any movement anywhere around me. I walked over to the bike rack, and saw that it was locked to the rack with a simple cable lock. It wasn't a heavy duty cable; I suspect that the bike owner figured that the security at the building would prevent theft.

The bicycle was my best bet for transportation at the moment. And since there didn't seem to be anyone around, I decided that I needed it more than whoever it belonged to.

I'm usually pretty respectful of other people's property. But I figured that I this was a special situation and I was in survival mode. So I took out my multi-tool, and opened up the hacksaw-like blade, and knelt down to saw through the cable. As I worked on the cable, I did keep an eye out for any movement.

A few minutes of sawing broke through the cable, and I took it off the bike, and moved the bike off the bike rack.

The bike was a 26-inch frame, with knobby street tires, looked like 15 speeds, front/rear caliper brakes, a water bottle holder, LED lights (white on front, red on rear), and, most importantly, a sturdy carrier rack over the rear wheels.

I took off my backpack and secured it to the rack with a short length of rope that I had in the backpack. I then put the smaller backpack on my back, adjusted the gun and holster, and climbed on the bike.

Before I started pedaling, I took a last look around the building. It was still quiet, and no movement.

Wait. There was one bird. Perched at the top of a tall pine tree over at the edge of the office park.

I took a closer look. It was black; looked like a crow or raven. No, too big for a crow, so I guessed raven.

It was at the top of the tree, just sitting there. Well, perhaps not 'sitting'. But staying in one spot, with the occasional wing-flap to maintain balance. No noise from the bird. Just sitting there.

Looking at me. Not moving. Not 'cawing' like you would expect. Just 'sitting' there on the top of the pine tree. Watching.

I took another look at the raven. Then I then started pedaling to the business park exit.

The business park consists of four buildings around a common public parking area, with the parking garage off in one corner. The whole place took up a large city-size block, and there were exits on two sides.

My normal commute pattern was to take the north exit to the street. I'd then follow the street to the main street, made a turn to a westbound street that would take me to the highway out of town towards my home. My house is roughly northwest of the city. The highway goes in that general direction.

The highway is a four-lane divided road with stoplights until it gets to the edge of town, and then becomes a mostly two lane road. About 8 miles out of town is a crossroad where another two-lane road heads to the hills to the east of town.

I pedaled out of the business park, watchful for any movement. I got to the street by the north exit, and stopped at the stop sign. The street, called Robertson Avenue, was a four-lane road; two lanes each direction, with a center turn lane. The street went through a mix of business and small homes; this is a smaller town. There are several stoplights along the way, with the usual mix of strip malls, gas stations, mini-marts, and a few banks.

I figured I could average about 10-15 MPH, a bit faster on the flatlands, and slower as I get up into the hills and mountains. I may need to walk the bike a lot as I get closer to the cabin; walking speed is about 2 to 2 ½ MPH. It is 60 miles to the cabin. I figured about three days to get to the cabin, barring any delays, assuming the roads are all clear, etc.

The food and water supplies in my backpack were not going to be enough. I needed to stock up my food supplies. So a visit to the nearest quick market would need to be the first stop.

I was thinking of this as I turned onto Robertson Avenue. And then I noticed the cars in the street. They weren't moving at all. I rode up next to one of them, stopped, and looked inside.

It was a newer Camry. The windows weren't tinted. The doors were all closed. The car was empty. Well, there was no person inside. I did see on the passenger seat an undisturbed purse. But the driver's seat was empty. And the seat belt was fastened.

That was unusual. The seat belt was fastened and sort of loose where the belts would be positioned around a body. I looked at the center console; the gear shift selector was in the Drive position. And the keys were in the ignition in what appeared to be the 'on' position.

I looked on the road around the tires, and didn't see any apparent skid marks. The car was just sitting there. Empty. Keys in the ignition. Transmission selector in Drive. An undisturbed purse on the passenger seat. Doors shut. No skid marks.

It was like the car had just stopped, like someone had hit a 'pause' button. As I looked around, I noticed that there were other cars stopped in the street. I pedaled to the next car. It was a small SUV. Doors closed; car empty; seat belt fastened; keys in the ignition; no skid marks. A soda cup with straw in the cup holder.

But nobody was home.

As I pedaled down the street, each car that I looked inside was the same. I was still keeping an eye out for any movement, but there was none. The air was still (other than that low-pitched humming sound), with the strange yellow-gray light. The Mammatus clouds were still in the sky, stretching as far as I could see.

As I pedaled to the next intersection, I noticed the signal lights were green. And they stayed green. They were lit, but they were not changing.

It was like I was pedaling through a street that had been frozen in place by some master pause button. I was the only moving object that I could see anywhere.

I shook my head a couple of times, and put the strangeness of the whole thing in the back of my head. I needed to get back into survival mode. That required more supplies than I had, so went through the intersection (the light was still green, although I swiveled my head to check the cross-street out of habit), I headed to the corner with the quick market.

I rode up to the front door, making sure that my holstered gun was accessible. I got off the bike, and moved it up to the front sidewalk of the market building, but I stayed away from in front of the windows.

I got off the bike, set the kickstand down, and placed my right hand on the butt of the gun in the holster. I moved the gun handle a bit to make sure that the gun would be easy to pull out of the holster, just in case.

With my back to the brick wall of the store, I looked around. No movement that I could tell. I edged over to the store window, and looked inside.

It was your typical quick market. There was a cash register area, refrigerated cases along the back wall, and a couple of rows of shelves. After a quick look at the shelf areas, I looked towards the cashiers counter. The usual collection of impulse items, a cash register, and some behind-the-counter stuff was all I could see. But I didn't see the store worker behind the counter.

The lack of people was starting to feel almost normal. I was still watching for any movement, but when I didn't see anyone, it didn't surprise me.

I again looked around the outside of the building, and then headed for the door of the quick market. It was a standard two-door arrangement, with a metal door handle to pull open either door. A quick look through the door's window, and I pulled open the door to enter, my right hand still on the handle of the gun in my holster.

~ 10~

I entered the store.

To my left was the cash register area with the typical counter clutter of impulse items, two cash registers, a lottery dispenser, and the ATM/credit card readers and PIN pads. Over the counter was a high shelf opening to the employee side for stacks of cigarettes. In back of the counter were some prepaid cell phones and cards.

To the right of the counter area was the soda dispensing machines, with about 20 different flavors, an ice dispenser, straws, lids, cups, etc. Next to that, the Plexiglas cabinets with doughnuts, and then the roller-tray heaters for the overcooked hot dogs.

The back wall was entirely refrigerated cases for cold drinks of all types, plus a few pre-made sandwiches. There was one door that had frozen foods inside, along with ice cream bars.

The center of the store was shelves full of other non-refrigerated food items - lots of snack foods, candy bars, gum, nuts and chips. There were some basic food items like small (and overpriced) soups and cereals, boxed cookies. Another aisle had small packages of medicines like pain relievers, antacids, toothpaste, and the like. There was one aisle with some basic auto and hardware items.

It was the typical quick market selection of overpriced and undersized items. If you were looking for bargains, this was not the place. It is a place for quick selection of what you need, plus lots of stuff that you don't really need but get anyhow.

And that was my plan – get the stuff I need, quick exit.

I took off my small backpack, opened it up, and started stuffing things in there. I went to the snack aisle first and grabbed a bunch of the beef jerky and energy bars. Then over to the grocery area. They had some packaged dried soups; I quickly opened one of boxes and dumped in the small packets of soup. I didn't go for any of the ramen soups; they were too bulky.

Around to the next aisle of medicinal stuff. I got some antibiotic cream tubes, pain relievers, bandages, and a couple of small travel-size hand sanitizer bottles. A couple of those flat packs of baby wipes made it into the backpack.

Then over to the auto section, where I picked up another small duct tape roll, a couple of space blankets, and a small coil of nylon rope.

Then back to the cooler wall, into the water section, for about 6 bottles of water. And on the way out, a stop at the cashier's counter for a handful of BIC lighters.

All of that went into my small backpack, which was getting quite full. I zipped it shut, and put it on my back.

As I quickly hurried to the door, I put my right hand back on the gun, looked outside for any movement, then pushed open the door and headed over to the bike and hopped on. I kicked up the kickstand, and quickly pedaled off of the outside sidewalk out towards the street, heading off into the same direction on Robertson Avenue.

All the while keeping a sharp lookout for any movement as I pedaled down the street, past all of the empty cars and trucks that were seemingly frozen in place, empty.

My current plan was to head for home. About 60 miles away, but usually a 80 minute drive, because of the mostly two-lane roads after you get out of the city. The elevation at the cabin is around 3200 feet elevation, and the city I am in is at about 800 feet.

The city I work in is a typical medium size town, situated in a small valley about 200 miles from the coast. Between here and the coast is a small mountain range, with peaks ranging up to 7500 feet. Away from the coast (to the east) is another larger mountain range, with peaks up to 9500 feet. In between is the valley floor, which is about 45 miles wide. The valley floor is mostly flat, with an elevation change of around 200 feet between the lowest and highest area.

As you go towards either set of mountains, the topography changes from mostly flat to small rolling hills which gradually increase in size and density as you approach the mountain range.

The area around the town is mostly rural, with small farms interspersed with small residential enclaves. The area has been able to escape the wholesale 'residentialization' of most areas.

Besides the typical retail infrastructure of grocery stores and other small businesses (WalMart hasn't gotten here yet, although there is a Target), there is the business park area with some light industrial mixed in with other businesses. There are the contractors, suppliers, and other retail support businesses. There are the small quick-stop type markets on some corners, with strip malls for other small businesses and the usual mix of fast food joints.

The downtown or central area is well established, with some older buildings, the city governmental offices, banks, the town library, and a large park. Schools (elementary through high school) are in the mix.

It's a typical small to medium size town. It's not a place where 'everyone knows your name', but you are likely to see someone you know as you wander around town.

There is a railroad running through the town area, over on the east side. A small railroad switching yard, with a 'tank farm' that is a distribution point for fuel for other areas, including a propane distributor.

The area is not unusual for a mid-sized town. It is rather bucolic, even. It's a nice place to live and work.

Or it was.

As I rode down the street, going around the empty vehicles on the road, watching for any movement, the sky was still the yellow-gray color with the Mammatus clouds over the entire sky. The ambient light was a similar yellow-gray color. And there were still no sounds, other than the background low-level low-pitched humming sound.

I looked at my watch. My excursion out of my office building, getting my basic supplies from my SUV, grabbing the bike, then getting more supplies from the quick market on the corner, had taken up some time.

It was now 7:45 pm. The time when you would expect things to start to get dark as the sun went down for the day – it was the middle of summer. I hadn't noticed it during my preparations, but that wasn't happening either. The light level outside was the same as when I first went outside the office building about two hours ago.

The normal stress of the work day (I had been busy), plus the added stress of the last couple of hours, was making me a bit tired. Not to mention the out-of-normal bicycle riding I had been doing.

I had covered about 4 miles, and it was time to figure out where to go for the night. Although 'night' wasn't a word that you would use to describe the current situation. It didn't look like there was going to be a normal night.

But even if there wasn't any 'night', I needed some rest. And I needed it to be in a safe place. So I considered my options.

I could go back to the office building. I had left a way into that building, and into my office, and would be in a fairly protected area, one that could be easily defended. But I had gone about 4 miles, and the prospect of biking back 4 miles (then doing the same 4 miles tomorrow) was a factor.

Or I could try to find a secure place nearby.

As I thought about the alternatives, I kept pedaling. And watching.

~ 12 ~

I was approaching the center of the town. And the library building – which starting to look like a good possibility for an overnight stay.

The library is on a city block next to a mid-sized park. There is an elementary school on the street in back of it. In back of that is the local high school. The park is mostly open space, with some mature trees (elm, I think) around the periphery to provide some shade. Picnic benches are placed near some of the trees. Each picnic area has a little charcoal grill that can be used by picnickers.

On most Friday evenings, there would be small groups of people lounging around in the shade of the trees. Families would be bustling about preparing a simple evening dinner of BBQ hot dogs or burgers. Some would have the obligatory red and white checkered plastic tablecloth on the table, with some sodas and chips and maybe a potato salad. There would be a bit of smoke in the air from the grills, with a smell of the burgers and dogs being grilled.

Kids, along with a few parents, would be playing out on the grass. A pickup touch football game would usually be in progress, with much yelling and screaming by participants and onlookers. A few people would be walking their leashed dogs, plastic bags in hand for the inevitable chore. There are knots of people here and there talking and visiting. And a few birds flying and darting around, looking for errant bits of food.

But not tonight.

The park was empty. No people. No dog walkers. No football games. No checker-boarded tables loaded with food. No smell of burgers and dogs on the grill. No birds looking for food scraps. No breeze blowing, making the leaves on the tree rustle a bit. No noise.

Nothing.

Nothing but the now ever-present yellow gray clouds, the yellow-gray light, and that background low frequency humming noise.

I pedaled past the park, up to the doors of the library, ever watchful for movement. I stopped the bike next to brick wall next to the front doors. I got off the bike, and put down the kickstand. I kept my small backpack on my back, and left the big backpack on the bike. I leaned back against the brick wall of the library.

I grabbed the water bottle out of the holder on the bike and took a small swallow, swishing around my mouth. I was ready to spit it out, but decided to swallow instead. No sense wasting any. I took a couple of more swallows, then closed the cap and put the bottle back into its holder on the bike.

All the while, I was keeping ever watchful. And I used my left hand for the water bottle, keeping my right hand free and near the gun holster.

The entrance to the library was the standard glass door, no automatic opener, just a double door with handles to pull it open. A glass panel, with the embedded wire grid, was on either side of the door.

I moved from the brick front wall towards the entrance. I carefully peeked through the window to the inside. The lights were on, but there didn't appear to be anyone home. The entrance lobby was empty other than the display of books. The check-out desk was in the center-back of the lobby area, and had a few books scattered on the countertop. There was no movement inside that I could see. The library lights were on, as they would normally be.

I went back to the bike and kicked up the kickstand, wheeling it to the front door. I pulled open the door, which opened easily. I wheeled the bike through the door, closing the door behind me. I moved over to the side of the lobby area, parking the bike against the wall.

I looked all around, and did not see any movement. I also didn't hear any noise. Even though a library is supposed to be quiet, you could usually hear some murmured conversations, but I heard nothing.

Now that I was inside, I could see more of the library. It was a one-floor building. To the left of the lobby were the restrooms and drinking fountain. To the right was the door to a small public meeting room. In the center, the library checkout and work area.

To the right of the library desk was an open seating area, with several chairs and a couple of couches, with some small tables scattered around. Behind that seating area were more tables and chairs. The tables were rounded, and could seat four to eight people, depending on the size of the table.

To the right of that seating area were windows that looked out onto the park. In the back was book shelves perpendicular to the back wall, with the back wall containing more shelves for books.

Over on the left side were a smaller seating area, and a larger number of bookshelves. The left side wall was brick floor to ceiling, with bookshelves running the entire length of the left side.

I didn't see another exit door in the back, although it may have been hidden by some of the bookshelves.

And throughout the library, there was no movement, no people, nothing. The library was empty of patrons, and empty of employees. It looked safe; the only thing I could see was the furniture and the books that were silently resting on the shelves.

I went over to the open seating area. I moved one of the couches so that it was facing both the window area and the main entrance door. I placed my backpack on the floor next to the couch. I kept my coat on, and adjusted the gun holster on my right side as I sat down on the couch.

I looked over to the windows, and noticed that the blinds were open a bit. I could see out, but an outsider might have trouble looking in unless they were right next to the window.

It was starting to get darker, but not entirely dark outside. The strange yellow-brown light was still in the sky, so there was some illumination outside. It was sort of like a full moonlit night, but with the strange color from the sky rather than the white light of the moon.

But the inside lights were a bit too bright. I imagined that you could see the inside if you were standing outside. And although I hadn't seen any people since the lights blinked in the office, I didn't want to take a chance on anyone or anything being able to see inside. I didn't want the inside to be totally dark, though, as I wanted to be able to see things myself.

So I got up from the couch, and looked around for the main light switches. There was a bank of them by the front entrance, so I went to them and turned them off until there was one set of lights in the main entrance. It was about what you would expect to see when the library was closed – enough light to see inside, but not an overpowering amount of light. Sort of a night-light type of effect.

I went back to the couch, which was now in a mostly dark area. Sitting on the couch again, I could see everywhere inside the building. And, since there was a minimal amount of light inside, I could easily see outside.

Then I decided that I needed to secure my temporary abode. The front door was the only way in, and the door was easily opened. I needed to secure that door, and I didn't have the door key.

But I did have the duct tape. I got it out of the backpack, went over to the door, and ripped off a length of tape long enough to wrap around both push-bar handles of the double door a couple of times. Not the best security; someone could break the door glass. But it would be enough that I could hear any attempts to enter the library.

That bit of security done, I went back to the couch. I reached into my backpack, and grabbed some beef jerky and a bottle of water. The water was lukewarm, but tasted OK. And the beef jerky was enough to keep my hunger at bay for a while.

I finished my little meal, putting the bottle on the floor next to me, and the package of beef jerky back into the backpack. I would need to refill the water bottle before I left the library. And it was then that I realized that I would need to do what they hardly ever show on a TV show, or that is mentioned in fictional books.

I needed to get some sleep. And I needed to visit the bathroom before going to sleep.

I zipped up the backpack, and was going to leave it next to the couch while I went to the restroom at the front of the building near the entrance. Then I remembered all of those TV shows and movies where a simple mistake of leaving something behind was usually proven not to be a good idea. So I grabbed the backpack with my left hand, and headed towards the restroom, right hand on my gun.

As I approached the restroom, I kept my peripheral vision active, watching for any sort of movement. I got to the door, and stood to the left side, and placed the backpack behind me on the floor. The door swung open to the inside, with the hinges on the left. With my back to the wall, realizing I might be a bit paranoid, I reached with my left hand and pushed open the door, watching and listening for any movement. The door swung open. I didn't hear any noise, nor did I see any movement. The door slowly closed.

I repeated the action, with the same results. I put on my backpack, and then opened the door with my left hand, keeping my right hand on the gun in the holster. Holding the door open with my left hand, I took two short steps into the restroom.

It was your standard restroom. Tile floors, neutral color paint, a sink, two urinals (it was the Men's restroom, after all), and two toilet stalls. The stall walls were open at the bottom like you would usually see. A short divider between the sink and the urinal. The doors to the stalls were half-open. I cautiously took two more steps, letting the entrance door shut behind me.

With my back to the wall, I moved closer to the stall until I was able to see that it was empty. The only movement I could see was me in the mirror over the sink. I was a bit pale and disheveled from the bike ride from the office.

I stepped up to the urinal, did the usual, but didn't flush. No need for extra noise yet. ("If it's yellow, let it mellow...") Then over to the sink, where I turned on the water to wash my hands. Water came out of the faucet in a normal manner, which was an interesting data point. Just like the electricity working, the water supply seemed to be normal. I washed my hands, ran my fingers through my hair to tame it down a bit, and then dried off with paper towels from the dispenser. I tossed the towels into the wastebasket.

So far, so good.

I adjusted the backpack on my back, and walked towards the restroom door. I opened it with my left hand slowly, and looked back into the library. No changes in anything that I could see. I opened the door all the way, and then walked back into the entrance area.

The door to the outside was still secure with the duct tape. The light outside was still that strange yellow-gray color. Even though it was getting late, it wasn't getting any darker. It wasn't getting any lighter either. The light levels outside seemed the same as when I first went outside my office building a couple of hours ago. And still no movement anywhere that I could see.

I decided to lean the bike against the exit doors. If anyone tried to enter, the bike might get in their way, and make a noise. And I remembered a scene from the old "Conspiracy Theory" movie.

I took a water bottle out of my backpack, and placed it on the door handle. Just like in the movie: any movement of the door would cause the bottle to fall on the floor. That noise would be a simple alarm. I wasn't normally a deep sleeper, so the noise of the falling bottle on the tile entrance floor might alert me. I took the other pack off of the bike's rack, and brought it back to the couch area.

I took off my backpack and set it on the floor next to the couch. I decided to take off my coat; the temperature inside seemed normal.

I arranged one of the couch cushions at the end of the couch to form a pillow. I laid down with my left side against the couch back, leaving the right side (with the gun holster) on the open side of the couch. I put my coat over me like a blanket, and wiggled a bit to get as comfortable as I could. My backpacks were in reach next to the couch.

I reached for my gun with my right hand, and took it out. I checked the safety (on) and the load (full). I put it back in the holster, making sure it was loose but not too loose. I arranged my coat so that it wouldn't get in the way.

I didn't expect any trouble. I hadn't seen anyone or anything since the lights blinked. But it was good to be ready. I'd seen enough mystery/thriller shows to know that being ready was a good thing. And even though this wasn't a movie or TV show, the whole experience was unusual. And that meant I needed to be ready for anything.

As I laid there on the couch in the library, with the lights mostly off, and a view towards the windows with the mostly-closed blinds, I reflected on the day's experiences.

And I started to think about tomorrow.

~ 13~

I must have dozed off, but something caused my eyes to open wide. I am a light sleeper, especially in a different environment.

It took a few seconds for me to figure out where I was: on the couch in a strange place. A bit of fogginess cleared, and I remembered that I was in the library.

I lay still, as I assimilated my environment. I made some quick checks without moving. All body parts seemed to be functioning properly. I looked around, and saw no apparent change in the area directly around me. I slowly moved my head to the right, and saw that my backpack was still in its place. I sensed the weight of the gun in my right hand.

There was still the one light in the back of the library, so I could see things. There was also the light from the outside through the windows. I could see that the outside light was still that same yellow-gray color; with the amount of light what you would see just after the sun set, so it wasn't totally dark.

As I looked towards the window, it was still quiet, except for that very faint low frequency thrumming sound.

Still without moving my head, I could see that there was no other movement inside the library or outside. At least, none that I could sense. But there was something that caused me to wake up.

The couch that I was laying on was facing at an angle towards the front door entrance area. It wasn't a clear shot to that area; there were some chairs and tables between me and the front. But I had enough of a view to see that the front door was still closed, and that my duct tape lock was still in place.

I moved my head a bit to look at other areas of the library. No movement that I could tell, but something caused me to wake up. Nothing inside or outside seemed to have changed.

I looked again to the front door area. There was a small creaking sound like from a hinge on a door. My eyes were well adjusted to the ambient light. The creaking sound stopped, and then started again.

I tightened the grip on my gun, making sure the safety was off, but keeping my index finger outside the trigger guard. I still didn't move from the couch, but I made sure that I was ready to if necessary.

Then I decided that lying on the couch wasn't the best position to be in. I slowly moved my legs off the couch, getting my feet on the floor. I slid my butt off the couch onto the floor, at the same time moving to a sitting position on the floor, steadying myself with my left hand.

I sat on the floor with my back to the couch, watching the area towards the front door. I still couldn't see any movement, and the noise from a door hinge had stopped.

Then, once again, I heard the sound of a door hinge. I looked at the front door, but there was no movement there. I could see through the glass door to the outside, and there was nothing next to the door that I could see.

And then I saw a bit of movement. I sat still in front of the couch. The movement came from one of the restroom doors at the side of the library entrance area. There was just a bit of ambient light there, but not enough to clearly see what was causing the movement.

The movement from the restroom door – it was the ladies' restroom – continued. I could see that the shape was a person, but not much more detail than that.

The restroom door opened inward to the restroom, and there was no light inside the room. So all I could see was the shape of a person tentatively peeking into the library entrance area, still inside the restroom. I could see that the person was taking a cautionary look into the library, while still staying inside.

I didn't move, but I was focusing all of my senses towards that restroom door. I wasn't sure what was there, but I wanted to analyze any potential threat before I made any sudden moves.

I could see the person still peeking out of the restroom door. Then she – it was the ladies' restroom after all - took a single step outside the door, but still held the door open as if they wanted to make sure they could quickly go back inside. The person stood by the door, and I could see them swiveling their head, looking first inside the library, then towards the door. Then another step away from the restroom door, and I could see the restroom door slowly closing, with the same sound of the hinge creaking as it closed.

I had a random thought of why a library would not fix a squeaky door hinge.

I still didn't move. I had a clear line of sight to the person by the restroom door. But of course that meant that they had a clear line of sight to me. I was still sitting on the floor in front of the couch, so I was reasonably sure that the person couldn't see me because of my position.

I watched as the person took another step away from the door. The steps were tentative, like they weren't sure where they were.

Then I heard the person speak.

"Hello? Is anyone there?"

The voice sounded tentative, like they were not sure if anyone was there. Sort of like you would say if you were entering a strange room, and were looking for someone else.

I kept quiet, wanting to ensure that it was safe to answer. And I didn't move, but I did concentrate on the front area of the library, watching the person while still keeping my peripheral vision active for any other movement.

The person took another three steps towards the library entrance area. The ambient light was a bit better, so I started to see details of how the person looked.

The person was about five-feet-six-inches tall. Standard human configuration – arms, legs, torso, head. That might seem funny to think of, but the events since the lights blinked while I was in the office made that thought seem appropriate.

I thought of my next move. It was probably important to establish my presence, while also establishing my authority and control over the situation.

Still sitting on the floor, I used my 'authority' voice.

"Stand right there, don't move, this is the FBI!"

Well, that seemed like it would be authoritative, even though I wasn't FBI.

The person jumped a bit, with a small scream of surprise.

"Who is that? Where are you?"

I still didn't move from my position on the floor.

"Don't move, stay right there!" I said.

The person's head swiveled in my direction, but that was the only movement I could see. There was nobody else there but the two of us, as far as I could tell.

"Where are you?" said the person, moving their head towards the sound of my voice.

I again repeated, "Don't move. I do have a weapon, but as long as you don't move, you will be safe."

I slowly got up to a standing position, watching the person as I stood up.

As the person started to see me stand up, they took a small step backwards, but there was no threat to that movement that I could see.

"I'm not moving!", said the person. "Who are you, and where am I?" The voice sounded a bit more frightened than aggressive.

"Who are you?" I said again.

"My name is Audrelle."

"Where did you come from?"

"I am not sure, I just came out of that room over there" said Audrelle, pointing towards the restroom door.

Again I noticed that her voice did not sound threatening. Still watching for any other threats, but not seeing any.

"I want you to walk towards me carefully. I still have my weapon, but as long as you don't make any sudden moves, you are safe" I said.

Audrelle took a few small steps towards me. As she walked, I could see her a bit more clearly. She was about 5 ½ feet tall, dressed in jeans and a T-shirt, and had blonde hair that reached down to her shoulders. She appeared to be in her mid teens. She was wearing tennis shoes that made a slight squeak on the library tile floor as she walked towards me.

I could see that she wasn't a threat. She looked like a normal teenage girl, although I could tell that she was a bit frightened.

I looked around the library; saw no other movement other than Audrelle slowly walking towards me. I relaxed my grip on the gun, turning the safety back on. I lowered the gun so it was hanging by my side.

"Come on over here" I said.

She walked towards me. There was enough light that we could see each other's features. She wasn't carrying anything; her hands were empty.

Still standing next to the couch, I motioned to one of the chairs next to the couch.

"Sit down" I said.

She looked around somewhat nervously, and then sat down in a stuffed chair opposite the couch.

"Who are you? Why do you have a gun? And what is happening?"

I took another look around the library, and then looked out the windows. No changes inside or outside that I could see. Except that now there were two people in the library.

I relaxed a bit, and sat down on the couch facing her. I put my hands in my lap, still holding the gun, but not in a threatening way. Although I suspect that having a gun is a bit threatening. I thought that a good approach may be to be a bit less threatening, although watchful.

"Your name is Audrelle, right?" I asked.

"Yes."

"My name is Glen – Glen Barbor."

"Hi."

"I am not here to hurt you. In fact, I am a bit confused like you probably are. The gun I have is for my protection. Things have been a bit strange lately."

I could see that she had relaxed a bit in the chair, but she still looked a bit wary. I could see that I would have to be careful in what I would say so she would become more at ease.

"Things have been a bit strange," I continued. "You may notice how things look outside."

She looked around the library, and then looked out the window. I could see the gears working, and the slow realization that it looked a bit different outside than normal.

"I don't understand. What is happening?" she said.

"I am not sure myself", I replied. "What do you see outside?"

"It looks sort of strange out there. It looks like it's evening, but the light color is different. "

I could then see a bit more puzzlement on her face.

"There's nobody outside" she said. "And the clouds look weird."

"Yes," I said.

It was a bit strange talking to someone, after not seeing anyone since the lights blinked.

"What were you doing in the restroom?" I asked. "Besides, the obvious" I added with a small smile.

"I am not sure. I don't remember going in there. In fact, now that I think of it, I don't remember much of anything that has happened, maybe in the last couple of hours. What is going on?"

I waited a moment before replying. I decided that I needed more information before I started answering all her questions.

"Let's get to that in a minute. What do you last remember?" I said.

Audrelle thought for a minute. She looked around the room, as if realizing that she was in the library.

"I remember being in the library. I came here after school to study a bit. I have a term paper that I need to write, and I wanted to do a bit of research."

"You mean actual research, instead of Googling or looking at WikiPedia?"

She smiled just a bit. "Yeah. I mean we have a computer at home, and all that, but it can get a bit noisy at home with my two little brothers."

"So you were at the library after school. Then what happened?"

"It was like quiet in the library. Yeah, I know the library is supposed to be quiet, but there is always some noise, you know, like people whispering or noises from chairs moving and stuff like that. But all of a sudden it got quieter than usual.

"I was in the back of the library, over there," she said, pointing to the back corner. "It's usually quieter back there, and I can concentrate better. There weren't very many people in the room. The librarian person was at the front desk, and there was just a couple of people in the font part, sort of where we are now.

"I was concentrating on a book I found, and I sort of noticed that it was pretty quiet. I didn't think much about that, because I was concentrating on the book.

"And then the lights sort of blinked," she said. "I looked up, and I saw a sort of shimmer inside the library. But it wasn't the whole room shimmering, just the other people that were in the library."

She paused. She was looking off into the distance, not really focused on me. Her voice got quiet.

"The other people in the library - they shimmered. And then they were gone. The lights blinked, I looked up, and the other people shimmered. And then they were gone."

She got very quiet, and was sitting very still. She was still looking off into the distance, her eyes unfocused. I didn't say anything.

She tilted her head a bit, and the action seemed to snap her back into the present. Her eyes got focused again, looking right at me. I waited for her to continue.

"I don't remember anything after that. I don't remember anything until I found myself in the restroom, in the corner, on the floor. It was like I was waking up, but I was on the floor. I looked around, realized where I was, and stood up. I went to the door.

"As I walked to the door, I remembered a bit of what happened, but not how I got inside the restroom. I was getting a bit scared, because I didn't know what was outside the door. When I got to the door, I stood there for a few minutes trying to decide what to do.

"Then I thought I was being silly. Like I had watched too many of those teenager horror movies. That was silly, I thought. But I still didn't feel quite right. But I decided that staying the in the restroom was silly.

"So I pulled open the door. Slowly. I looked out the door, and didn't see anything, so I started walking out into the front area.

"And that's when I heard you telling me to stop. So I did."

She stopped again. Her eyes started to do that long-distance focus thing, but she shook her head and looked back at me.

"What is happening?"

~ 14~

Audrelle looked at me. Her eyes were wide open, and her face had that sort of deer-in-the-headlight look. She was scared of something. It wasn't me. It was everything around us.

We were the only people in the library. In fact, as far as I could tell, we were the only people in the whole town.

I looked at my watch. It was still working. I was going to say 'ticking', but my watch was digital, so there was no ticking involved. I could see the seconds counter changing, so it was still working. The numbers on the watch said 1:48, and it showed as "AM".

So it was the middle of the night. A time when you would think that it would be dark outside.

I looked out the window of the library. It wasn't dark outside. There was that yellowish light in the air. The trees in the park had a faint yellow glow on the leaves and branches. Even the grass on the park was yellowish, not green at all.

And there was no movement. The leaves on the tree, as far as I could tell, weren't moving at all. If I was outside, I would recognize the stillness of the air, like it was when I was on my bike after leaving the office.

And there was that faint low frequency humming sound. Not loud enough to be bothersome, but loud enough that you could hear it. The sound didn't seem to come from any particular direction. The sound seemed to be all around.

I turned away from the window, and looked back at Audrelle. She was waiting for the answer to her question.

"What is happening?" she repeated.

"I don't know," I said. I started to tell her my story.

"All I know is that the lights blinked while I was in the office. And after they blinked, there was nobody in the office. It was at the end of the work day, so I just figured everyone else had left early. Fridays are sort of a slow day at work, so it is not unusual for people to sneak out a bit before the normal closing time.

"So I grabbed my stuff and figured I would leave too. But things were strange enough that I didn't just walk out the door. For some reason I made sure that I could get back into the office if I needed too. I had a strange feeling about the whole thing. Although the office was empty, and I had been the last person in the office before, things were different."

I stopped for a minute, remembering.

"As I went through the office, I noticed that my coworker's personal things were still in their cubicles. A few coats and sweaters were still on the chairs or coat hooks. There were purses and bags still in the cubicles. And a few notebook computers."

I paused again.

"It was like people had left, but they didn't leave like they normally did."

I turned towards the back of the library, where the reading tables were.

"It's like here. There are backpacks and sweaters still on the tables. There were people here before.

"And now there isn't anyone here. Except for you and me."

I turned back towards Audrelle.

"As far as I know, it's just you and me. And I don't know why."

Audrelle looked at me. "What did you do next?" she asked.

"Well. I guess that I also watch too many late night horror movies. And I had that disquieting feeling of 'something is wrong'. So I was a bit careful about what I did, and where I went.

"I decided that it was time to leave. Before the lights blinked, I was planning on heading to my home in the mountains for a long weekend.

"I wasn't sure of what was happening. I still don't know. But I thought that it was important for me to get to my home."

I stopped again. Audrelle looked at me, her face softening away from the scared look she had before. I could tell she was waiting for me to continue.

"So, I gathered together my stuff, including the flashlight I kept in my desk drawer, and the multi-tool I had for my belt. I grabbed my backpack and coat. And I carefully left the office by the back way, using a book to prop the door open so I could get back in if I needed to."

I explained how my office was in the basement of the office park building, and that I used the stairs instead of the elevator to go to the main level. And how, when I got to the lobby, I found that it was empty of people also. Even the security guard area was empty.

I explained how I had gone to my car, but it didn't work. And how I had gathered up my supplies into my other backpack that was in the car, and then I had gotten the bike.

"After riding away from the office on the bicycle, I thought of the need to get some basic supplies – food, water, stuff like that. So I went to the nearby convenience store.

"I didn't see anyone the whole time. Not while pedaling the bike, and not in the store. And even though there were cars on the street, they had stopped. And they were empty.

"And the strange thing about that is that the driver's seat belt was always fastened. But nobody was in the car. A few cars had child car seats, with buckles fastened, but the seats were empty."

I stopped again. "That was strange. And then there was the noise. Or lack of noise. No birds chirping. No insects buzzing. No dogs barking. No noise at all, except for that low thrumming sound you can hear now.

"And the light. The yellowish glow in the air. And the clouds that look like yellow-gray bubble wrap. It was like nothing I had seen before."

Another pause. Audrelle was still looking at me, her features softening a bit more. But still with a sort of scared look lurking beneath.

"So I got the stuff from the convenience store. I packed it all into my backpacks. And got on the bike and pedaled until I got here. It was getting late, and I thought that I needed to be inside somewhere when it got dark. So I found the library, and came in here to stay for the night.

"And I locked the library door, ate a bit, and then stretched out on the couch here. I was sort of asleep when I heard a sound that woke me up. That's when I saw you.

"And here we are."

I looked at her.

"What is happening?" she repeated. "And what do we do?"

I had no answer for either of those questions.

~ 15~

We both sat in the library. I was on the couch, and she was in an overstuffed chair that was at a 90 degree angle to the couch. Her chair faced away from the windows. The couch was facing the front of the library, where I could see the front doors. They were still closed, with my duct tape locking the push bar handles. And the water bottle propped on the door bar handle was still in place.

I was sitting at the end of the couch away from the windows. I could see out both the front door and the windows on the side of the library.

I looked at my watch again. It showed 2:49 am. We had been talking for a while, sharing our experiences since the lights had blinked. Even though it was the middle of the night, it wasn't really 'night' outside.

There was that same gray-yellow ambient light outside, sort of like what you would get just after the sun went down. There was enough light outside that I could see the strange cloud formations. The clouds were also a yellow-gray color, and covered the entire sky. They had large bumped out cloud pockets hanging underneath, like bubble-wrap. I had seen those types of clouds before in pictures, but had never experienced them until now. And the pictures just showed a small cloud formation that was only in a small portion of the sky. I remembered them being called Mammatus clouds. They weren't very common, but they also weren't like these clouds.

These clouds stretched over the entire sky. And the yellow-gray color was also something I had never seen. I had also never seen it being this light outside in the middle of the night. Perhaps people that lived in the Polar Regions would see a light sky in the middle of the night, but I didn't live in the Polar Regions. So the middle-of-the-night light wasn't something that you would normally find in this area.

It was quiet in the library. That was the normal intent of a library, but this was a different type of quiet. You would normally hear a little bit of noise when there were people in the library. But it was just me and Audrelle.

Actually, you could hear something other than the quiet. Ever since the lights blinked, I had heard this low pitched and low volume humming sound. During the evening as I rode my bike that was all that you could hear. There were no birds' sounds. No traffic sounds, since every vehicle I had seen was frozen in place in the roads. No dogs barking, no insects humming. The only humming was that low frequency humming that seemed to come from every direction.

"Hmmm."

I looked at Audrelle. She still had that faraway look on her face, staring off into the back of the library, but not really focusing on anything.

I realized it was Audrelle that said "Hmmm". But it didn't look like she was aware that she said it.

"Audrelle?"

She was still looking at the back of the library, and didn't seem to notice that I had spoken.

I tried again. "Audrelle?" I said in a normal voice.

She suddenly moved her head and looked at me. "Hmmm," she said. But it didn't seem like she knew that she said anything.

"We should probably get some rest. Perhaps things will be better in the morning."

I didn't really believe what I said, but my protector instincts figured that that was probably the best thing to say.

"Yeah, I guess," she said quietly.

"Do you want the couch?" I asked.

She looked at the couch. "No. I'll just stay here in the chair."

She scrunched down a bit in the chair, drawing her legs underneath her. She leaned her head against the back of the chair. She turned her head to look at the back of the library. Then snuggled down a bit more, crossing her arms and sort of hugging herself.

"Hmmm."

I watched for a minute as her eyes slid shut.

"Hmmm," she said, a bit quieter than last time. And then it looked like she was sleeping.

I moved back in the couch, laying down with my head at the one end, and moved my feet up on the other end. I was facing the window again, looking through the window over the top of my feet.

I made sure my backpack was on the floor next to my head. I realized I was still holding the gun. I double-checked that the safety was on, and then placed the gun back in the holster that I still wore.

I wiggled a bit, trying to get comfortable on the couch. I looked over at Audrelle. She hadn't moved, and appeared to be asleep.

As I started to close my eyes, I heard it again.

"Hmmm."

Hmmm, indeed.

~ 16 ~

My eyes were closed. There was something happening, but I wasn't sure what it was. But I was sure that if I kept my eyes closed, it would go away. So I kept my eyes closed.

I thought I could hear something. But I figured that I would just keep my eyes closed. The alarm would go off in a few minutes, and I would reach over and smack the clock to turn off the alarm. I would lay in bed for just a few more minutes, then I would get up and stumble to the bathroom and take a shower and shave and get dressed and go out to the kitchen and toast a bagel and pour myself some orange juice and check my email and take the bagel out of the toaster and put some butter on it and grab my juice and sit down at the counter and check my email and eat my bagel and drink my juice and then I would go to work.

But for now, I would just lie in my bed with my eyes closed and wait for the alarm to go off.

I twisted around in my bed a bit, grabbing for the covers. But they weren't there. No covers.

And then I turned the other way and my arm smacked against something that was sort of soft but sort of hard. It felt like the wall, or maybe the headboard. But the headboard of my bed wasn't soft. It was hard wood. That wasn't hard wood that I felt.

So I turned over a bit more, and my whole body was up against that hard but soft surface. That was strange. I still wanted to keep my eyes closed. But I decided to open them just a little bit.

I looked through my half-open eyes through a fuzzy view of wherever I was. And the 'wherever I was' wasn't on my bed. It wasn't even my bedroom.

I opened my eyes a bit more, rubbing them to clear out the haze of sleeping. And I looked around.

And realized I wasn't in my bedroom. The great detective in me realized that I was on a couch. But it wasn't the couch in my living room.

I opened my eyes more. The fogginess of sleep dropped away from my eyes. And I started remembering where I was, and how I got there.

And that I needed to make sure that I was safe.

I remembered the gun in the holster. I reached down with my right hand and grabbed on to the gun, leaving it in the holster.

I was still lying down on the couch. And as I looked around, I remembered that I was in the town library.

I looked past my feet to the window to the outside. The light outside was just the same as it was before. It wasn't the brightness of the morning light; it was the same dull yellow-gray light as it had been since… what?

As my brain started processing my environment, it started coming back to me.

The lights had blinked.

And ever since the lights had blinked, things had been not quite normal.

I then looked to my right.

The chair was empty.

I sat up a bit on the couch. I blinked, and looked up at the chair again.

Still empty.

I looked over towards the library windows. There seemed to be no change out there. It was light outside, but the strange yellow-gray light, not the normal morning sunshine kind of light.

There was still no movement that I could see out the window. The leaves on the tree weren't moving, as far as I could tell.

I looked above the trees at the sky. The clouds were still there, their yellow-gray color unchanged, although perhaps a bit brighter than yesterday. But that could have been an imagination on my part. The clouds still had that hanging bubble look, and the clouds covered all of the sky that I could see.

I pulled back the focus of my eyes into the library, moving my head to the right towards the chair where Audrelle had been last night. The chair was still empty.

I looked at the watch on my left wrist. The display showed "8:47". I figured it was AM, and the little AM/PM indicator on the watch face did indeed show "AM". So, based on all apparent observations, it was 8:47am. Ain't I the great detective?

As I looked at my watch, I listened a bit harder, straining to hear any sounds. Nothing. Except for that low humming sound that I had heard since the lights blinked. And even that sound was fading into the background of my mind, like the sound of a train would for someone that lived close to the train tracks. After a while, those types of background sounds move to the background of your mind, so you don't hear them.

Sort of like not smelling the odors of a stockyard if you work there, I guess. If that odor can get to the background of your senses, then I suppose that the same thing can happen to sounds after you have been hearing them for a while. If you think about the sound, you hear it, but those background sounds get softer if you aren't paying attention to them.

So the light outside was about the same. And the sounds were about the same. The library appeared to be the same, empty except for me.

And Audrelle was gone.

As I sat there on the couch, I wondered if I had been imagining the whole thing. Perhaps Audrelle hadn't been there at all.

That would normally be improbable, but then things hadn't been normal for since yesterday when the lights blinked.

I sat up on the couch, swinging my feet to the floor. As I did, my feet bumped up against the backpack that was on the floor next to the couch. I leaned forward a bit, and saw that the backpack hadn't been disturbed, at least as far as I could tell.

I leaned back into the couch, my hands brushing against my sides. My right hand brushed against something hard and metallic, and I looked to see what it was. It was the gun in the holster, of course.

I reached up to scratch my head, pushing my hair around a bit, and then using my fingers to straighten up what I figured was a bit of 'bed-head'.

I looked at the end table next to the couch. My bottle of water was still there where I had left it last night. I grabbed the bottle, unscrewed the cap, and took a small swallow. It tasted normal, like bottled water usually did.

I held the bottle in my left hand for a minute, then screwed the cap back on and put the bottle on the end table again.

I again looked around the library. No change, as far as I can tell. I appeared to be the only one there.

~ 17 ~

As I sat on the couch after waking up, I realized that I needed to do the usual morning routine. I looked over towards the front door, and then remembered that was where the rest rooms were.

Well, of course. Everyone needs to do the 'morning ritual' thing after waking up, so that's probably where Audrelle was. I took a breath, which was probably more of a sigh of relief, as I figured out why the chair was empty.

"No time like the present," I thought. So I pushed myself up off the couch, did a little stretch and twisted left and right to work out a few kinks in my muscles, and headed towards the rest rooms.

The doors to both restrooms were closed, of course, the automatic door closers doing their job. I knocked once on the door marked "Women", and said "I'm heading into the Men's room for a minute". I figured that was better than barging in to say hello.

I pushed open the Men's room door, and went inside. No surprises in there. I did the usual, and then I washed and dried my hands and pulled open the door.

As I exited the 'facilities', I looked towards the inside of the library. I saw no movement anywhere to indicate where Audrelle was. I knocked on the door to the Women's restroom: "Everything OK in there?" There was no response.

I waited a moment, and knocked again. "Audrelle, are you OK?"

Still no response. So I knocked again: "I'm coming in to check on you."

Feeling a bit embarrassed at what I might be interrupting, I opened the door and poked my head inside, but still no fully entering.

"Audrelle? Are you in there?"

No response.

"I'm coming in."

I pulled the door open the rest of the way, and took two steps inside. The room was as you would expect. A sink area with two wash basins and a mirror was on one wall. On the other wall there were two stalls, and a small chair in the corner by the door, but far enough away that the door opening wouldn't hit the chair.

"Anyone home?" I called out.

No response.

I looked at the sink area, then at the mirror. Then I squatted down a bit, and looked for feet in the stall area.

The room was empty. The lights are on, nobody is home.

I took a few more steps into the room, and gently pushed open the door of the first stall.

Nothing there.

I did the same with the second stall, and got the same result.

I looked around the room, I even looked up at the ceiling, not that I expected anything – or anybody - to be there. And there wasn't anything there but the light fixture.

I turned and walked towards the door, pulling it open and walked back into the front entrance area of the library.

I walked over to the door, and saw that the duct tape I had wrapped around the push bar door handles was still in place and undisturbed. And the water bottle was still on top of the door bar handles.

I looked outside through the front door glass, and saw nothing unusual. Well, at least nothing new since the lights had blinked.

I turned away from the door, getting a bit nervous. I placed my right hand on the gun in the holster. I walked back towards the center of the library.

"Audrelle? Are you here?"

Still nothing.

I walked to the library checkout counter, and then looked into the area behind the counter.

Nothing there.

I made a circuit around the interior of the library. I looked down each row of book shelves. I got to the back of the library, then continued to the right and walked towards the first set of windows in the back.

I stopped for a moment, again looking around the library. The only thing moving in the library was me.

I looked out the window to the park next door. There was the yellow-gray light outside, the leaves on the tree not moving, nothing moving out there.

I continued walking past the windows, keeping an eye on the outside, but there was nothing moving anywhere. I walked over to the couch, took one last look around the library, and then looked at the chair where I had seen Audrelle sitting then sleeping last night.

Nothing there. Nothing anywhere.

I sat down on the couch again.

And thought to myself "That was weird."

Then I remembered that this whole thing has been weird. Ever since the lights blinked, it has been weird.

I sat on the couch in the library. I grabbed an energy bar out of my backpack, and slowly ate it. I finished it, and grabbed a piece of beef jerky. Between sips of water from the water bottle, I mentally reviewed the past 12 hours.

I looked at my watch. Well, maybe the last 15 hours. All of them weird.

As I sat there chewing on the beef jerky (teriyaki-flavored, in case you were wondering), I figured that what I really needed to do was to was to plan my next move.

I couldn't stay in the library. I needed to get to the cabin – my home. That had been my plan just after the lights blinked, and everything I had done so far was part of that plan.

I had my own survival equipment. I had enough food and water for the several days it would take me to get to the cabin, whether I got there by using the bicycle, or by walking. I had the clothing I would need for all but extreme cold. And since this area was not in the frozen north, the clothing I had should be sufficient.

I had simple sheltering equipment; a couple of space blankets and plastic garbage bags I could use to protect me from the basic elements of cold and rain.

And I had the gun, plus enough ammunition that should protect me from man or beast, as long as there weren't too many of them.

So I needed to get going.

I packed up my backpacks, arranging things so that the important items are readily available. I had two backpacks. The smaller one would be on my back, and the larger one on the bike rack.

I moved to the front of the library, into the entrance area. As I did, I kept a look out the windows to the side, and through the glass doors. As far as I could tell, nothing had changed outside.

I grabbed the water bottle from the door bar handles. The duct tape lock I had fashioned last night when I got inside the library was still in place, so I used the knife of my multi-tool and cut the tape. I put the tool back in its leather holster on my belt (left side, out of the way).

I carefully removed the duct tape, putting it on the outside of the back pack, in case it was needed later. No sense in wasting duct tape.

I went over to the bike, and fastened the larger backpack to the bike rack, securing it with a couple of bungee cords I had gotten from the store. I checked my gun, making sure it was loaded and the safety was on.

A final check of the bike, and I kicked up the kickstand and walked towards the door. One more look outside in all directions, carefully looking for anything out of place. That was fairly easy, since there wasn't anyone out there. And one more look inside the library.

All clear.

I pushed open the door, and wheeled the bike outside. The library door slowly closed behind me.

And I was outside.

~ 18~

There wasn't much change from yesterday, as far as I could tell. There was still nobody around that I could see. There were cars out in the street, but they were not moving, and there still appeared to be nobody inside the cars. It was like they had frozen in place like a snapshot.

Even though it was morning (I could tell by my watch), there wasn't any sunlight to be seen. Just that same yellow-gray light throughout that I had seen since yesterday.

There was no sound, other than the background low-frequency humming sound that I was starting not to even notice. No birds chirping in the trees; no dogs barking in the distance, no hum of car tires on roadways. There was none of the normal city sounds anywhere.

And there was no movement, at least as far as I could see. No critters anywhere in the park next to the library. No kids playing on the playground at the school across the street.

Wait. There was some movement. In one of the trees in the park next to the library.

I looked towards the tree where I had sensed some movement. There was a black shape there. I took a closer look. It was a raven again.

As I looked, the raven fluttered its wings a bit. Then folded them back into its body. Its head turned to the side a bit, so its eyes – well, one of its eyes – faced me.

It looked at me for a bit. And I looked at it.

Then the raven fluttered its wings a bit. Settled its wings back.

Then the raven pixelated.

You know how when you are watching a DVD, and the picture stutters a bit? And the image pixels sort of flutter in blocky shapes for a second or two until the picture stabilizes back to normal?

That's what the raven did. Pixelated. Just the raven, not the tree it was in.

The raven pixelated. And then it was gone.

I looked all around. There was no other movement anywhere.

The raven was in the tree. It turned its head to look at me. Then a wing flutter. Then a pixelation.

Then it was gone.

I stood there next to my bike, looking at the tree where the raven had appeared, then pixelated, then disappeared.

I shook my head a bit.

And there was no reason that I could think of to stay where I was. It was time to get on the road.

I tucked my pant leg in my sock on my right foot so that it wouldn't get caught in the bicycle chain. I put my left foot on the left pedal, pushed off with my right foot, and swung my right leg over the bike seat. I got my right foot on the right pedal, and pushed down, steering the bike towards the street, pumping the pedals, doing the bike riding thing.

And I kept a close eye out where I was going, and where I had been. I wasn't focusing just ahead; I kept alert in all directions as I pedaled down the street towards the mountains and my cabin.

Riding a bicycle can be sort of peaceful. It's not entirely quiet. There is the faint humming sound of the bike tires on the street. The sound changes a bit depending on the surface you are riding on.

Sometimes you will hear a slight crack as you hit a small rock and it goes shooting off to the side of you. When you are riding on a street, the sound is a bit different when you hit the painted lines of a crosswalk.

Some streets have small cracks, so there can be a little 'thump-thump' as your bike tires hit the cracks in the road.

There's also the sound of the wind rushing past your ears. As you ride down the street, and turn your head a bit as you are looking around, the wind sounds a bit differently.

Then there are the sounds of the chain running through the sprockets on your bike. When you use the brakes to slow down or stop, there is that almost squeaking sound as the brake pads hit the bike rim.

There are also the sounds that you, the bike rider, make. The steady in-out rhythm of your breathing. The little grunts that you might make as you pedal a bit harder to go up an incline.

All those sounds are not always noticed as you ride your bicycle. After a few minutes of riding along, those sounds sort of fade into the background. You start hearing the other sounds that are near you.

Like the sounds of cars approaching, or a dog barking off in the distance, or bird sounds. Maybe a car horn honking or a truck engine accelerating, or the truck's air brakes.

There is some rattling of cars as they pass by; maybe an open trailer of something also rattling.

Since those sounds are not a part of yourself as you pedal along, you tend to hear them as you are riding. Those sounds will fade into the background a bit, although you are aware of them.

So various sounds are a part of your bike ride, whether you are riding along a city street, or a urban trail, or wherever.

Most of those sounds I didn't hear.

There were the sounds that were made by my bike as I rode along the city streets. I could hear my breathing as I pedaled along. There was the sound of the wind past my ears. Occasionally the slightly different sounds of the bike tires on the various surfaces of the street.

But that was all.

No traffic sounds. No dogs barking. No car or truck engines. No people talking.

Just the sound of me and my bike.

And that low-pitched, thrumming sound that was just audible. A constant 'thrum'. Not enough to irritate you. Not loud enough to be uncomfortable.

Just loud enough to know that it was there.

The sights as I was riding along were the usual, but *not* the usual. There were buildings, and cars, and trucks, and I even saw a baby stroller and a tricycle.

But all of those sights were like in a three-dimensional painting that I was traveling through.

Everything was frozen in place. Nothing was moving, except for me and my bike.

There was not even a slight breeze that was causing the leaves and branches of a tree to move.

Store signs that would have been rotating were not moving. Electronic billboards displaying ever-changing messages were stuck on one display. Cars and trucks were frozen in place. Street signal lights were not changing.

And then there is the sky.

The sky was covered with a light-gray cloud cover. It was clouds like you would see on a day that it might rain, but probably wouldn't. The clouds were all the same color.

And they had the most unusual pattern. It was like the clouds were covered (on the underneath, of course; I had no idea what they looked like on top) with sheets of bubble wrap. Large-bubbled bubble wrap.

Each 'cloud bubble' was the same size, as far as I could tell. It was like looking at those old 'popcorn' ceilings in older homes, but with large uniformly-shaped chunks, in a pattern that made them all look the same.

It was like if you had a big area of rocks, each rock exactly the same size and height. Every rock the same color without any color variation. And each rock placed in an exact pattern, all lined up in both directions as far as you can see. But they are clouds.

And the clouds weren't exactly gray. They had a yellowish cast to them. Not yellow, not gray, not bright, but a dull yellow-gray color. And the same color throughout the whole bubble-cloud-filled sky.

It was really strange as I rode through the town.

Riding through a three-dimensional painting, everything around me is frozen in place. The bubble-clouds in the sky stretching as to the horizon. No sound, other than the sound of me and my bike, and that low-pitched humming sound that seemed to be coming from all directions.

Really strange, and really quiet.

And empty of any other living thing but me.

And that one raven I had seen before it disappeared in a pixelation.

~ 19 ~

I was pedaling steadily, heading towards the edge of town, towards the mountains, towards my home, and hopefully, towards something normal.

Other than that, I was not sure what I was heading for, and what I would find along the way.

So I was not riding with 'tunnel vision'. I was pedaling at a steady pace, but I was not just focused on what was directly ahead, with a background awareness of things that were around me.

It was not a normal bike ride.

I was constantly looking around. Ahead of me, of course, to make sure that I didn't run into something. To my sides, to make sure that something didn't run into me. I was even looking in back of me, to make sure there wasn't anyone – or anything – sneaking up on me.

I was passing cars and trucks on the street. I was mostly keeping to the right side of the road, out of habit. I didn't want to be hit by a car going down the street. Again, a habitual thing, since there was no movement anywhere that I could see except me pedaling down the street.

As I would pass a car or truck, I would glance inside. Nothing in there, living or dead, as far as I could see. I could see the evidence of someone that was once in the car. Some shopping bags in the back seat, or a purse on the passenger seat. Perhaps a child car seat or two in the back seat.

But nothing living. No people. No kids. No dogs.

Nothing.

I was riding in the general direction of the main road out of town. I had been pedaling for about 25 minutes. I decided to stop for a couple of minutes to rest and rehydrate.

I picked an open spot on the road, passing through an intersection with cars stopped for a red light, and no traffic on the cross street. It used to be irritating to be stopped at a red light and there were no cars using the green light of the other direction. Now, it was just cars stopped.

I went through the intersection, running the red light, watching for any cross traffic. Not that I expected to see any cross-traffic, but old habits die hard.

I went through the intersection, and then pulled to the side of the road next to an empty bus stop bench. I put my right foot up on the bench as I reached for my water bottle for a drink.

I grabbed the bottle, but took a good look in every direction. It was kind of spooky to be in the middle of a city, with frozen cars in the road, and no movement to be seen in any direction, and no sound to be heard other than my breathing.

I appeared to be all alone, but my survival senses told me that I should be ever-aware of my surroundings, looking for any possible threat to my well-being.

So I didn't take a drink of water when I first stopped. I looked in all directions.

It was a typical intersection. Some strip malls on the corners along with one gas station. You've probably seen something similar numerous times on any day. But I still looked around to ensure that there were no impending threats.

I twisted around in the bike seat to check all directions; you have to watch your 'six'. I did a quick look first as I turned my head to the left and then all the way around to look in back of me. I turned my head back to the front, moving a bit slower this time, looking carefully near and far for anything that might be a threat. Or anything that might look 'normal'.

I did the same thing as I turned to the right. A quick look as I turned my head all the way back to my 'six', then a slower and more thorough look as I turned my head back to the front.

No threats, as far as I could tell. No changes to anything. No movement, no 'normal' sounds.

Still watching around me, I unscrewed the cap of the water bottle, and took a slow drink. I reached around into the backpack, and grabbed an energy bar out of my stashed supply.

I put the water bottle back into the holder on the bike frame, and unwrapped the energy bar, and slowly took a bite and chewed.

The sound of my chewing seemed unnaturally loud in the overall silence. As I ate the energy bar, I noticed that the taste seemed a bit subdued. There were nuts and raisins and chocolate chips in the bar, but their taste was a bit flat. It wasn't an unpleasant taste, but just wasn't 'normal'.

I grabbed the water bottle, unscrewed the cap, and took another drink as I swallowed the first bite of the energy bar. And I noticed that the water tasted a bit 'flat' also. It was like the 'taste level' was subdued for both the water and the energy bar. Not enough to taste strange, but different enough that it wasn't a normal taste.

As I sat there on the bike, my left foot on the left pedal, and my right root on the bus bench, I continued to eat the energy bar, along with sips of water. I knew that one energy bar was probably not enough, so I grabbed a piece of beef jerky to chew on.

The beef jerky also had a subdued taste. It was not old or expired, but didn't have the usual beef jerky taste. It was like there was a dimension of taste that was missing from the energy bar and the beef jerky and even the water. I hadn't noticed that in the library, but I noticed it now.

But I knew that I needed the energy and hydration, so I finished the beef jerky. I also emptied the water bottle.

I was about to toss the disposable water bottle in the trash can that was next to the bus bench, but stopped. I seemed to realize that a container, even though it was empty, would be useful at some point. Even though I had several full bottles of water in the backpack.

As I sat there on the bike with my empty water bottle, I recalled watching old TV westerns. There would be the cowboy traveling across the desert, trying to ration his water as he walked along or rode his horse, and eventually getting to the point that the canteen of water was empty.

The cowboy would always hold the canteen upside down over his mouth, trying to get the last drop of water out to parch his thirst. And then he realized that there was no more water to be found inside the canteen.

The cowboy would always toss the empty canteen aside, and then start walking or riding again.

Yeah, I knew it was just a movie. But it always seemed like the wrong thing to do. An empty canteen doesn't weigh that much, and it would be useful if the cowboy got to a water source so he could fill up his canteen again.

If you throw away the canteen, then get to a water hole, what are you going to put your water in for the next part of your journey?

That's what I flashed on while I was sitting on the bike, about ready to throw away the empty water bottle into the trash can by the bus stop bench.

The empty water bottle might come in useful later on in my journey. Or it might not be needed. But I was not going to throw it away like the cowboy in the desert in the old western movie.

I put the cap back on the bottle, and put the empty water bottle back into the bottle holder on the bike frame.

I sat there for a few more minutes. Always looking around in all directions. Left. Right. Forward. Back. Even up.

And over on a light pole in the parking lot across the street was a black object. I looked closer. A raven, just sitting there on top of the light pole. Looking at me; at least, that's what it appeared to be looking at.

And, again, a wing flutter or two. Looking at me.

And then, the raven pixelated. And disappeared without a sound.

Other than the raven appearing and then pixelating away, I didn't see anything different around me.

But knew that keeping a sharp eye out for anything, normal or not, was a good idea.

The raven – appearing, then pixelating, then gone – was not normal. Along with everything else that had happened after the lights blinked.

This was not 'normal'.

~ 20~

If you have been paying attention, you might notice that this is my second day of bike riding. The first day started out after the lights blinked. That was in the afternoon. I was heading to my ultimate destination of my cabin in the mountains. I biked for several hours after the 'blink', and after getting some supplies at one of the quick markets near my office.

It was starting to get dark after that first session of bike riding. "Dark" being a relative term, because it never got totally dark last night. I got to the library a bit before 9:00 pm, which means that I was biking for about 3 hours before I got to the library.

I spent the night in the town library. The library is located near the center of the town, surrounded by a nice park. The library's doors were open, so I spent the night inside, after securing the entrance as best as I could.

It was there that I met Audrelle, which was a bit startling, since that was the first person, or even living thing, that I had seen since the lights blinked. After the initial shock of meeting each other, we discussed what was happening, coming to no specific conclusions.

Both of us were tired at that point, so we each went to sleep. I was on a couch, and Audrelle chose a comfortable oversized chair.

When I woke up, Audrelle was gone.

I had searched throughout the library, but Audrelle was nowhere to be found. I eventually left the library, got back on my bike, and started my journey to the cabin.

Now it was around noon. I had left the library about four hours ago. I was still on my route out of town. I hadn't taken any long breaks (well, there was that one by the tree that was necessary).

I'm not a big bike rider. I don't go out for long-distance bike rides with others. I don't have the funny 'clown clothes' – bright shirts with logos, tight shorts that extend to my knees, short socks, and special shoes – that many bikers wear.

But I do like to take short rides on the back roads near my cabin. So I am not uncomfortable riding a bike.

When I go to my mountain cabin, I'll take half-day hikes around the area. And I'll go to a state or national park, and take short day hikes there.

Riding a bike doesn't give me muscle aches or cramps. I probably couldn't do a 50 miler in 3 hours, but I do usually maintain a respectable pace of around 7-10 mph.

So here I was, taking a rest stop around noon on the second day after the 'blink'. I had been biking for about 8-9 hours total – about 4 hours each yesterday and today.

I thought about that for a moment.

At a pace of around 7-8 mph, that would mean that I had gone about 60 miles. That's a pretty good distance, I thought.

Until I thought about that some more.

Our town is not that big. It's not a small town. But it is, I'd guess, about 25-30 miles in diameter.

You see where I am going with this?

My office is on the south side of town. Not at the edge of town limits, but on the south side. I am headed north-westerly, towards the mountains and my cabin.

So the edge of town, from my office, should be about 30 miles at the most.

I had been pedaling for, say, 60 miles. And I was still in town.

That's a bit strange, don't you think?

I am on the bus bench, my bike right next to me, taking a short break after biking about 60 miles since the blink. At least, about 60 miles for the 8 hours I've been biking.

And I am still in my town, which is only about 30 miles from one side to another. My route has been mostly a straight line.

I have traveled 60 miles. And I am not anywhere near the 'edge' of town.

In fact, if I have gone 60 miles, I should be at the cabin by now.

This is a bit hard to process.

I haven't noticed any repeating landmarks or intersections as I have traveled towards my cabin.

I look around. Everything looks normal. At least, the buildings and trees don't look compressed or stretched out. Letters on signs, such as the bus stop sign right next to the bench, are all normal sized.

There are no people or animals or birds, of course. I haven't seen any of those, except for Audrelle in the library, since the lights blinked. No dogs. No birds flying through the air. And, come to think of it, no flies or mosquitos. Not even any flies buzzing around the trash can next to the bus bench.

No crows or sparrows hopping around, looking for food scraps. No birds flying through the air. Well, except for those two sights of a raven – that then pixelated and disappeared.

And no sounds, except for that very low humming sound that I have heard since the lights blinked. I've gotten used to the sound, so don't hear it unless I think about sounds.

No cars going by on the street in front of me. In fact, all the vehicles I have seen are motionless; at least they seem to be.

And the sky is still strange. Those Mammatus-like clouds, looking like large yellow-gray bubble wrap stretching to all horizons. The ambient light is also a strange yellow-gray color, like what you would get with a smoky sky.

I take a deep breath through my nose. And then I notice that there is no odor in the air. You can usually smell something when you are outside. Sometimes it's the 'wetness' of the air during a rainstorm, or the more clean smell that you get after a rainstorm.

But I don't smell anything. Well, there is my body odor. I have been pedaling a bike for a while. But it's not as pronounced as you would think. I'm not a really smelly guy when I get some exercise, and I don't sweat a whole lot. But after biking since the lights blinked, yesterday and half of today, you would think that there would be a bit of body odor. And there isn't. Just a slight amount.

So, not only is there no air movement, or any living things of any size that I can see, or anything moving other than me, plus the weird light, and the low-pitched humming sound, there is basically no odor.

And the fact that I have pedaled my bike for about 60 miles, and am still inside my small town.

~ 21 ~

I finally got to the edge of town, and kept on the two-lane highway. The road had a nice paved shoulder, so I kept there. It was easier than having to go around the occasional vehicle that was stopped in the middle of the road.

As I passed the various cars and trucks, I looked inside. Nobody home, of course. I got to the point where I didn't look inside any of the cars as I passed them. Nobody would be in any of them.

Biking is a quiet activity now. In the normal world, you have to be aware of cars coming in both directions, and assume that the car drivers might not be paying close attention. So you learn to listen for the sound of an approaching car, and take a glance over your left shoulder to make sure they are giving you enough room.

When a big truck approached, you had to learn to anticipate and adjust for that wave of air that they push in front of them, and the draft of air that pushes at you when they pass. If you don't pay attention, you can get a bit wobbly and lose control.

Except now there was no sound of approaching cars from either direction. The only thing I had to worry about was the cars that were stuck in the road, not moving at all.

I kept a steady cadence on the road. According to the bike speedometer, my speed was about 8 mph. At least, that was the measurement it showed.

As I left town, the road had changed from the city streets (two lanes in each direction, with a center turn lane) to a two-lane road – one lane in each direction, with the occasional widening for the left turn lane. Still, the shoulder area was nice and wide, and I only had to look out for the occasional bit of trash on the road shoulder.

There was a bit of a breeze. Or at least air movement caused by my movement. I could see no indication of wind in the trees or grass on the side of the road.

As I passed the town limits, there were fewer houses and no commercial buildings. The countryside changed into actual countryside. There are open fields on both sides of the road as the valley area continued. The rolling fields were mostly planted in hay, or fenced for cattle grazing.

I had traveled this road many times. You would see small herds of cattle out in the fenced pastures, or a few horses, all of them just hanging around eating the grass. Some fields would have tractors doing their hay-harvesting thing.

There are a few streams in the area. You'd see some waterfowl – geese or ducks – paddling about in the streams. Sometimes you would see a couple of kids with fishing poles.

Today was different.

The road had several lazy turns in between straighter sections. It was at the side of a small long valley. The valley was small farms of hay fields and fenced pasture areas. The valley was about 5 miles wide, on average. On the other side of the valley, a small ridge of gently rolling hills. Some of the hilly areas were cleared pasture areas, because they were too steep for farming any type of crop. Simple barbed wire fencing delineated some of the pasture areas, but many areas were large open areas where no fencing was immediately visible. I suppose there could have been fences hidden in the trees.

On those hilly areas, there were some forested areas. Mostly tall trees like pines and whatever. The ground underneath the trees appeared to be covered with some bushes and large clumps of berry bushes. The area looked like a good area for various types of wildlife to live in.

The road I was in was mostly level, but followed the contours of similar hilly areas. One side of the road was open fields and farming areas and the other side was more forestry.

The forest next to the road had the same types of trees - various pines and other types. Some of the trees were quite dense, with sometimes dense underbrush. There were large areas of berry bushes that looked to be blackberry, although there wasn't much fruit on them.

In the forest underbrush were occasional cleared areas that looked like some small-scale logging had been done there. Some of the logging looked to be clear-cut, but not recently. There were still piles of 'slash' or debris from the logging activities. Most areas had recovered from the logging with the growth of large bushes and other underbrush, again with the areas of berry bushes that got there, I suppose, by berry-eating birds and animals.

The forest area looked like it would support a good wildlife population of deer; bobcats, foxes, squirrels, birds, and other animals would typically be in the forest.

The forest area continued back quite a ways, although it was hard to tell due to the darkness of the wooded area. It didn't look like there was much human habitat in there, although there was the occasional road that branched of and wandered into the forest area.

If you were to stop at the side of the road next to a forested area, you would probably see, after a while, some critters in the forest. Probably small birds, since they would be more likely to show themselves. I suspect if you waited long enough, you might see squirrels, or maybe a few deer. Other animals, like bobcat or fox or bear, would be less likely to make themselves visible near the road.

Over on the left side, in the farm and pasture area, you would see an occasional house with the usual outbuildings of barns or stables or smaller fenced in areas. The houses in general were back off of the road several hundred feet. The houses were generally small and single story, and generally older.

The outbuildings were typically a barn of various sizes, sometimes with a separate stall building, sometimes with small fenced paddocks next to the barn. A couple of places had a short outbuilding farther away from the main barn, surrounded by a mostly muddy small fenced field. Those looked to be areas for pigs, based on the muddy field with little to no standing grass.

Around many of the barns was a varied collection of old vehicles, some that looked like they hadn't moved for decades.

As I rode down the slightly curvy road, the basics of the farming areas on the left didn't change much. And the forested area on the right was mostly similar. All in all, the area looked like a fairly typical rural/farm valley with several residences. Outlying fields for small herds of cattle, or a few horses, or more flat areas that looked to have some sort of hay growing. On the other side of the valley, a mostly forested area, with slopes that looked to be too steep for crops or grazing areas.

Next to the road was a forested area too steep for rural use.

If you have ever spent any time wandering around a rural area, those areas would look similar to this area.

Except it wasn't.

Pastures and fields and fenced areas, small streams or irrigation ditches. All of it empty.

No living critters of any kind could be seen. No cows in the field. No horses slowly walking from one patch of grass to another, or standing next to each other swatting flies with their tails.

No dogs sitting on the front porch in the shade, or cats wandering around looking for a free rodent meal.

Nobody out riding a tractor, cultivating the fields, or mowing the hay. No birds flying from one spot to another. No blue jays or crows making their noises in the forest. No evidence of squirrels or any other critter.

No flies buzzing about or mosquitos next to a damp area, no bugs flying into me as I rode down the road.

No eagles or hawks in the air making lazy circles as they find the thermal drafts. No airplanes buzzing high in the air. No cars going down the road; any car that I saw was just sitting in place in the middle of the road as if someone had taken a picture of the road, freezing the cars and trucks in place. Nobody in the cars driving or riding.

No clouds drifting lazily through the air. No breeze rustling the leaves on the tree in the forest, or moving the weed by the side of the road.

No sounds of crickets buzzing, or frogs croaking in the small ponds. No kids fishing in the ponds. No fish jumping, making small concentric ripples in the water.

No shadows from tree branches overhanging the road.

There were only two sources of sound. One was me and the bike, the tires humming a bit on the road, the occasional clicking of the chain as I changed to a different gear on the bike.

The other was the low-frequency humming sound, slightly pulsating, and appearing to come from all directions.

The clouds in the sky, with their strange, bubble-wrap shapes, colored a yellow-gray, not moving in the sky, and covering the entire visible sky. No shades of color in the cloud, just one single color. No patches of blue sky.

The ambient light was diffuse. There were no shadows. Even on a cloudy day, you would see dim shadows.

But not now.

~ 22~

I kept on pedaling, taking the occasional drink from my water bottle, and an energy bar or piece of beef jerky. My watch said it was 5:42 pm. But my watch was on 'normal' time. It would soon be time to find a place to stay for the night.

Although I wasn't sure there would be a 'night'. All day long, the ambient light had been the same. No brighter or dimmer than when I got up this morning.

But I had been riding for quite a while, and need to rest somewhere.

As I rode down the road, I saw another house off to the left. It was similar to the others that I had seen since this morning. Looked like a good place to stop. I didn't want to camp in the forest – there was a sense of danger appearing to lurk inside even the small meadows in the forest on the right side of the road. I didn't sense that from the rural/farming areas on the left side of the road.

I slowed down the bike, and turned into the road to the house. There was a slight downhill slope on the paved road, with a few small potholes to avoid.

The paved part of the road ended, transitioning to a mostly dirt-packed area in front of the house and barn. The house was a typical ranch-style; single story, a simple front door, and one big window on the left that looked to be for the living room area. There were two bedroom-sized windows to the right of the front door, with a smaller frosted window between them.

The house was stucco; a faded brown color that looked like it hadn't been painted since the house was first built. The roof was asphalt shingles that looked to be in decent shape. There was a brick fireplace chimney on the left end of the house, on the living room side.

The house had a small lawn that had seen better days. It was mowed, but had more crabgrass than lawn. A small maple tree was in the middle of the lawn, and a flat stone walkway led up to the simple concrete steps at the front door.

There were a few children's bikes strewn on the lawn, along with a few miscellaneous toys.

To the left of the house was a medium-sized barn, red, of course, although the paint was somewhat faded. There was a big double door on the left front side of the barn, and a couple of dirt-streaked windows to the left of it. It looked like the other end of the barn on the right side had some horse stalls.

An old riding lawnmower was near the barn door. To the left of the barn was another patch of dirt. I saw an old truck there; from its appearance it hadn't moved from that spot for many years. Leaning up against it was a small dirt bike, caked with a bit of mud on the tires and fenders.

An old van that looked to be at least 15 years old was between the house and the barn. Although old, it appeared to be serviceable and used. The glass was streaked a bit with dirt, but overall looked like it had been in use lately.

Next to it was a newer truck. Well, newer than the van; the truck looked to be 5 years old. You could tell it was the work truck for the family. An old white toolbox spanned the width of the truck bed. The back bumper was that stamped steel type, with a bit of rust color, but not enough rust to damage the steel. A ball hitch on the back looked like it had been well-used over the years.

I stopped in the driveway area in front of the house, and called out "Hello? Anyone home?"

I didn't expect an answer, since I hadn't seen anyone or anything since the lights blinked. Well, except for the visitor in the library the first night.

And the raven.

You would expect to see a couple of dogs running up to investigate a visitor. Or at least the barking of a couple of dogs in a dog pen. You'd also expect to see a few chickens scratching in the dirt of the driveway, or in the cleared area in front of the barn.

There was no answer to my call. No dogs running up to guard their territory. No parting of the window curtains to see who was outside. No kids barging through the front door to greet a visitor.

I yelled out again towards the house, and still no answer or any movement. I turned towards the barn and yelled again.

Nothing.

I got off the bike, and wheeled it to the front door. I rang the doorbell several times, but no answer, even when I knocked.

I walked the bike over to the barn, to the partially opened double doors, again yelling out "Hello? Anyone around?" and not getting any response. I looked around in all directions for any movement and saw none.

I put down the kickstand of the bike, made sure it wouldn't fall over with any shifting weight of the pack on the back rack.

Although I didn't feel any direct threat, I arranged the gun holster on my belt so it would be easily accessible. I didn't draw the gun, but kept my right hand near it. There wasn't any specific threat to my safety that I could sense, just the general unease of getting to a house that was obviously someone's home, but not seeing anyone or anything around.

Keeping my right hand near the gun holster, I walked slowly towards the barn door. I kept my eye focus in a general area, watching for any movement in my peripheral vision.

After about ten slow steps, I reached the barn door. I grabbed the right-side door by the handle and slowly opened it wider, still yelling out my "Hello – Is anyone home?" and getting no response.

The door creaked open on rusty hinges. A normal sound, but a bit spooky in my current circumstance. I got the door open all the way, it moved slowly to the fully open position, slamming gently against the barn.

The inside floor of the barn appeared to be cement, although dusty. I could see tire and foot tracks in the dust on the floor. And a few paw prints from several dogs.

There was a bit of light inside the barn from the outside, so the inside wasn't totally dark. There were no shadows on the floor like you would expect. It was as if the outside light had diffused into the inside of the barn so that the light appeared to be coming from interior lights.

I got to the entrance of the barn, and looked inside, again with the "Hello" thing. Just like before, the only voice I heard was my own.

I looked to the left side inside the barn, and there appeared to be a workshop area. A workbench was cluttered with an assortment of tools on the bench, with more hanging from a pegboard over the workbench. On the wall around the workbench were shelves with various paint cans, and other boxes of various stuff.

The work area took up the left end of the barn. In the center, there was another double door to the outside; it was closed. To the right appeared to be three stalls, for horses, although (of course) there were no horses in there. Above the stalls was a hay loft area. A simple set of boards arranged into a ladder led up to the loft. I could see an opening on the back right side of the loft that looked like it would be used to get hay bales up there.

On the front wall next to the stalls to the right of the door I entered were some horse tack – some bridles and ropes, a shelf with brushes and stuff, and a sawhorse that had one well-used saddle. Over the saddle were a few dusty horse blankets. And there was the usual assortment of rakes and shovels and brooms hanging from or leaning against the wall.

It was a typical barn, at least as far as I knew. Except for the part about the only living creature in it being me.

After looking around in the barn, all the while trying the "Hello – Is anyone home?" thing, I went back outside to my bike.

I walked my bike between the house and the barn towards the back yard area. I didn't want to leave my bike – and all my supplies – unattended, even though there didn't appear to be anyone around.

The back yard was not fenced, other than the fence to the pasture area and the fenced area around the stalls of the barn. There was a trampoline there, and a big old oak tree. There was an old tire swing hanging from a branch of the tree, with a scuffed area in the dirt underneath the swing.

There was the usual 'kid clutter' of toys randomly scattered around on the somewhat weedy but mowed lawn. Over there was a Frisbee waiting for someone to grab and throw it.

At the back of the house was a back door. To the right of the back door was what looked like a kitchen window, and another larger window for the dining room. To the left of the back door were two more bedroom-type windows. A small cement stoop with a couple of steps was in front of the door.

To the side was a clothesline attached to metal post and T-bar, with four lines of rope going to the T-bar that was the other end of the clothesline. There were a few clothes on the line, not moving at all because there was no wind. The clothes were kid-sized, probably under 12 years old, and looked to be three different sizes. So I assumed that the family included three kids.

And the family also included three dogs, as there was a rough lean-to fastened to the house next to the back door, with three dog dishes for water and food. But no dogs anywhere in sight or in hearing.

Still doing the "Hello" thing, and getting no response, I walked up to the back door and knocked loudly. Several times. And no response.

The lower part of the door had a well-used medium sized doggie door. The upper part of the back door had a window, but no curtain. I cupped my hands and placed them on the window and looked inside. As I had surmised, there was a dining room to the right, and a kitchen area to the right of that. Towards the front of the house I could see the living room area, which was open to the kitchen/dining room area.

The dining room table had some dirty dishes from the last meal on it, as if the meal had been finished, but nobody had cleared off the table. There were three half-empty glasses of milk for the kids and two water glasses for the parents, which confirmed my guess of a family of five.

I knocked on the door several more times, still with no response. I figured that there might be a slim chance of something nefarious inside, and that I should investigate. I couldn't call 911 since my cell phone hadn't worked since the lights blinked, even though the phone had shown several signal bars on the display.

So I grabbed the door handle, and twisted it, and felt no resistance like the door was locked. Once again yelling out "Hello!" I opened the back door with my left hand, keeping my right hand near the gun in the holster attached to my belt.

The door opened with a bit of a creaking sound from the hinges, and a slight scraping sound from the bottom edge of the door on the floor.

Again, a "Hello?", again no response, so I entered the house. The first thing that I noticed was that even though the dishes appeared to have been left on the table for a while, there were no flies buzzing around the leftover food. You would think that a farm would have a few flies around, but not here.

I left the door open (for any needed quick escape), and walked into the dining room. I looked to the right to an empty kitchen past the dining room table.

I walked a few steps ahead into the family room, past the hallway that went to my left. The family room was empty. Well, there was furniture there, and kid clutter, and a large-screen TV on the wall next to the fireplace. The TV was dark, and the fireplace had only cold ashes.

I looked to the left down the hallway, all the time calling out "Hello?" and getting no response. There were three doors on the right side; I assumed for the bedroom, a bathroom, and another bedroom. On the left side of the hall were three doors; two for bedrooms, and one that I assumed was a hall closet, since the outside of the house only showed two windows on that side.

I slowly walked down the hallway, my right hand resting on the gun in its holster. Although there were no lights on in the house, there was an ambience of light coming from the outside through the un-curtained windows.

I got to the first set of doors, which were on opposite sides of the hall. Each looked to be a children's room: one bed, a dresser, a small closet, and a small clutter of toys and dirty clothes. Still no sounds or responses to my continual "Hello?".

I walked down the hall past the first two bedrooms, and looked in the bathroom on the right. Empty, except for a few towels on the floor.

A few more steps brought me to the last two doors at the end of the hall. The one on the right was another kid's bedroom. The one on the left was apparently the parent's room. It had a larger bed and larger dresser, and a larger closet. There didn't appear to be a bathroom off of the master bedroom.

And there didn't appear to be anyone home. Or anything home.

I turned and walked back down the hallway to the family room and dining room area. I went through the back door and pulled it shut behind me.

~ 24 ~

I had left my bike next to the picnic table in the back yard. I went over to the bike and got a bottle of water and an energy bar out of the backpack. I went over to the table, sat down, and opened the water and took a few swallows. I opened up the energy bar wrapper, and sat there, looking around, while I ate the energy bar interspersed with swallows of water.

It wasn't hot outside. There was no sun to heat things up. It wasn't windy. The temperature seemed to be about 65F.

This was all quite puzzling. Ever since the lights blinked, I am the only living creature that I can see anywhere. Time and distance seem to be a bit off of normal.

I looked at my watch, it was 6:32. Since it was early fall – or at least, it was the fall season before the lights blinked – the sky should be getting a bit darker as it got towards sunset. But I could sense no difference in the brightness (or lack thereof) of the sky. The clouds were still there, the light was still that yellow-gray color, and there was no movement of anything.

Even though it didn't seem to be getting darker like it normally would, I decided it might be a good idea to prepare for sleep. I looked at the house, and decided that sleeping inside there didn't seem right. But I also decided that an energy bar and some water was not enough of a meal.

I got up from the picnic table, grabbed the empty energy bar wrapper and water bottle, and went back to the house. Even though I had some food supplies that I had grabbed from the quick-stop store after leaving work, I thought that there might be some food inside the house that I could eat.

I went back to the house through the back that I had left open. One more "Hello?", although I knew there would be no response. I walked into the house and headed towards the kitchen.

I did a search of the cupboards, and found the usual collection of boxed and canned foods for various meals. I figured that any boxed food might be suspect, so looked on the shelf for some canned food. I found a couple of cans of chili, and some soup cans.

In another cupboard I found a small saucepan, so grabbed that and put two cans of chili and two cans of soup inside it. And two cans of canned peaches. I looked to make sure all the cans were not damaged; I didn't need a bout of botulism.

There was a medium-sized spoon in a silverware drawer next to the stove, so I grabbed that also. I figured some chili for dinner would taste good. I also found a clean kitchen towel in another drawer, so I grabbed that. And there were two bananas on a bowl on the counter, so grabbed those.

I turned on the burners of the stove – it was electric – but nothing happened. The burner elements didn't light up, or give off any heat. I turned the controls back to the off position.

Armed with my gourmet dinner ingredients, I walked back out the back door. I went to my bike, and balanced the pot with the cans inside and the bananas on top on the pack on the back of the bike, kicked up the kickstand, and headed for the barn. I figured that the barn area would be an acceptable place to spend the night.

I walked over to the open barn door, and wheeled my bike into the center of the barn, and leaned it up against one of the stall doors on the right. I grabbed the pot and one can of chili. I went back out the door to where I had seen an old charcoal grill. I dragged the grill to the front of the barn door. There was a pile of wood next to the house, so I grabbed some wood and sticks and brought them back to the grill.

I went into the barn to the workshop area, and poked around until I saw a small hand ax. I grabbed it and a handful of dry (and clean) hay and went out to the grill and built a small fire inside the grill. I used one of the lighters I got from the quick-stop store to start the fire, and got that going.

Then I used my multi-tool to open up one can of chili and spooned it into the saucepan and placed it on the grill over the fire. While that started cooking, a grabbed one of the cans of sliced peaches and opened it with the can opener on my multi-tool, and bent back the lid. I used the knife on the tool to grab a peach slice to eat. It was quite tasty.

There were a couple of old wooden crates in the barn, so I grabbed those for a simple table and chair. I sat down and ate my peaches, stirring the chili pot a couple of times. When I was done with the peaches, the chili was ready, so I took the pan off the fire and placed it on my wooden box table.

I let the chili cool down a bit, then ate that. Yes, I know that chili is the 'musical fruit', but I figured that it wouldn't bother anyone but me. Besides, I like chili. I prefer it with crackers and shredded cheese, but plain was OK too.

As I sat there eating, I kept a lookout. You could see a couple of miles, and in all that area, I didn't see any movement as I ate.

Dinner finished, I took the pan over to the outside water faucet I saw next to the back door, tossing the empty can of peaches in the trash can next to the back door. I did a quick rinse of the pan – the water still worked - and then brought it back to my dinner spot.

I grabbed my empty water bottles (there were two more empties in my pack) and went to the water faucet to fill them up. As I did, I again remembered those old westerns when the hapless cowboy used up the last water from his canteen, and then tossed the empty canteen away. A dramatic moment that emphasized that the cowboy had run out of water, but it always appeared stupid to me. I figured that an empty canteen – or water bottle – might come in useful later one, and didn't weigh that much to carry.

Taking my full water bottles back to my bike, I put all but one in the pack on the bike. The other I stuck in my back pocket.

I had decided to spend the night inside the barn. With the bike and backpacks inside the barn, I poked around for a good sleeping spot. I figured that a bed of hay would work OK. There wasn't any clean hay in the stalls (of course), but it looked like there was some up in the hay loft.

I slowly climbed up the hay loft ladder until my head was just below the hay loft floor. One more step, looking carefully all around for anyone or anything that might appear.

Suddenly, I heard a flutter of wings. Two ravens flew out of the hay and headed for the hay loft opening to outside. My heart racing, I watched the birds circle once inside the barn, then go outside through the open hay loft door.

As I watched them go outside, they suddenly pixelated. Just like you would see on TV when the picture freezes into disjointed pixels, which is what happened to the birds. There were two birds flying out the window, then a mess of disorganized pixels images where the birds were. Then nothing.

I stood there on the hay loft ladder trying to get my heart rate back to normal. The birds were inside the hay loft area, and I startled them (and they startled me). They flew out of the barn through the hay loft door.

And then pixelated and disappeared.

I climbed the rest of the way up into the loft and moved over to the stacked hay bales and sat down on one. I looked out of the hay loft door on the upper level. At least, that's what I call it. Not a farm boy, so don't know the technical term. But 'hay loft door' seems good enough.

Out the hay loft door I could see the nearby fields, and the forested hills in the distance. And the sky with the strange bubble-wrap yellow-gray clouds.

As I waited to get my heart rate back to normal, I thought on what I had seen. The birds were apparently alive – and present – inside the hay loft area. It was only when I startled them and they flew out the hay loft door that they pixelated and disappeared.

It was like they went into an invisible worm hole, or maybe a black hole. I was never into science fiction movies, although I did sometimes watch the old Star Trek reruns on the cable channels. The special effects of the transporter scenes came to mind. When the 'away team' was transported to another place, they used a shimmer effect to show the characters being 'transmitted' (OK, 'transported').

The birds' disappearing was sort of like that, but more of a pixilation like you see when your TV picture freezes for a second and then recovers. Only the birds didn't reappear, at least as far as I could tell.

I got up and walked over to the hay loft door and stood at the edge of it.

The view to the fields appeared normal. But as I studied the view, a longer look at the distance than I had done before, I could see a bit of fuzziness in the distance. It was like the distant forested area was not quite in focus.

Now I have good eyesight, close and distant. I had never had a problem with distance vision. I could see and read a highway sign in the distance before anyone else in a car.

I also don't have any color blindness. My last eye checkup showed I had 20/16 vision, so my vision is sharper than most. I can see distant objects clearer than most.

So when I looked at the forest area across the field, which is about 3 miles wide, I should be able to see the forest quite clearly. I can see individual trees, but not the detail of the leaves. That is my normal vision clarity.

From the hay loft door, the distant trees looked a bit fuzzy. I kept looking at the trees, and I started noticing an abnormality in the shapes of the trees. They edges were not as distinct as they would normally appear to me. They weren't fuzzy; the edges were more 'blocky'.

And then it occurred to me that the edges weren't 'blocky' as much as they appeared to be pixelated. Sort of like a digital picture when you zoom in past the optical part of the zoom to the digital part of the zoom, so you can see distinct edges, rather than more fuzzy edges.

I am probably not explaining this very well. But perhaps you get the idea. The forest, 3 miles away, didn't look like I expected it to look. I hadn't noticed that as I was biking along since the lights blinked.

I looked to another area down across the valley toward as forested area that was probably 10 miles away. As I concentrated on that spot, I started to notice it was a bit pixelated. It wasn't a definite pixilation, but it was noticeable as not looking normal.

I walked back to the hay bales, and used a hay hook that was on one of them to drag a hay bale to the edge near the ladder. After making sure that there wasn't anything in the way on the floor, I shoved the hay bale over the edge to the barn floor. I then shoved another hay bale over the edge, which bounced off of the first one to a spot next to it.

I went over to the ladder, and climbed down with the hay hook. Back on the barn floor, I used the hay hook to drag the bale over to the door of one of the stalls. I used the hay hook to twist around the hay bale string until it broke, and then repeated the process with the other two strings.

The bale flaked apart a bit, and I broke apart the hay bale flakes to make a bedding area. I used all of one bale and part of the second one until I had a reasonably soft area to sleep.

I grabbed two of the blankets off the shelf on the wall. They were fairly clean and didn't smell too much. I put one over the hay bed, and left the other one folded on top of it for now.

I looked around at my handiwork, and figured it was good enough as a sleeping area. It wasn't that cold; in fact, the temperature hadn't changed much ever since the lights blinked. So I wasn't worried about being too cold at night. Besides, I didn't think it was a really good idea to build a fire inside the barn, even if I did use the old BBQ I used for dinner.

As I looked at my sleeping area, I glanced over to the workbench area. Hanging from a nail on the wall was a pair of binoculars. Looking towards the forest with those might be interesting.

I walked over to the workbench and grabbed the binoculars. The lenses were a bit dusty, so I wiped them with the tail of my shirt. I then walked over to the barn doors and stood there.

I used the binoculars to scan all around. The field areas were empty; I could see no sign of any movement of anything.

I looked towards the forested area across the fields. I could see the trees a bit better. The trees weren't that thick, so I could see a bit deeper into the forest. The binoculars were 10x50, according to the numbers stamped on them. So I was getting a 10x magnification.

Through the binoculars, the trees in the forest looked normal. That was a bit puzzling. I looked towards the same area that seemed pixelated from the hay loft opening, and even through the binoculars the trees looked normal. I looked all along the line of trees of the forest, and as far as I could see, everything looked normal.

I pulled the binoculars away from my eyes, and looked around. No changes in anything that I could see. I looked towards the barn and the hay loft opening.

And then I thought I should look at the forest from the hay loft opening. I walked back into the barn, hung the binoculars around by neck with the neck strap, and climbed up the hay loft ladder.

I got to the hay loft and walked over to the hay loft opening. I stood where I stood before, and looked out at the forest. I could see the same slight pixilation of the trees. It was different from when I looked at the forest from the ground level.

I brought the binoculars up to my eyes and pointed them at the forest. I looked at the trees. A definite pixilation effect on the trees, more pronounced now that I was seeing them at the 10x magnification of the binoculars.

I made sure the lenses were clean, and that the focus was set properly. I looked again. Still the definite pixilation effect of the trees in the forest.

I estimated that distance to that part of the forest to be about 3 miles. I then looked towards the other area of the forest, the part that was about 10 miles away. And I could see a definite pixilation effect on the trees of that part of the forest.

~ 25~

I tracked from the 10-mile distant forest back to the 3-mile distant forest spot. As I moved from 10 to 3 miles, I saw less pixilation.

I then tracked from the 3-mile spot across the fields to almost in front of me. I did it very slowly, looking carefully at the edges of things, like fence posts, larger bushes, and isolated trees.

The closer I looked to where I was, the less pixilation I could see.

I took the binoculars away from my eyes, and stood there on the edge of the hay loft opening, trying to figure out what it all meant.

And I had no idea. It was all different than normal. And that difference sort of tracked with the differences in things since the lights blinked. Like the disconnect of normal time and distance. Or the lack of any other living thing anywhere, other than the birds that flew out of the hay loft.

Or the empty cars and trucks. And the empty stores. And the empty building where I worked – not even the security guards were there and they were normally there all the time.

Or the lack of any critter – dog, cat, insect, bird, squirrel, whatever.

And the environment – no breeze, no shadows, the weird cloud formation and colors, the strange ambient light.

All of that is not normal. So the pixilation is just another 'not normal'.

And I had no idea why.

The only idea I had was to get to my cabin. And it was getting late.

I stood there in the hay loft opening. I looked at my watch. It said 9:32 pm.

It had been about three hours since I at dinner. At least 3 hours of time as calculated by my watch. Although it didn't seem that long. Time is weird here too.

At that time of night, it should be fairly dark. And it wasn't. There was no appreciable change in the ambient light since I got here at the farm or even from before as I was biking out of town.

Either my watch was going goofy, or time was going goofy.

Probably both.

In any event, I was getting tired. Although I am in fair physical shape, all of that biking since this morning was taking a physical toll on my body. Not to mention the mental toll of all the strange things that have been – and still are – going on.

It was time to get some rest.

I looked out the hay loft door, and still didn't see any movement of anything anywhere. I put the binocular strap back around my neck and walked back to the ladder. I climbed down, and walked to the barn door. I looked at the house and saw no change. I did one more "Hello – anyone home?" yell, but without much enthusiasm or expecting any answer.

No answer, of course.

I decided to pull the barn doors shut for the night. Although I hadn't seen any critters (except the ravens in the loft) since the lights blinked, closing the doors seemed like a good idea.

I went back to the bike, and took the pack off of the bike and brought it over to my straw bed, placing it at one end to use as a sort of pillow. I grabbed my jacket out of the pack, along with the water bottle I had filled from the tap next to the house. I placed the jacket over the pack for a bit of padding as a pillow, and leaned back into my pillow, lying on top of the bottom blanket.

I took the other blanket and arranged it over my legs. I opened up the water bottle, took a few swallows, and put the cap back on, putting the bottle on the ground next to me.

I lay there for quite a while, trying to figure things out. Even though I was very tired, it was difficult to sleep.

Things were very puzzling.

I lay there in the barn, listening to the night noises. Of which there were none. Only the low humming sound I had heard since the lights blinked.

And it wasn't dark. There was this weird yellow-gray light that had been around since the lights blinked. And it seemed to be 'inside' the barn as well as outside.

The inside light wasn't like you would normally get. There seemed to be a light 'presence' that was inside the barn, not light that was coming from the outside.

The inside light didn't appear to be any stronger in one area of the barn or the other. It just seemed to be all around me, visible in every corner of the barn. There were no shadows coming from outside, like you would see on a clear night with a full moon. In fact, there were no shadows at all that I could see.

I burrowed into my makeshift hay bed, pulling the dusty blankets that I had found around me. The temperature inside the barn wasn't cold; in fact, the temperature hadn't seemed to change at all.

After lying on my hay bed for a while, I looked at my watch. It showed 10:35 pm. I turned over on my other side, rearranged the blanket, and closed my eyes again.

My eyes popped open again. Something had happened that woke me up.

I looked at my watch: 2:17 am. I must have slept for a bit, assuming my watch was accurately measuring time. At least, I could use my watch as an indication of time passing, although it didn't seem to be entirely accurate.

I lay still on my hay bed. The light was still in the barn, as well as outside. I could hear no sounds, other than my own breathing, and the usual humming sound. I'd tuned out the humming sounds, not noticing them anymore unless I remembered to notice them. Sort of like a background noise that you don't consciously hear, but the sound is always there.

I slowly moved the blanket off of me. I reached around for the gun in my holster, which I had placed next to the backpack I was using as a pillow.

You know that feeling you get when you sense someone is around but you can't see them? Or that something is 'out there', but it is hard to tell what that 'something' is?

Yeah. That.

I took the gun out of the holster with my right hand. I felt for the safety, it was still on. But I put my finger next to the safety, ready to turn off the safety if needed and take my index finger down to the trigger.

I used my left hand to push up to a sitting position. I looked all around the inside of the barn. The ambient light hadn't changed at all, even though, according to my watch, it was the middle of the night.

Can't see anything different. I turned my head in all directions, looking carefully at the barn interior. I looked up to the opening to the hay loft, and saw nothing different there.

But I still had the feeling of 'something' being there. If I was a dog, the hair would be standing up on the back of my neck.

Just like it would be on the dog that was over there by the barn door.

~ 26 ~

The dog just sat there by the barn door, looking at me. No sound, no growling, no panting. Just sitting back on its haunches, looking directly at me, taking it all in.

I've had some different dogs over the years. My first dog was a cocker spaniel when I was about 4 years old. As much as I can remember from that long ago, we were constant companions, although he was an outside dog.

I've had other dogs – a poodle, an Irish setter, a few mutts of indiscriminate origin. People outlast dogs, unfortunately. Currently, I was 'dog-less', at least, before the lights blinked.

The dog and I looked at each other for a couple of minutes, neither one of us moving. It looked to be a border collie, with a black and white mixed coat. It looked to be fairly well taken care of. Its coat looked as if it had been brushed regularly, although maybe a bit dirty; it was hard to tell in this light.

His (hers?) ears stood straight up and alert, with a bit of twitching as he/she (let's just say 'he' for now) apparently tried to pick up any sounds. His eyes were bright and alert, and his tail was still. His mouth was open just a bit, but he wasn't panting like he had run into the place.

Besides, I had closed the barn door. And it was still closed.

The dog's tail moved just a bit. Not a full wag, but sort of a preliminary and hesitant wag. Now that we had both had a minute or two looking at each other, it appeared that we both had decided the other one was not a threat. The dog thumped his tail on the barn concrete floor just once, then once more.

I realized I was still holding the gun, so I slowly un-tensed and moved the gun back to the holster. I was still sitting up on the floor.

The dog seemed to notice that I was less of a threat (if I was a threat at all) now that the gun had been put away. The dog turned his head to the side just a bit, as if questioning things. His tail thumped twice more, with a little bit more energy.

"Hey, boy! What are you doing here?" I said softly. I tried to remove any tension from my voice.

The dog turned his head the other way, as if trying to understand how he got there. I was thinking the same thing.

"How did you get here? Where are you from?" I asked.

The dog dropped his head a bit, and stood up slowly. His tail started wagging, just a small wag, but a more friendly wag. His ears drooped down a bit like he was letting down his guard.

I slowly pulled my legs up and got in a kneeling position. I outstretched my left hand to him, palm down. I think that's how you present your hand to a dog in a non-threatening manner.

The dog looked at me, tilting his head slightly, his ears twitched forward. After a moment, he got up from the sitting position he was in, tilted his head the other way, and then walked slowly over to me.

As he got closer, I didn't get any feeling of danger. Rather, it was a feeling that 'we were in this together', whatever 'this' is. Sort of compatriots, although that might be too strong a word since we just met. But the dog got close enough to sniff my hand. He gave my outstretched hand a couple of sniffs, then sat down like he was expecting something.

So far, so good. The dog didn't seem to be a threat, although I was still unsure how he got into the barn with the door closed.

I slowly moved my hand to his head, and gave his head a few scratches. "Hey, there" I said as I scratched. His tail thumped once, then twice.

Now, I am not any kind of 'dog whisperer'. It had been a while since I had my own dog. But it seemed that the dog had concluded that there was no danger here.

I slowly got up, and grabbed a water bottle out of my pack. I went over to the corner where I had placed the cooking pot. I poured some water into the pot, and set it on the ground next to the dog.

He looked at me, then went over to the water and lapped it up. He then looked up at me again, with a look that I suppose was a "Thank you". He slowly padded over to the hay bed that I had made.

He turned around twice (why do dogs always do that?) and then lay down with his head on his paws, still looking at me. His tail thumped three times, and he closed his eyes and appeared to quickly go to sleep.

I stood there, trying to take it all in. When I first got to the barn, I looked all around, and could see nothing else. Up in the loft, there were the two ravens that I startled, who flew away out the hay loft door, and flew up into the sky and pixelated into nothingness.

I had looked in all corners of the barn, and had found no other living thing. I had prepared by bed of hay, cooked and eaten dinner outside the barn. I had gone back into the barn after dinner, closing the barn doors. I had gone to sleep, and had been awoken by something.

Whatever it is that woke me up resulted in the dog appearing in front of the shut barn door.

And it appeared that I had a new friend.

~ 27 ~

I went back over to my hay bed, and sat down, leaning against my backpack. The dog was still sleeping, his eyes closed, and slowly breathing. I must have also slept for a while.

When I woke up, I looked at my watch. According to 'normal time', it was 5:45am. Time for the sun to come up. The third day after the lights blinked.

I looked out the windows. It didn't appear to be any lighter outside, or even inside. Not any darker, either. The inside light was still there, about at the same level as the outside light. No sunlight that I could see.

I sat there for a while, contemplating things. I shifted positions. The dog opened his eyes and raised his head, tilted it, and looked at me. He seemed to be asking "What now?"

I looked at him, shrugged my shoulders and said "I don't know. But it looks like I should resume my journey."

I got up from the bed and gathered things together. I put the gun holster back on my belt and grabbed the backpack and brought it over to the bike, strapping it on.

"It looks like we ought to find something to eat for breakfast." The dog seemed to agree, walking over to the barn door then looking back at me as if to say "Well, let's get going!"

"Yep. Let's go outside," I said.

I opened up the barn door carefully, swinging it out halfway. I looked around, and could see no difference. The house was over there, with the car still next to the house.

I looked all around. Nothing moving, no critters, no people, no insects, no birds, no breeze, no sound except for the humming sound.

The sky was still the same. The clouds with their yellow-gray bubble wrap appearance covered the entire sky. The ambient light was still the same level.

I stretched a bit. So did the dog. And I yelled out "Hello! Anyone home?" No response of course, although the dog looked at me when I yelled. No response from him, either.

The dog stayed close to my side as I walked towards the house. I went to the front door and knocked, not expecting an answer and getting none. I walked around the back of the house and knocked on the back door.

As I waited for any answer, not expecting one, the dog looked at me like I was wasting time.

"Time to find something to eat" I said to the dog. Since the family that used to live here – or used to be here – had a couple of dogs, as evidenced by the dog houses by the back porch, I figured that I might find something for both of us to eat inside.

I knocked once more, and then opened the door. Nothing had changed inside. The dishes were still on the table, but no flies buzzing around like you would expect to see.

"Let's see what we can find," I said to the dog – and myself. I went to the kitchen pantry and rummaged around on the shelf. The dog, with its more sensitive nose, immediately found a bag of dry dog food on the floor of the pantry, and nudged my leg.

I grabbed the bag and found a clean bowl on the counter and poured a bit into it and set it on the floor. The dog sniffed at it a bit, and looked up at me, as if asking permission to eat.

"Go ahead – it's all yours" I said. The dog nuzzled into the bowl of dry dog foot and started eating. I found another empty bowl and used the kitchen sink faucet to put some water in it, and set the water bowl next to the dog.

"Now that you are eating, I guess that I'll see what I can find." I poked around in the panty, and found some canned fruit. I also grabbed a couple of cans of chicken noodle soup, and a couple of cans of spam for later. There were some granola bars, and some unopened bags of beef jerky, so I added those to my collection. And I grabbed a clean fork out of a drawer.

There was a fabric bag in the pantry, the kind that you use for groceries, so I put the cans in it. The dog had finished the dry dog food, and some water, and he looked at me with an "OK, I've eaten. What now?"

"OK. We'll head outside." I turned away from the pantry, and then turned back to get a couple of rolls of TP. I figured they would come in useful at some point.

I grabbed the bag of food, and we both walked to the back door and went outside. I closed the door behind us. We walked back over to the barn, where I sat on the old crate and opened up a can of peaches with my multi-tool, using the fork to eat them. I also opened one of the granola bars.

The dog sat down next to me, watching me eat, but not begging. Apparently he was full from his breakfast. I finished off one can of peaches and started on a second one, along with another granola bar.

While eating, I looked around. Nothing much to see, of course. I stopped eating for a minute, and went into the barn to get the binoculars. I came back outside, sat on the wooden crate, and grabbed another bite of peaches.

While chewing, I looked through the binoculars. I started with near things, looking at fields and fence posts, and some bushes. I went slow, looking closely at everything. I didn't find any critters or birds, nor was anything moving – not even a slight breeze. The air wasn't humid or oppressive, it was just still.

I took the binoculars away from my eyes while taking a bite of granola bar. While chewing, I started looking at things that were farther away.

As I looked towards the forested hills across the small valley, about 3 miles away, the trees looked similar to how they looked last evening. They were pixelated with large blocky squares of color. It was hard to guess the size of each pixel area, but I'd guess they were a couple of feet in size. Not exactly square, but there were definite hard edges.

I moved my view to the hills that were farther away, to the ones about 10 miles out. I could see the same pixilation of the trees, although it was harder to tell the pixel size. But you could definitely see the pixilation of the trees.

I moved the binoculars back to the closer forested area, the one that was about 3 miles across the valley. With my back to the wall of the barn, I braced myself so that any movement of the image in the binocular was minimized. Then I concentrated on one area of the ground below the trees.

It may have been just a trick of my eyes because I was concentrating on one spot, but I thought I could see some movement in there. The movement wasn't a specific shape, like you would see if a large animal like a deer was walking through the woods. It was more of a slow vibrating shape, with indistinct edges. But there was definite movement on the ground under the pixelating trees.

I took the binoculars away from my eyes, and looked at the ground under the trees. I think that I mentioned that my vision was a bit better than most, especially my distance vision.

Although not as clear as through the binoculars, I thought I could see that sort of throbbing movement in the trees. As I looked, I could see that the movement was not one small area, but all through the forested area.

And I noticed that the dog was looking off in the same direction, sitting very quietly, but I could sense the intensity in him.

I brought the binoculars back up to my eyes and focused on the same area. Now that I knew what I was looking for, I could definitely see the throbbing movement throughout the forested area across the valley.

"That is really strange," I remarked to myself. Apparently I spoke out loud, as the dog looked at me with a bit of questioning eyes.

"It looked to me that you are seeing the same thing over there," I said to the dog. Not expecting an answer, of course. And I didn't get one, of course. Unless you think that the dog looking at me with his head tilted to one side was an answer.

Whatever it was out there, it wasn't normal. The pixelating trees; the indistinct shapes that appeared to be moving in the trees across the valley – these are not things that seemed normal.

And me sitting on a wooden crate, leaning against a barn, on a property that appeared to be recently abandoned. That wasn't normal, either.

It was time to move on. I went back into the barn, and packed things into the backpack to put back on the bike. I decided to leave the blanket there, but I did take the binoculars. I'd return here when things got to normal and give them back to the owner of this place.

Assuming that things would get back to normal.

~ 28 ~

With the backpack on the bike, I wheeled the bike to the front of the house, the dog following me. I took another drink of water, and used the hose next to the front door to refill it so I could place it in the water bottle holder on the bike.

There was a dog's water dish by the front door, so I filled that with some fresh water. The dog took a drink from it, and then looked at me as starting walking the bike back up the driveway to the main road.

I got about halfway up the driveway when the dog started a slow trot towards me, catching up to me when I got to the top of the driveway.

"Well, take care of yourself," I said to the dog. I climbed on the bike, and started slowly biking towards my cabin destination.

I looked back, and the dog was following me, a few yards behind me as I pedaled. I wasn't going very fast, but the dog was keeping up quite nicely.

In fact, the dog looked like he was enjoying the exercise. I guess that border collies (his breed, as far as I could tell) don't mind a bit of exercise. And I didn't really mind having a bit of company along.

So we both kept on going down the road.

As we both – me and the dog – left the farm where we had met, I took a look at my watch. It read 8:22 am.

At that time of the morning, you'd expect a bit of sunshine. I hadn't seen the sun since the day the lights blinked. But the ambient light hadn't changed since I had dinner last night. It was like an Alaskan summer night without the sunlight. I've never been there, so I'm just guessing.

Anyway, the dog and I (I suppose that I should think about a name) were biking down the road. I've never been biking with a dog before, so wasn't sure what to expect.

But the dog was keeping up with me. I wasn't speeding, mind you, probably going about 5 mph at the most. There were a few cars on the road that I would slow down a bit so I could peek inside as I went past, but I never saw anybody – or anything – inside the cars.

The road itself was mostly flat, with some slight hills. On the hills, I would get off the bike to walk up the hill. No sense in over-exerting myself – or the dog.

The dog didn't appear to have any problem keeping up with me. When we were walking up the hill, I would notice that he would keep an eye out on his surroundings. He didn't stop anywhere to sniff around, but kept up with me whether I was walking or riding.

At the top of one hill that was a bit steeper than others, I decided to rest a bit. I wasn't that tired, but was a bit concerned that the dog was getting overworked. He didn't look like he was having any problem keeping up, though. But it was a good excuse to rest and figure out where I was.

There had been several small hills since we had left the farm this morning. I'd estimate that we had gained about a 1200 foot elevation since then.

The road was a bit wider here. There was a gravel road off to the left side of the road. Four mailboxes here, so four houses down the road. Next to the mailboxes, the road was a bit wider, and paved, to allow the mail vehicle to get out of the way of traffic while stopping to deliver the mail.

It looked like this was also a school bus stop. There was a bench made out of two short logs, and a long log. The logs had their bark removed, and you could tell that it had been there for a while; the surface was a bit smooth, and there were initials and stuff carved into the log. It was sort of like those rough benches you might find on a hiking trail rest stop.

Since we (the dog and I) had just walked up this hill, I walked the bike over to the log bench and put down the kick stand. I grabbed a water bottle and a package of beef jerky out of the backpack and sat down on the bench.

The dog had followed me over to the log bench, and started to get a bit interested when he picked up the scent of the beef jerky. I first opened up the water bottle, and poured a bit into my cupped hand and held it out to the dog.

"Here, boy! Want a little drink?"

The dog looked at me, again with his head cocked to one side, then moved next to me and sniffed my hand. I kept my hand still. The dog sniffed again, and then started lapping up the water. I poured a bit more in my hand for him to drink.

I then grabbed a couple of swallows for myself. Then I set the bottle down and opened the beef jerky package. It was the teriyaki one, not spicy, so I figured that it would be OK for the dog.

I grabbed one piece of jerky, tore it in half (which is not always very easy), and held out half to the dog.

"Here, do you want some of this?"

The dog again looked at me with his head cocked to one side. Then he sniffed at my hand, and gently removed the piece of beef jerky. A couple of chews, and he was done. Dogs don't chew their food very much.

"You want some more? Let me get a bit for myself first."

I took a bite of beef jerky, and then held out the rest of the piece to the dog. He didn't hesitate much this time, and again gently removed the piece from my hand.

While I was chewing on my piece (I don't chew and swallow as fast as a dog), I got the water bottle and poured some into my cupped hand, holding it out for the dog.

This time, he didn't hesitate, and drank up, and I added a bit more to my hand as he lapped it up.

"Well, what should we do now? Have you got any ideas what is happening? And how you managed to be here with me when there are apparently no other critters around?"

He looked at me, again with the head tilted sideways. He didn't respond. This is what I expected, since he hadn't talked to me before.

What he did do was to walk a couple of steps back towards the road, then stop and look back at me.

"You want to get going again? You aren't much for long rest stops, are you?"

He turned around to face me, and turned his head back to the road, then back to me.

"OK, if you insist. Let's figure out a plan. Although you appear to already have a plan.

"Let's continue heading for my cabin. I think that there are a few more hills ahead of us, and then we ought to be at the turnoff for my house. My place is back away from the road a bit, so we'll still have some traveling to do."

I looked around. On the other side of the road were more trees. The trees were widely spaced next to the road, but appeared to get more dense farther back. There didn't appear to be much light back deeper into the woods.

"Let's just look around here a bit to see what we can see."

The dog trotted back over to me while I reached into the backpack for the binoculars I had borrowed from the farm house. He must have figured we weren't leaving yet, because he circled twice and lay down facing me with his heads on his paws. Sort of like he was thinking "Well, go ahead and look. I'll just wait here while you do that."

I straddled the log bench so I could look back across the valley that was on the left side of the road. The valley was a bit wider here, maybe 8 miles, I guess. Mostly farm fields, either for pasture or crops.

The gravel road that we were next to went off towards the hills on the other side of the valley. It meandered a bit for the slope of the land, but was mostly in one direction. I could see two houses on either side of the road about halfway across the valley, and the road continued past those houses until it disappeared into the trees on the other side of the valley.

I started looking through the binoculars at the closer houses. They were a bit lower than my spot on the road, maybe 75 feet difference. Typical farms, as far as I could tell. Except I couldn't see any movement anywhere. No critters of any kind, no smoke from the chimney on the house. No dogs loitering on the front porch. Not even any chickens pecking at the dirt.

"Looks like nobody's home, boy," I said to the dog. He didn't move, just opened his eyes a bit and looked at me.

I moved the binoculars view farther along the road, towards the hills on the other side of the mountain, until the view got into the trees on the hill.

There it was. The same pixilation in the trees I saw from the loft of the barn. Something deeper in the forest also; those same slightly shifting dark shapes in the woods that I saw before. Sort of fog-like, but a bit more defined in the edges.

The more I looked into the tree area with the binoculars, the clearer that I could see the pixilation and the shifting dark shapes. They were much more pronounced than what I had seen in the hay loft.

I moved the binoculars away from my eyes, and then looked through them again. Still the pixilation and the dark shapes.

I moved the binocular view to the area of the road behind me. The valley was longer than it was wide, so I could see quite a ways back where I had been.

Off in the distant view through the binoculars, I could now see the same sort of pixilation. No dark shapes, but the same sort of pixilation that I saw in the woods across the valley. I hadn't noticed that before, although I hadn't really looked. And I didn't have the binoculars then.

But the pixilation was back there where I used to be.

I turned around on the log, facing the direction of where we were headed, and looked through the binoculars. All looked normal. Well, except for the lack of any other living thing.

I turned to my right, and looked across the road into the forested area. I couldn't see much through the forest, in fact, it was mostly black. No pixilation or dark shapes in there. This was probably a good thing.

So whatever was causing the pixilation was in back of me and to the left side across the valley.

This was probably a bad thing.

Time to get back on the road.

I stood up, and placed the binoculars back in the backpack on the bike rack. As I stood up, the dog stood up also, with one of those dog stretches that they do. Then he trotted over to the road, and looked back at me.

I walked the bike over to the road. We were at the top of a hill. It was a short downslope, but a bit steep, and the road made a turn to the right out of sight.

"Looks like a downhill ride, so I'll coast a bit. Might have to use the brakes to keep from going too fast. I'll try not to go to fast for you."

The dog looked at me. It almost looked like he understood, as he moved to the center of the road to give me room to get going.

I climbed on the bike, pointed it down the hill, and gave a few pushes on the pedal to get going. That was all that was needed, as I picked up speed going down the hill.

It was nice to feel the wind that was caused by my speed. Not that it had been hot; in fact, the temperature hadn't changed at all that I could tell since this morning. But the breeze, such as it was, was refreshing, since I hadn't felt any natural wind since the lights blinked.

I was nearing the bottom of the hill, using the brakes a bit, but still going faster than normal. There were no stopped cars on this part of the road, so I had a clear shot.

I turned around a bit to see where the dog was. He was behind me about 35 feet, running, but having no problem that I could see keeping up.

I turned back forward, and just then noticed the rock. It wasn't a very big rock, I think, but it was right in front of me. I started to turn away from it, but hit it dead on with the front wheel of the bike.

And that's the last thing I remembered.

~ 29~

Dark.

It was dark. There was no sound. I didn't even hear the humming sound that I had been hearing since the lights blinked.

I was laying on something hard. Well, almost hard. Mostly hard.

It was really dark.

Did I have my eyes open? I blinked a couple of times. I could feel the blinking – something you normally ignore, but when you pay attention, you can feel the slight movement of the muscles around your eyes moving when you blink.

I scrunched my eyelids closed. I can feel that.

I un-scrunched. Still dark.

This is not good.

I decided to 'inventory'.

Move fingers. Check

Move arm up, then down. I can feel the ground. Check.

Wiggle toes. Feels fine.

Move foot. Left foot good. Right foot good.

Lift leg and drop gently. Left leg, good. Right leg, Good.

Move head left and right. Good.

Inventory seems OK. Good.

Breathing. Good. (Real good.) Although I probably should have checked that first.

Closed my eyes then opened them. Still dark.

I appeared to be on my back, mostly. I moved my left hand to my left side, and felt around. Seems a bit dirty here. Maybe some gravel; small pieces.

No, no gravel. Grass? Clods of dirt with grass? Yeah, that's it.

Let's check out the right side. Right hand, down. Feel around. Grass. Dirt clods. A few hard things. Feels like small sticks.

Wait. Sore spot on my left shoulder. Move my right hand to the shoulder. Feel around.

Urk. Sticky spot here. Sort of moist. Sore there. Left arm moves around OK, but left shoulder stiff. Right arm moves around OK.

I took my right hand and held it on the sticky part of my shoulder.

Dark.

Still dark. Sounds. What are they? Something poking me. No, not poking. More of a prodding thing. Where? Right side. Hip? No, right thigh.

Opened eyes. Dark still. Left shoulder hurts. Something sticky there.

Quit poking me!

Poking stopped. Then started again. This time on my face. Something cold. Wet, maybe. On my face. Right cheek.

Sound. What is that sound. Not loud. But seems to be coming from the prodding. Cold.

Wait. Cold. Snuffling sound. Wet thing.

Ah. Dog.

I moved my right hand away from my left shoulder towards my face. Found something soft and fuzzy.

Yep. Dog.

Still dark. Eyes open, right? Right.

"OK, I'm awake. Stop licking me!"

I gently pushed the dog's head away from mine, but gave it a couple of scratches with my fingers.

"Yeah. OK."

Maybe sit up?

Hands back down to my side. Push down with hands. Lift body. Sitting position.

"Urf". My "urf", not the dog's. But I got into a sitting position. Moved my legs a bit. Stiff. But doesn't hurt to move legs. That's good.

Dark. Wait, not quite as dark as before.

I'll just sit here for a minute. Reached my right hand to my left shoulder. Still sore there. Something sticky, too. And wet.

Not quite as dark. Shapes? Some vertical ones over there. Dark shapes. Something lighter between them.

Getting a bit lighter.

Focus. Yeah, that's a good thing to try. Concentrate on one spot. Vertical shapes. A bit sharper.

Wait. They are trees. Tree trunks. Focusing more. Can see a bit more light.

Shape to my right. Not a tree. A critter. Wait. The dog. Of course.

I turned my head to the right.

Yep. The dog. I reached over towards him, and scratched him behind his ears.

I moved my legs again, still sitting. Legs in 'Indian' style. Or 'Native American' style. Or 'Indigenous People' style.

Whatever. Legs crossed. Still sitting.

Eyes working. Focus.

Yep, focusing. Can see shades of light and darkness.

Trees in front of me. To the sides also. Not right next to me, but around me. Dog to my right.

Focusing. Done. Vision. Appears to be normal.

This is good.

~ 30~

So I am sitting among some trees in the forest. Eyes seem to be working OK now. Looks like I am at the side of the road. There's a bit of a berm next to the road, only a foot or two high. Then the forested area next to it.

Not a thick forest, though. Which is good, I guess. Because I landed between the trees, not in a tree.

Wait. Left shoulder still hurts. Right hip, now that I think of it.

Shoulder first.

I turn my head and look at my left shoulder. Yep. Tore the shirt. A bit of 'road rash'. Some blood, but not flowing though. Looks like a surface scratch. Hurts a bit, though. Will need to clean that up.

Right hip sore. I look down, and see that my gun is still in the belt holster. Right where it is sore.

I feel around there. Nothing sticky, so no blood. Sore, though. Bruised, I guess when I landed.

Wait. Landed.

Bike.

I was riding the bike. Right. The rock. Must have hit the rock with the front wheel of the bike. Then crashed.

Where is the bike? I looked around. Over there. Next to the tree. Well, more 'into' the tree. Doesn't look right, though.

Time to stand up. I looked at the dog; he was still next to me. Sitting now. Waiting. For me, I guess.

I slowly maneuvered myself into a standing position. Some soreness. I put my weight on my left leg. Good. Weight on right leg. Also good. I flexed at the knees with a bit of a squat. A bit stiff. But good.

I walked the few steps over to the bike.

Not good.

It appeared that when I hit the rock, the bike and I headed to the side of the road, hit that small dirt berm, and crashed into the forest.

I landed on a soft spot. The bike didn't. The front wheel is bent, with a couple of broken spokes. The handlebars are a bit offset. Front of the bike is not good.

Wait. The backpack. Not on the bike.

I felt a bit of panic. The backpack contains food, water, and lots more. Gotta have the backpack.

I looked past the tree that the bike hit. Ah, there's the backpack. Must have come off the bike when the bike hit the tree.

The bike was totaled. No way was I going to be able to repair that front wheel, with the bent rim and broken spokes.

I went over and got the backpack from where it landed, and brought it back to my landing spot. I dug into the backpack, and got another bottle of water.

And the brown bag of the bandages and antiseptic and other stuff that I grabbed from the quick-stop store.

I sat down, with my back against the bike-eating tree. It was a pretty good sized tree.

Time for a bit of first aid. Hey, I was a Boy Scout. Get a clean rag, one of my T-shirts should do. I used the knife on my multi-tool to get a piece big enough to clean the road rash on my shoulder. I took off my shirt, and used a bit of the water on the cloth to dab against the road rash.

"Ow!"

The dog had sat down across from my feet, with his head on his paws. He looked up when I yelled, but didn't appear to be alarmed. He put his head back down on his paws and waited patiently.

A bit more water, and a bit of gentle scrubbing, and the road rash was cleaning up nicely. I grabbed the tube of antiseptic cream from my stash, wiped it into the road rash. That should help.

I took a clean piece of my T-shirt, and folded it into a bandage. I had a piece of gauze from the stash I got from the store. I covered the road rash with the gauze; it was just below my shoulder on my upper arm. Then I took the strip of t-shirt cloth and wrapped it around my arm. Not too tight, just tight enough to keep the bandage in place.

That will work for now.

I took another sip of water, and then offered some to the dog. He got up and slurped a bit, then sat back down again. Head on paws, as usual.

I put my shirt back on, carefully. Shoulder (arm?) was still a bit stiff, but nothing more than road rash. I could handle that.

OK. First aid work done. I gathered up the first aid stuff, put it back in the paper bag, and put it and the remains of my t-shirt into the backpack.

And I got a piece of beef jerky for me. And one for the dog.

I stood up again, chewing on the jerky. I looked at the bike. Yep, still unusable. But there were things on the bike that might come in useful.

I remembered watching one of those survival shows. You know, the one where the guy with only a camera and his multi-tool goes off somewhere for a week to survive on only the few things that he had with him.

On one of the shows, he had a bike. Broken, just like mine. But he figured that several bike parts would be useful for his survival in the wilderness.

I figured the same thing. So I got out my own multi-tool. I removed half of the spokes from the wheel, the spokes that weren't bent. I came up with about 20 of them.

Let's see. Rubber inner tube: useful. Brake cables: also useful. That rubber thing that sits between the inner tube and the wheel: useful. Bungee cords that held the backpack on the bike rack: useful.

More useful things: white reflectors on the front wheel; bike light. Probably useful. The metal bars that go from the bike rack to the bike frame for support of the rack. Useful. Wait. The rack: useful. The back inner tube: useful. Maybe some more bike spokes; they don't weigh much: useful. The handlebar tape stuff: maybe useful.

So I ended up with a bunch of bike spokes, two inner tubes, the rubber strip thing that goes over the ends of the spokes inside the rim, the bike rack, the bungee cords, the brake and gear cables, the handlebar tape, and the reflectors.

I tied all the spokes together with the rubber strip thing. I coiled up the cables. Then I fastened all of that to the bike rack with the other rubber strip thing, folding up the rack support legs so that everything was flat. All one neat package of useful stuff. Didn't weigh more than two pounds, I'd guess.

I stuffed the reflectors into the backpack. Then I used the bungee cords to attach the bike rack package to the backpack between the backpack frame and pack.

I lifted up everything. Not too bad, I've gone on hikes with heavier packs. Even with my sore shoulder, it should be OK.

I took one more drink of water, and another handful for the dog, who had been watching my efforts with one eye closed. Or maybe two. I put the half-full water bottle back in the pack, fastened everything up, put my multi-tool back into its pouch on my belt, and put on the backpack.

I shifted around a bit to get the backpack settled properly, adjusting the straps.

And I found a nice walking stick.

Ready to go.

~ 31 ~

With one last look at the damaged bike, I shifted my backpack to a comfortable position and headed back to the road. I went down the dirt berm, and saw the bike tire tracks that apparently launched the bike into the tree, and me onto the ground. And the stupid rock that I hit.

I was about to kick the rock to the side of the road, but caught myself. No sense breaking a toe over the silly thing. So I nudged it over to the side of the road.

Not that anyone would notice the rock in the middle of the road. There wasn't anyone around that I could see. Just me and the dog.

The dog had followed me back down to the road, and then walked ahead a bit before stopping and turning his head back to me.

"Yeah, I'm coming."

One foot in front of the other. A bit of stiffness in my right hip, but nothing that caused a limp.

I put the walking stick in my right hand. My left upper arm was still a bit tender, so I hooked my hand in the pack support strap. I didn't need the support of the walking stick, but thought it might come in useful for something.

We were about at the bottom of the hill, where the road curved to the right. As I approached the curve, I kept a good lookout to the front, ready to drop the walking stick and grab my gun if needed.

The forest was still on my right, but as I rounded the curve I saw that the road had a long straight stretch. And the hill on my right flattened out, with the trees thinning out and stopping.

After a few minutes, there was a clear area on both sides of me. The dog and I kept walking down the road; the dog a few steps in front of me. I could see that he was quite alert, moving his head from side to side as he watched the area around him.

I figured that was a good thing to do – keep alert all around me. I even checked in back of me at times.

The dog and I didn't see any threats. Well, the forest across the valley on the right was still there. But we were in a less-developed area. No houses up ahead that I could see. Nothing moving, either, except me and the dog.

I've been down this road before, of course, it is my regular commute-to-and-from-work route. So the surroundings were familiar. The road is straight for a bit, then makes a wide sweeping S-curve to the left as the road gets closer to the far side of the valley. Two miles after the S-curve is the turnoff for my cabin. The main road continues on for about 25 miles before it gets to the next town.

The turnoff for the cabin - that's the destination for me. And the dog, apparently.

The dog and I settle into an easy rhythm. I am keeping an eye out as we walk. Our pace is not fast, even though I would rather get to the cabin as soon as possible. But I don't want to over-exert, so we are walking at a pace of about 20 minutes to cover a mile. Let's see, that would be about 3 mph? That's a good average speed.

From where we are now to the cabin turnoff, is about 14 miles. So how long will it take to get to the cabin turnoff?

That brought to mind those old math problems in school. Never was very good at those, but this one seems a bit easier.

Just to hear the sound of my voice, I said "A man and his dog are walking at an average rate of 3 miles per hour. Their destination is 14 miles away. How long will it take them to get to their destination?"

At the sound of my voice, the dog looked back at me. He kept on walking, so I did too. He didn't answer me, though.

"So I guess I'll have to figure this one out myself. Ought to be pretty easy. Fourteen divided by three is a bit under 5. So the answer is about 5 hours. That will take into account a few rest stops and maybe a stop for lunch."

The dog ignored me.

"After we get to the turnoff to the cabin, the cabin is about 6 miles from the road. There are a few more hills in the way, which will probably slow us down a bit. So let's say that our speed drops to 2 mph."

Another word problem. "If a man and his dog are walking about 2 mph, and their destination is 6 miles away, how long will they walk before they get to their destination?"

"Well, this one is not that hard. Six divided by 2 is three. So three hours down the cabin road."

Nothing from the dog. Not even a short bark of encouragement. Although perhaps Mr. Justin, my high school math teacher, might be impressed. Or not.

"So, five hours to the turn off, and three hours from there to the cabin. That's eight hours. And it is about 10:30 now. So we should get to the cabin about 6:30 pm.

"That sound about right to you?" I asked the dog.

No answer.

"Well, it sounds about right to me."

The dog kept walking.

So did I.

~ 32~

We'd been walking for a while when we came to the river and the bridge.

"This looks like a good a place as any to take a lunch stop. What do you think?"

It appeared that the dog recognized the word "lunch". His ears perked up a bit at the sound of that word.

We got to the bridge. There was a little parking area next to the bridge, with a metal guard railing around the parking lot. A gap in the railing led to a trail down to the river.

The river wasn't that big. I suppose it is more like a large stream. The river meandered on either side of the bridge. The water level was lower than I remember, so there were a few exposed sandbars in the river.

We walked over to the guardrail, and I took off the backpack and leaned it up against the guardrail. I sat next to it on one of the supporting posts.

The dog went through the opening in the guard rail onto the short path to the river. Or stream. He went down the path slowly, stopping to sniff now and again. He must have found a good spot, because he paused a bit to lift his leg and leave his mark.

Finished with that important piece of business, the dog slowly walked down the slight incline to the river, looking around as he did so. Apparently, there were no threats, because he went to the river. A few steps in the river, which wasn't flowing very, fast at all, and he took a few laps of the water.

As I watched him, I realized I probably should do the same thing. Since there was nobody around – I hadn't seen anyone since the lights blinked – I got up and walked about 10 steps from the bridge, more to the side of the parking area. I looked around, found a good spot, and took care of my business.

Zipping up, I went back to the backpack, sat back down on the guardrail post, and grabbed a bottle of water out of the backpack. Unscrewing the cap, I drank about half of the bottle. Not all at once, but slowly.

Finishing the bottle, I decide it might be useful to fill up the empty ones. I had three of them now. I grabbed all three from the backpack, and then put on the backpack. I suppose I could leave it here while I go down to the river; it's not like there is anyone around that would take it. But the back of my mind tells me that it's probably best to keep the backpack near me at all times.

I head over to the break in the guardrail, and head down the path to the river. The dog is out of the water now, lying on the gravelly beach next to the water. His head perks up when he hears me coming down the path, but he doesn't get up.

"Resting while you can, eh?"

The dog just looked at me. Not a big conversationalist, I guess.

I got to the gravel next to the dog, and set down the backpack. I took off my shoes and socks, and rolled up my pant legs a bit. I took the bottles and went to the river a few steps.

It wasn't deep here, just a few inches above my ankles. The river was flowing, gently, so the water wasn't stagnant, it was clear as far as I can see. I took the cap off of one bottle and filled it up, then did the same with the other two empty bottles.

I stepped back onto the gravel sandbar – the 'beach' – and put the bottles down. Then I stepped back into the river and used my bandana – every hiker has a bandana, right? – to wash off some of the grime on my face and neck and hands.

While I was doing that, I noticed a little bit of movement in the river. That was a bit startling, as I hadn't seen anything moving except me and the dog, and the water of the stream as it went by.

Wait. "Stream" or "River"? Could be both. No matter. I'll just call it a river. Even though it is not much of one, the water seems to be clear.

Wait. Got sidetracked. The movement in the river.

I was standing in the river, mid-calf high, and saw a flash of movement. This was unusual, since the movement was going upstream, not downstream. Not a log or branch. Looked like a fish.

"Wait, there it is again!"

That seemed to wake up the dog. He stood up and looked at me.

"There's another one! What do you think about fish for lunch?"

The word 'lunch' seemed to resonate with the dog. His tail wagged a bit. He seemed to agree with me.

Now, how to catch a fish. Fishing pole? Nope, don't have one. Chase it into the shallow part of the river. Yeah, that will work. Not.

"Wait a minute. Spear-fishing! That ought to do it!"

The dog tilted his head to the side.

"Of course, I need a spear to do that."

And then I remembered why I had taken apart the bike. I saw it on that survivor-guy TV show. Bike spokes, stick, inner tube. Yeah, that's it.

Fish would be good for lunch. So I set about to build a fish spear.

I got out of the river back to my backpack. I grabbed my walking stick and got out my multi-tool and opened up the knife.

So here's how you build a fish spear out of bicycle wheel spokes. Take about eight of the bike spokes. Sharpen one end of each spoke a bit; I used the concrete of the bridge.

I took the walking stick and used the knife to split it down about four inches, in an 'x' shape. The stick was pretty green, so I didn't have to worry about it breaking of splitting in half.

I grabbed a small rock, and stuffed it in the 'x' of the stick to spread out the four parts of the stick a bit. Now to fasten the bike spokes to the stick.

I got the rubber bike tube protector thing – the rubber strip that goes around the inside of the rim to protect the tube from the spokes. I cut off about a third of it, and then used it to hold the bike spokes parallel to each of the split areas of the stick. I stretched the rubber a bit so that it would hold the spokes. And I made sure the non-sharp end of the spoke was past the split part of the walking stick, taking another third of the rubber strip to fasten the spokes.

So the spokes are fastened in two spots. Once at the split part of the stick, and once just above where the small rock spreads out the four stick parts. Hard to describe, but maybe you get the idea.

The idea is that the spokes are spread out a bit to increase my chances of stabbing a fish. They are sharp on the one end, and the stick is long enough that I can hold it with two hands while attempting to spear a fish.

"Looks pretty good, doesn't it? Almost like I know what I am doing! That time spent being a couch potato and watching those survivor shows might pay off!"

The dog had been watching me carefully while I made the fish spear. I put away the extra pieces and folded up my knife back into the case on my belt.

I was ready to go. Since I might have to wade out into the river a bit, I took off the gun and holster and put both in the backpack and closed it up.

"Ready? Let's go fishing!"

I waded out into the river a bit farther, just about to my knees. I got the spear ready, and started watching for fish.

I was pretty wet now. Lots of splashing around in the water – by me, not the dog. Lots of stabs into the water with the spear.

And lots of misses.

"This is not as easy as I thought."

By this time, the dog was back on shore, laying down, sleeping probably. He didn't respond to what I was doing, or saying.

"Well, I'll try for a bit more. It's only been 20 minutes."

A few more stabs into the water.

And I got one!

"Whoa! Look at that!"

I held up the fish, which was wriggling on the end of a couple of bike spoke spears. I walked back to shore carefully, making sure that I didn't drop the fish. I moved up onto the short about 10 feet to where the backpack was leaning against a big rock.

The dog's eyes opened, and he brought his head up a bit, and turned it sideways again. Like he was waiting for dinner to be served.

I took the fish off of the spears, and whacked its head on the rock, which stopped the wiggling. Looked like a rainbow trout, about 3 pounds, I guess. A nice, healthy looking fish. And a nice meal.

But not raw. Don't like sushi. Time to build a fire.

There was a small stand of trees just past the parking lot area. I put the fish on top of the rock and covered it with the rest of the t-shirt that I had used to bandage my arm after the bike crash.

"You leave that fish alone. We have to build a fire to cook it. So we need to gather some wood."

The dog looked at me, still lying down. It looks like I'll be doing all of the work.

I went over to the stand of trees. There was some dead wood from one of the trees that had blown down, from a windstorm, I guess. I broke off several of the branches and brought them back to the rock.

The dog was watching, but not moving. I went back to the stand of trees and got a bunch of smaller sticks and twigs.

Bringing it back to the rock on the beach, I used my hands to scoop out a small depression for the fire. I grabbed some smaller rocks from the beach and made a small fire ring. Then I built the fire: small sticks at the bottom, cross-hatched for air movement, and some larger sticks broken apart and placed next to the rock to add to the fire.

I cleaned out the fish, removing the head and tail, but leaving the skin on. I rinsed the insides with a bit of the water from the water bottle I filled from the river earlier.

I started the fire. You probably expected me to use a flint and steel, or rub two sticks together. I was a little better prepared than that.

I dug out one of the small lighters that I had gotten from the quick-stop store. Cheating perhaps, but effective.

I got a small fire going in the fire ring. The fire ring was next to the big rock, so I moved the fire to one side away from the rock. That left some room between the fire and the rock for a cooking area.

I put the cleaned fish back on the fishing spear carefully, making sure it wouldn't move around. I didn't have any foil or seasoning, so would have to rely on the natural taste of the fish.

Then I placed the fish between the fire and the rock, resting both ends of the spear on the rocks of the fire ring. The rock will reflect some of the heat from the fire, so I should get a more even cooking of the fish.

With the fish cooking, I went down to the river and rinsed off my hands, along with rinsing out the remains of my t-shirt.

I went back to the fire and rotated the fish so that the other side of the fish was near the fire. It wasn't a big fire, but it was big enough.

I've had rainbow trout before at the cabin, so I knew about how long it would take. Ten minutes ought to do it. So I sat down next to the fire and waited, rotating the fish a few times to get it evenly cooked.

By this time, the dog had perked up and trotted over to the fire. He sat down and watched the fish cook. It appeared that he expected to share the meal with me.

So we did. The fish was done. I put it up on the rock to cool a bit – I had rinsed off the area where I cleaned the fish.

I used my knife to open up the fish, skin-side down. I poked it a bit to make sure it was all cooked. I removed the bones carefully, putting them to the side. Then I cut a small piece and tried it out.

Tasty. Even without any seasonings.

The dog had moved over a bit into my line of sight. His tail wagging, he patiently waited for his bit. I cut off a piece for him, making sure it was free of any bones, and held it out in the palm of my hand. He carefully nosed into the fish, and then took it gently. A couple of chews and it was gone.

"OK. One for you, then one for me. Patience; I tend to chew my food a bit more than you."

So we ate the fish. All of it, except the skin and bones, of course.

"Good fish, right?"

The dog wagged his tail a few times. I guess he agreed.

"Well, we ought to get going."

I drank a bit of water, and then took my fish spear down to the water, along with the skin and bones. I tossed the skin and bones into the water, and they floated away. I rinsed off the fish spear, stabbing it into the gravelly dirt next to the stream a few times to get any leftover fish off of it.

With the spear well-rinsed, I went back to the rock. I held the bike spokes over the fire a few seconds for a final cleaning. I waited a minute for the bike spokes to cool, and then I took apart my spear. After all, the spear is also my walking stick, and it would be much easier to use without the bike spokes.

I kicked some dirt on the fire and made sure it was out. I put the bike spokes back into their spot on the bike rack, fastened everything together again. I took the flat rubber spoke cover thing and wrapped it around the spear parts of the stick (I had taken out the rock already). That made sort of a handle that I could use while walking.

I took the gun and holster out of the backpack and put it back on my belt. I got the backpack closed and secure, and hoisted it up and on, adjusting the straps for a good fit.

With everything cleaned up, water bottles filled, walking stick ready, it was time to go.

~ 33~

Time. It marches on. By the time we got back on the road, it was 1:50 pm according to my watch.

The ambient light was still the same level. You couldn't tell time by the position of the sun in the sky – those bubble-wrap clouds still covered all of the sky – nor could you tell by the brightness of the light. The light was still the same as yesterday. And last night, too.

As we crossed the bridge, I looked up and down the river. The only movement I saw was the water flowing in the river. No wind, no birds, no bugs, no critters – wild or tame – except me and the dog. I didn't see any fish now, either. That was weird.

And no sound, other than the soft padding of my shoes on the road, and the occasional tap of my walking stick on the road.

The rubber cover on the handle of the walking stick made it more pleasant to use, though, so that was a good idea.

This part of the road was curving gently to the left, nearer the forested hills on that side of the valley. It was more flat here, so the dog and I were able to keep a good pace.

We would walk for an hour, and then stopped on the side of the road for a short rest and water break. There were a few small streams crossing the road, and the dog took advantage of those for his water breaks. I'd just slow down a bit, and maybe stop, while he walked off the road to a stream for a short drink.

I kept to the right side of the road, mostly in the paved area right next to the road shoulder. The dog walked mostly on the shoulder, which was a mixture of dirt and small gravel, I guess it was easier on his paws. He didn't seem to mind the walking; I guess his paws were used to being outside.

And he had plenty of energy, but seemed to be smart enough not to use it all up running back and forth. Mostly, he just kept at the same walking speed at me, sometimes a little bit ahead of me, and sometimes a bit behind. But never too far ahead or behind me.

We walked most of the afternoon. After about 3 hours, we got to the road that turned off to my cabin.

I stopped at the turn off, which was off to the left. The road was a bit wider here, with a wider dirt shoulder area. The road to my cabin was a bit lower than the main road.

I turned down the road. The dog looked at me, tilting his head to one side.

"This is the road to my cabin," I said. "That's where I was headed. You are welcome to come along."

The dog tilted his head in the other direction.

"Well, I'm going to the cabin. Are you coming with me, or not?"

I headed down the gravel road. I looked back at the dog, and he looked at me. Then he looked down the road in both directions, and then back at me.

Decision made, he turned and walked down the gravel road with me.

"Glad to have you along," I said as I kept walking.

The road was gravel, wide enough for two cars to pass, and a decent shoulder. This area wasn't really good farmland, so the fields on either side had been barb-wire fenced for grazing. Nothing in the fields, of course.

The road was a bit above the level of the fields, so a small ditch ran along either side. The weeds in the ditch weren't very high.

The road was generally downhill, but just a slight grade. A bit short of a mile, there was a small bridge over a stream. The bridge was made out of concrete, with a short concrete wall on either side, and guard rails running up to the bridge on both sides of the bridge and road. On the other side of the bridge, the road went uphill, winding into the trees after about 2 miles. The cabin is about 3 miles through the forest after that, in a small cleared valley almost 5 miles square.

A small stream, much smaller than the river we went over before, flowed under the bridge. I took advantage of the two and a half foot concrete wall of the bridge to take a break. I shrugged off the backpack and leaned it against the bridge wall on the road. I stretched a bit, and then sat down on the wall, grabbing a bottle of water out of the backpack.

I also grabbed the beef jerky. The rainbow trout was good, but I needed some more protein because of all the walking. I tossed one piece of beef jerky to the dog, and took a bite of my piece.

The dog ate his piece, and then wandered around the bridge a bit. He found a useful bush, and then went down to the stream to get a drink.

The stream wasn't very wide or deep, there was not much water flowing, just a little bit. But the dog splashed around a bit, then came out, did that dog-shake-off-water thing, and came up to the bridge where I was sitting. He looked at me, then turned around twice and lay down, putting his head on his paws.

Waiting for me, I guess.

I took another drink of water, and then decided to use the binoculars again. I was a bit worried, as we were getting closer to the trees on that side of the valley.

The trees were about two miles away, as I remembered. So we were much closer to the trees than we had been before.

The road headed mostly to the tree area, then curved to the right to parallel the trees a short distance before heading into the forest.

I put the binoculars to my eyes and focused to where the road turned right. At that point, the forest was a couple hundred yards away from the road.

I looked into the trees. They weren't that thick, not much ground brush around the trees. Mostly just grass/weedy areas under the trees, with the trees getting a bit thicker deeper into forest.

And that was where I was looking. Into the forest. Where there was darkness.

And that dark, moving shapes. Sort of fog-like, but a bit more distinct.

I couldn't make out the composition of the fog-shape. The color was mostly dark shades of black and gray. There were some lighter areas, maybe yellow-gray in color, but a bit darker than that. Just not totally black.

Nothing that I had ever seen before.

There was no sound coming from the forest area that I could hear, but I was 2-3 miles away. There was still that low-frequency humming sound that I had been hearing – and not paying attention to – since the lights blinked. Most of the time I wasn't aware of that sound, unless I remembered it was around. I had sort of tuned it out.

Now that I was listening to it, the sound seemed a bit louder. Not much, but discernable.

I looked down at the dog. His eyes were closed. I guess the sound wasn't bothering him. Although I knew dogs had good hearing; better than humans. So I didn't understand why the sound was not bothering him. Maybe he had tuned it out like I had.

I put the binocular back up to my eyes. I turned on the bridge a bit, straddling the short bridge wall, so I could focus on the road to the cabin.

I slowly moved the binoculars up the road, looking for any movement. When I looked into the forest that the road paralleled, the dark, slowly moving indistinct shapes were still visible. But the shapes did not seem to come out of the forest towards the road.

The road was clear of any vehicles. That was not uncommon, it wasn't a well-traveled area. Even though the road was two cars wide, I hardly ever saw another car when I would go back and forth to work during normal times.

Of course, I didn't expect any cars to be moving anyway, now that this is not the 'normal times'.

I used the binoculars to follow the road where it paralleled the edge of the forest, then along the road until it disappeared into the forest. Other than those indistinct shapes moving in the forest, there was no other movement of man or beast that I could see. No wind; the air was as still as it has been since the lights blinked.

Whatever was out there in the forest, it was between me and my cabin.

I had gone this far since the lights blinked to get to my cabin. Although it had only been a three days, I was anxious to get to my destination.

Well, perhaps a bit more than anxious.

There was a little bit of uncertainty in what I would find when I got to the cabin.

Not to mention those shapes in the forest. Which were between me and my cabin.

I put the binoculars into my backpack. I grabbed an energy bar for me, and a piece of jerky for the dog.

The dog quickly finished his jerky, and then went down to the creek for a short drink. I took a couple of swallows of water from my water bottle, and put it back into the backpack.

I got up, stretched a bit, and put on the backpack. I grabbed the walking stick. The dog followed me.

We walked across the rest of the bridge, then up the slight incline of the road to where it turned and paralleled the forest.

It took about 45 minutes to get to the spot where the road turned to the right to parallel the forest. As we walked through the road's gentle turn to the right, I noticed a bit of difference in the dog.

He stopped for a bit, turned to the forest, his ears pointed towards the forest. He raised his nose a bit, sniffing the air. Since he stopped, I stopped too.

I transferred the walking stick to my left hand, and unfastened the gun holster with my right hand. I rested my hand on the gun, leaving it in the holster, but ready to use it if needed. And I made sure the safety was off, with my finger outside of the trigger guard.

The dog looked at me, then back at the forest. I looked there too.

There were still indistinct dark shapes moving in the forest. Getting closer to them did not make whatever they were clearer; the forms were still undefined and unfocused.

If you watched a particular shape as it moved, it sometimes seemed that the darkness was pixelating just a bit. That wasn't very evident, but more of a sense of pixelating. I tried to focus on a pixelated spot, but the spot would fade back into an unfocused blackness.

The dog looked back into the forest, but apparently did not see any immediate threat. He looked back at me and then ahead, taking a few steps forward. He looked back at me, in a 'Well, are we going or not?' look.

Still keeping my right hand on the gun in the holster, I took another look into the forest.

"Well, if you don't see anything there that looks threatening, I guess we'll be going."

The dog kept looking at me. I started walking forwards again, and after a few steps the dog turned his head back forward and started walking next to me.

We both kept walking. This part of the road parallels the edge of the forest on the left for about two miles. So we kept on walking.

The road had a slight uphill slope, so we walked for another 45 minutes. Both of us – me and the dog – kept glancing into the forest on the left. Both of us seemed to agree that there was no immediate threat in the forest.

But that didn't keep me from staying alert, with my right hand near the gun in the holster.

We got to the bend in the road where it went into the forest. The road was still two lanes, with a nice wide gravel shoulder sloping down a bit to a ditch on either side. On the other side of the ditch, which was dry, but obviously for rain runoff, there was a slight slope of about five feet high and maybe 20-30 yards wide. So the trees were not right next to the road. But it was a forest on both sides.

The dog and I had both stopped on the road just before it turned into the forested area. The dog had his ears parked forward, but with a bit of twitching to the sides. He had tilted his head a bit, like he was trying to concentrate on what was ahead.

I was also concentrating, with my head on a slow swivel. It was still mostly quiet, although that low humming sound was continuous; I had mostly tuned that out. The sound popped into my consciousness off and on as we had been walking.

Now, it appeared to be louder. No, not louder, but a bit more intense at the same volume as before. It was almost a sound that you could feel, but not quite feel. Hard to describe, but it was definitely different than before.

Although the dog wasn't talking to me, I could sense that he could also hear the difference in the sound. His ears were twitching a bit more, I guess trying to figure out the source of the sound. To me, the sound appeared to be coming from all directions, without coming from any specific direction.

As we both looked up the road to the front of us, I could see what appeared to be floating dark pixels. It was almost like you would see if you got a very small spot on your glasses. I didn't wear glasses, though. Maybe it was more like those 'floatie' things you see in your vision sometimes. But it wasn't inside my eye, like floaties would be, but off in the distance.

There were still the dark indistinct shapes in the forest on either side. They didn't focus into anything specific, just indistinct shapes. They didn't appear to be any closer than before, but were just 'in' the forest.

The shapes, now that I think about it, were more like small puffs of dark clouds. Denser than fog, though. They were the little puffs of cloud moisture that might be just about five hundred feet above you; lower than the rain clouds that might be at 5 to 10 thousand feet.

Now that they were a bit closer – but not physically closer- they looked like large fuzzy bubbles. The clouds in the sky were still had that bubble-wrap look. So maybe the dark shapes were 'bubbles' that had detached from the clouds, or at least were similar to the clouds. They weren't round; they didn't have a regular shape to them. But they were definitely moving around in the forest in irregular patterns.

The road was patiently waiting for us to continue our travels. I took a small sip from a water bottle.

"Well, we're not getting any closer to the cabin just standing here. We might as well get going."

The dog looked at me as I spoke. He didn't answer, of course. He just turned his head forward, and looked ready to go.

With my left hand on my walking stick, and my right still resting on the butt of the gun in my holster, I started walking. As did the dog.

~ 34~

We continued up the road through the trees. The road was mostly straight, with a slight uphill climb.

Off in the distance, I could still see the black pixel-like specks. They would randomly appear for a very short time, no more than a second. Then that pixel spot would fade out, and another one would appear in a different spot, and a different distance away.

We had been walking about ten minutes, watching the pixels blink in and out of view. And I was noticing that there seemed to be a bit more of the pixels in view. Not a lot, but noticeable if you compared it to what there had been when we started into the road.

Some more walking and the black pixels seemed to be more prevalent. Before, you might see one every 10 or 15 seconds. Now they seemed to appear every 5 seconds.

Along with the pixels appearing, the low humming sound, the same sound I had been hearing since the light blinked, seemed to be getting more intense. Not a lot, but noticeable. The volume of the sound was the same; it was just that the sound had more 'presence' to it. And that had been slowly increasing ever since we started on the part of the road through the forest.

We kept on walking. My head was on a slow swivel, mostly watching ahead, but also watching into the forest on either side. The dog was doing the same thing with his head. But also with his ears, which would also swivel in all directions.

Another few minutes, with a slight increase in the number of black pixels ahead of me, along with the slight increase in the intensity of the humming sound. The shapes in the forest seemed to be a bit more distinct, although still fuzzy.

While I was walking, looking mostly ahead, and to both sides, I glanced in back of me.

And I wasn't sure, but I thought I had seen some pixels in back of me.

I stopped. The dog took a few steps then stopped and looked back at me.

I slowly turned around; facing the direction we had come from.

Off in the distance were randomly appearing – and disappearing – black pixels.

I looked to the front – towards our destination – and there were also randomly appearing and disappearing black pixels.

The ones in the back – where we came from – didn't seem as numerous. So there were more pixels in front of me than in back of me.

Then I looked to the sides. On both sides, into the forest, I saw the black indistinct shapes, like small hunks of fog or clouds. Some of them had bubble-like shapes, like the clouds above I had seen since the lights blinked.

The shapes in the forest – on either side of the road – were a bit spooky, but they didn't seem to be getting any closer (or farther) away. They always seemed about the same distance back into the darkness of the forest.

The pixels in front of me – and in back of me – were spookier. There were more in front than in back.

I looked at the dog. He was doing almost the same thing as me. Looking in front – towards our destination – and then turning around and looking in back – from where we had come.

His ears were swiveling, like he was trying to sense or listen to what was going on. The only sound I heard was that low humming sound, but, on thinking about it, it was even more intense than before. Not overpowering-intense, but noticeably more intense than before.

"What's going on?" I asked the dog.

He glanced over at me as I spoke, and then continued to look back and forth.

"I got no idea, either." I replied to myself. The dog was still not answering me.

"You're a lot of help," I muttered.

The dog just looked back at me, twitched his ears, and then kept looking around.

"Well, let's get going, I guess. Not much else we can do; can't stay here."

I kept my left hand on my walking stick and my right hand on the gun in my holster. Although I am not sure how the gun would help in this situation.

Guess it couldn't hurt to have it ready.

We kept on walking on the road through the forest. I kept an eye on all points, including my 'six'. Not much change in what was happening.

After about 5 minutes of walking, I stopped. So did the dog. There appeared to be more black pixels in front of me. Not a solid wall, but I could tell there were more than before.

I turned my head to the back. More pixels there, but not as many as in front of me.

"Nothing to do but to keep going," I said.

The dog seemed to agree, as he started walking when I did. I did notice that he was staying close to me as we walked.

The road curved a bit through the forest. As we walked up the road, the number of black pixels appearing ahead of us increased. They would remain visible only for a second or two, and then disappear. They would never appear in the same spot, but randomly throughout my entire field of vision.

But they continued to appear in front of us. In back of us, they also seemed to become more numerous. Again, visible for only very short periods, but visible nonetheless.

The sides of the road had a slight rise in the ground level, with a clear spot of 10-15 yards before the forest started. The trees were sparse at the edges, with a few low bushes of some sort. The trees got thicker deeper into the woods, until there was blackness because of the number of trees and bushes.

And within that blackness of the dense part of the forest, there were those moving shapes. Not getting any closer, not getting farther or deeper into the forest, but always about the same distance into the forest.

As we walked, I kept looking all about. The dog was walking right next to me; he was not straying far from my side. His ears were swiveling, trying to catch any sound or perhaps threat.

Into the forest, the dark shapes were still moving. I could also see a few of the dark pixels appearing in the woods. And the pixels appearing all around me now. Not next to me; they appeared to be some distance away, although I couldn't tell how far they were. They would appear then disappear so rapidly that I couldn't figure out how far away they were.

It was like walking into a fog bank, but not as 'fuzzy'. The pixels were distinct objects, rather than the fuzziness of a fog.

The pixels got to a point where they almost appeared as snowflakes during a snow storm. It was not like walking through a snowstorm, since the black pixels would only be visible for a short second or two. But it had that effect; we were walking through a black pixel snowstorm.

The surface of the road, or the gravel on the road's shoulder, or the dirt and weeds and grass on the side of the road, didn't seem to be affected by any of the dark pixels. The pixels were just in the air, not in the surface of any object – natural or man-made – around us.

The pixel 'snow storm' continued around us as we walked. They never got dense enough that they were continuous. But I could tell that there were more, and they were becoming denser around all sides of us.

I could see a normal distance ahead. The road had very slight curves, but the pixels were not a full blockage of the view. I could see ahead of the pixels, and had a sense that they were a three dimensional object of minimal thickness, rather than a total blockage of everything in back of the pixel. It was not like a black spot on a picture; they seemed to be more floating in front of a picture.

This all continued for many minutes as we walked along the road. It was hard to tell where we were. I had driven this road many times as I went to the cabin, but I didn't have a good sense of where I was in relation to our destination.

The area around us was vaguely familiar, but it wasn't quite the same as I recalled. Of course, when you are driving, your view of your surroundings is much different than if you were to walk the same route. But I could sense a 'dissimilarity' in the surroundings, and it was not just because of the black 'pixel snow'.

We continued walking, the dog and me. Down the road, through the forest, and through the pixel snowstorm. Listening to the deep humming sound that had always been present since the lights blinked, but with the sound being more intense but not louder. The ambient light had not changed; it was still that yellow-gray light visible since the blink.

This continued for about 30 minutes of walking. I had lost most of the sense of where I was in relation to what I would see during a drive 'pre-blink'. The road continued its gentle curves through the forest.

The trees started to grow closer to the edge of the road, until they were right next to the narrowing gravel shoulder of the road. The trees were tall and growing closer together.

Even though it was a two-lane road, the trees were close enough to the road and tall enough that the branches closed off the view of the sky directly above the road.

It started getting darker because of the canopy of trees over the road, although not as dark as it normally would be. There was still the yellow-gray ambient light all around, even though the tree canopy should have blocked any light from the sun.

The dark pixel snowstorm continued to the point where it was like walking through a heavy snowstorm. The dark pixels never seemed to be right next to us. It was like there was an area around us that wasn't affected by the dark pixels.

Sort of like a cone of light if you were standing under a street lamp. As we walked through the dark pixel snowstorm, there was an absence of dark pixel 'snowflakes' directly around us, like that light from a street lamp.

The dog got closer to me as I walked. Well, we both slowed down a bit, watching the dark pixel snowstorm get thicker.

And really thick.

Dark.

Again.

Really dark.

Can't see my hand in front of my face.

The dog was pressed against my legs. We had stopped when the black pixel snowstorm intensified to near totality.

Then it got dark. Really dark.

The humming sound increased in intensity, but not in volume. You could feel the sound.

It was like standing in front of a massive bass speaker during a rock concert. But not loud. Only intense.

As the black pixel storm increased around me, I dropped to my knees. The dog got even closer, if that was possible.

I sat back on my feet, took off the backpack, and rummaged around for the flashlight, finding it in one of the side pockets where I had left it.

I pointed the flashlight forward. Pressed the button to turn it on.

Still dark.

No light from the flashlight.

I rummaged in the backpack for one of the small lighters. I flicked it, not even a spark. I could feel the thumb wheel thing striking against the flint.

No spark, no matter how many times I tried.

"This is not good," I told the dog. He whimpered and shook a bit as he leaned even closer to me.

Dark.

Really dark.

Have you ever been in a cave and turned out the lights? Or in a very dark room, maybe a closet, with no lights?

I've been in the Carlsbad Caverns, those caves in New Mexico. And the guide turns out the lights. And it gets really dark.

It was darker than that.

Much darker than that. You could almost *feel* the dark.

There was no light anywhere.

The sound intensified a bit. It didn't get louder; it was just more intense. More intense than any rock concert I had experienced.

Dark.

Intense sound.

No light from the flashlight or lighter.

I am not sure how long the dark lasted. I couldn't even see the watch on my wrist. And the watch's light didn't work anyway.

It seemed like a really long time.

The dog and I just sat there.

Waited.

Waited some more.

I don't know if my eyes were getting their night vision, but I still couldn't see anything.

Eyes wide open. Ears hearing the intense but not loud humming sound. And a bit of whimpering.

From the dog, too.

And it was still dark.

And then my night vision could see a bit of 'less dark'. It was not very distinct, just a very gradual lightening. Sort of when you think you can see something, but not really.

So we waited. Nothing else to do.

I still don't know how long the dark lasted. Maybe a minute. Maybe 15 minutes. Maybe an hour.

I had no sense of the amount of time that passed.

But it was getting lighter. No, not lighter. Less dark. Not much 'less dark', but almost perceptible.

So we waited. How long we waited, I don't know.

But it got lighter. No, not lighter, but less dark. The dark pixels were being replaced by lighter pixels.

As time passed – how much time, I don't know – the lighter pixels were replaced by pixels that looked like normal surroundings.

It was like the dark pixel snowstorm was getting less intense. You could start to see things.

The dog and I were still in the middle of the road. I could tell by feeling the hard surface against my knees as I kneeled.

The humming sound was getting less intense. The volume of the sound had not changed throughout the whole time it was dark. But it was less intense.

Time passed. The dog and I waited.

The black pixel snowstorm decreased. The intensity of the sound decreased.

The shaking and whimpering decreased. Both me and the dog.

I could see that we were still in the road. More towards the side of the road than I remember being when the black pixel blizzard started.

I could see the edge of the road, the edge of the forest next to it. The trees close together. The branches overhead, almost touching each other from the sides of the road to create a forested canopy.

I could see the road continue in front of me.

I turned around. It was dark back there, the black pixel snowstorm apparently behind me.

I looked into the forest. I didn't see the shifting dark indistinct shapes in the forest.

I didn't know what to say. Neither did the dog, apparently.

I looked at the dog; he was looking back, a bit calmer than I was, apparently.

I realized I was still holding the lighter in my hand. I flicked it once, and the flame started. I let go of the little flame lever on the lighter, and the flame went out. I flicked it again, and it worked. I put out the flame and stuck the lighter back in my shirt pocket.

Then I noticed the flashlight on the ground in front of me. The lamp was on. I pressed the button, the light turned off. Click the button, light on. Click the button, light off. So it was now working.

Making sure it was off, I put it back in the backpack. And got a bottle of water. I took a few swallows, and then poured some in my cupped hand for the dog, who lapped it up.

I had no energy. It was hard to move. Although I was pretty sure that I was still breathing.

I got an energy bar out of the backpack, opened it, and gave half to the dog as I ate the other half. A few sips of water for me, some for the dog, and I felt a bit of energy returning.

The dog must have gotten his energy back, as he stood up from his sitting position. He did that dog stretch thing, and then looked back at me, waiting.

"OK. I guess we ought to get going," I told the dog.

Right. Let's go.

"Yeah, we should go," I said.

Um, wait. Who said that?

The dog looked at me. He cocked his head a bit, like he had done before when he was waiting for me to do something.

"We should go?" I asked the dog?

No answer. Not that I could hear. Or even sense.

Not sure what just happened. I thought I had heard someone say "Right. Let's go." It wasn't me.

And it wasn't something that I heard out loud. It was more something that I heard within me.

I looked around. Just me and the dog.

I looked at the dog. He was in front of me a few steps, still looking back at me. Waiting, I guess. Not saying anything.

My imagination, I guess.

One more sip of water, then everything went back into the backpack. I reached over to my walking stick, and used it to stand up. I grabbed the back pack, strapping it on, and doing that little 'backpack jiggle' to get everything situated right.

With my walking stick in my left hand, I started walking. Silently.

As did the dog.

Silently.

As I walked; slowly at first, I tried to get my bearings. We were still on the road, which kept on gently curving uphill as it wound through the forest.

"We should be getting closer to the valley and the cabin," I said.

The dog ignored me, and just kept on walking.

"Shouldn't be too far now," I said.

Humph.

"A bit of an attitude, eh, boy?" I said. More to myself than anyone else. Since there wasn't anyone else around here.

No response. From anyone. Including the dog.

But I had heard the "Humph".

We walked silently for about 15 minutes. The trees in the forest started thinning out a bit. The mostly clear area between the road and the trees got a bit wider.

We started around one more curve in the road, this one to the left.

And I noticed that the black pixel snowflakes had gone. Not sure when, I had sort of gotten used to them. But now that I was paying attention, they were gone.

I looked in back of me. No black pixel snowflakes in back of me. Or anywhere.

"That's got to be a good sign, I guess," I said.

Hmmph.

Again with the "Humph." It was a clear response from someone. Or something.

But it was just me and the dog.

I was thinking of this, when we got around the left curve of the road.

And saw the valley.

Baxter Springs Valley is about 25 miles long and 8 miles wide, oriented roughly SW to NE. The road we were coming in on headed into the valley on the SW corner. It was the back way into the valley; most traffic came from the east side of the valley.

The valley elevations were about 1500-2000 feet, with the surrounding mountains ranging up to about 8500 feet. Most of the higher mountains were at the north to western side.

As we stood on the road overlooking the valley, we were facing about north. The road curved down from about the 2800 foot level along the foothills of the mountains that were on the western edge.

Clockwise from there you could see the mountain range going from about west to the north, with the mountains continuing east from there. The valley was mostly farm land; hay and grains, and some cattle ranges.

There wasn't much population in the valley, maybe a couple thousand altogether. Mostly it was a higher valley ranching area.

There was a small town at the eastern edge of the valley, with a main road continuing mostly east from the town, paralleling the mountain range. Going clockwise from the town location, there were smaller foothills that wrapped around to the south back to where the dog and I were on the road on the southwest corner. The foothills to the south and southeast of the valley, sort of southeast of where we were, rose to about 4000 feet into a high desert area.

There were a few streams coming down from the mountains on the northwest to northeast side, running together into a river that was mostly on the northern edge of the valley, with the river running to the east. There was a small lake about in the southeast of the valley.

My house was to the northwest of our current location, next to one of the small streams that fed into the river in the valley. There was a road to the main town area that was at the eastern end of the valley. But my house was nestled back into the foothills at the west end of the valley.

That was the normal view of my valley. The road we were on winding down to the western end of the valley, then continuing east to the other end where the town was. The road to my house was a bit northwest of where the road curved towards the town.

Since it was farm country, you would normally see some cows or horses out in the fields. Or some farmer in a field on a tractor. A few cars would be on the road as it wandered over to the town on the east end of the valley. Maybe some smoke curling from farmhouse chimneys, if the weather was a bit chillier.

That would be Baxter Springs Valley.

I took the binoculars out of the backpack, and looked around the valley. I couldn't see much detail; they weren't that powerful.

What I couldn't see was any movement. No animals, no cars or trucks, no smoke from chimneys, no farmers on tractors out in the fields. No birds flying through the air, no hawks, no eagles, no crows.

No sun. The same bubble-wrap gray-yellow clouds covering the entire sky.

No sounds. Except that low humming sound.

I looked towards the east end of the valley. And saw a few black pixels out there. None around me, but there were some off at the far end of the valley.

I looked at the mountain range as it went about west to east. A few black pixels up there.

But not as many as we both experienced before.

~ 37~

I took a drink of water and noticed that my water supply was getting a bit low. I would have to conserve a bit until we got to the house, even though there was a nice spring up my road before you got to the house. I gave a bit of water to the dog.

Walking stick in hand, we started up again, heading for the cabin.

The road was mostly downhill here, and the surrounding land was open fields, mostly fenced in for grazing. I didn't see any critters of any kind, though.

We walked a couple of hours until we got to the turnoff to the house.

"Here we are," I said out loud.

The road was a mixture of gravel and hard-packed dirt, and headed off to the left, roughly in a northerly direction from the road. Mine was the only house on this road.

A short walk and we crossed the first bridge. There was a free-flowing stream there, and the dog went over there to get a drink. I knew about a mountain spring a bit up the road, so didn't stop to fill my water bottles.

I just paused for a minute for the dog to finish sniffing around the stream. He apparently didn't find anything interesting, so he bounded up the slight embankment from the stream back to the road where I was standing.

"Not far now," I said.

The dog did one of his tilted-head looks back at me, and took a few steps forward.

"OK, let's go," I said, starting to walk again.

The dog seemed to agree, as he fell in beside me as we went up the slight incline of the road.

The road continued uphill, and the clear area next to the road gave way to a few more trees. The trees weren't very thick, and I didn't see any dark, shifting shapes back into the trees.

So that was good.

The road curved to the right a bit, then went downhill a very short distance. At the bottom of the hill was a stream that I knew was fed by a natural underground stream. The stream wasn't that big, more of a steady trickle of water that went down a natural stream bed.

The stream tumbled down the hill into a small wooden box that had been added years ago. The water inside the box was as clear as I had remembered it would be, with a bit of dirt and small rocks at the bottom. A notch in the side of the box let out the excess water.

The water from the box dropped into a small pile of rocks that someone had put there years ago to break the flow of water from the box. The water continued down the side of the road, and then eventually went away from the road.

There were a couple of old tin cups that were on hooks on the side of the wooden water box. I grabbed one, and used the overflow stream to rinse it out and fill it up with the cold and clear water.

The dog had found the small pool of water from the overflow of the water box. He didn't appear to need the other tin cup for his drink, as he lapped up the water from the small stream trickling away from the water box.

I drank the water from the tin cup. It was as I remembered – clear, cold, and very tasty due to the built-in minerals from the spring. This spring water box had been a favorite stop of mine as I hiked around the area. I would often stop here on the way home and get a drink.

Both of us rested for a few minutes, each of us taking small drinks of water. The dog sniffed around the area, taking in the smells of whatever dogs are looking for. He trotted over to a bush away from the water, and found that spot to his liking. I took one last drink of water, and then set the cup back on its hook on the wooden box. Then I looked around for a good spot away from the stream.

Once all that was taken care of, I went back to the wooden water box. I took my empty water bottles out of my backpack and filled them up where the water went into the water box. It was always good to keep the water supply refilled.

"Now that we have taken care of watering us and the landscape, are you ready to go on?" I asked the dog.

Yeah. Let's go.

There it was again, that voice that appeared to be answer to my question. I heard it, but it didn't appear to be from an external source, but from within me, although it wasn't like my 'internal' voice. It was a bit more high-pitched than my internal voice.

I know that you have heard your internal voice. You hear it when you are reading and at other times. You recognize it as an internal voice of something you were thinking. Not 'thinking out loud', but 'thinking out internally'.

But the answer to my question was not any internal voice that I recognized.

I looked at the dog, which was a few feet in front of me, sort of turned sideways to me. He was looking at me with that tilted head look again.

Surprisingly, hearing the voice didn't startle me. It wasn't like the voice of someone sneaking up in back of you. It wasn't an intense voice, nor was it loud. It was more of a conversational voice.

What? Are you coming or not? We've wasted enough time here.

"Uh, OK," I replied, realizing that I was talking with the dog. And I also realized, or sensed, that this was normal. Not that I had been talking to animals before; I'm no Doctor Dolittle. Well, I am like most people who talk to animals like they are people.

You know, when a friend comes over with their dog and the dog comes up to you for a scratch or head rub, and you talk to the dog while you are scratching or petting. Talking like that is normal.

Getting a verbal answer to your conversation with an animal – not so normal. But it didn't feel abnormal; it was like it was a normal thing to do. You ask a dog a question, and he answers. Just another conversation.

It didn't seem abnormal. But, then again, nothing had been quite normal since the lights blinked.

Because I told the dog it was time to go, and he apparently agreed, we went.

Off down the road to the house.

~ 38 ~

Not much further now. The road takes an slow uphill climb of about 500 feet in elevation, along with a couple of twists in the road.

The forest here was thin, with tall pine trees mostly, and a bit of underbrush. As we walked, I kept an eye on the forest on either side of the road. No dark shapes floating around that I could see, so that was a good thing, I guess.

The road sort of goes sideways up the hill, with the higher part of the hill on the right side, dropping away in a gentle slope on the other side of the road. There was a small ditch on the right side of the road to catch rain or snow melt; there was a trickle of water flowing down the ditch.

As the road wound around the hillside to the right, the area flattened out a bit, and the trees got less dense.

I rounded the last curve in the road, which had flattened out. There was the house, and the meadow next to it.

I stopped as the house came into view. I didn't expect anyone to be there, since my house was the only one on this road. Besides, I hadn't seen anyone since the night in the library after the lights blinked.

But it was good to be cautious, since this wasn't apparently a 'normal' time.

The dog stopped too, turning his head back to me, and then looking forward again. He raised his head a bit, and I could see him sniffing the air, with his ears twitching around a bit, trying to hear something, I guess.

There was nothing to hear, as usual, except that low humming sound that I had tuned out most of the time. The sky above was still covered with those gray-yellow bubble clouds, and you couldn't see where the sun was above the clouds. The air was as still as it had been since the lights blinked. No wind, no sound, no blue jays squawking, and no insect sounds.

The same as it had been.

I looked out towards the house. It was at the edge of a large meadow that was maybe about 50 acres in size. The meadow – I usually called it 'my valley' – was mostly flat, with a small stream that went past the house down one side of the meadow towards the end of it. This was the same stream that flowed under the bridge on the road that we had stopped at earlier.

The meadow was mostly low grass. Around the meadow was the forest, mostly of tall pine trees. There was a stand of berry bushes and a few alders around the lower (farther) end of the meadow next to the stream.

The stream had a good flow to it. It was mostly 10-20 feet in width, and meandered through the meadow on a streambed of some rocks interspersed with some larger boulders.

I had explored the stream many times on my day hikes on weekends; it sourced from an underground spring several miles above the house. There weren't any other houses or cabins in that area. So the water was quite fresh and clean, and it used it as the water source for the house when it was first built.

Over the years, I had power poles run to the cabin from lower in Baxter Springs valley, with the power poles mostly running through the forested area. I had a well put in near the cabin. It went down about 350 feet, and provided a good supply of clear and cold water. A septic system, away from the well area, of course, was used for waste water.

The house was a modest affair, originally built out of logs with a fireplace of stones gathered from the area. The fireplace was double-sided, with a separate fire pit on the inside and outside of the cabin, sharing a common rock-built chimney.

The house was two stories, but not that big. The ground floor had a living/dining area, with a small kitchen and bedroom off of the main living area. There were lots of windows for the view of the surrounding area.

Stairs in one corner led to an upstairs area of three bedrooms. The stairs led to the center bedroom, with one bedroom on either side of the center bedroom. Each bedroom had room for two twin beds, provided that you didn't need much headroom, as the cabin's tin roof sloped down next to the beds. It was more of a large attic than a full second floor.

There was only one bathroom, downstairs, off of the kitchen, which was off of the living/dining area. The bathroom was a small affair, a 'three-piece', I guess. Sink, toilet, and a shower that had just enough room for one person, so it was cozy. There was a door off of the kitchen to the back side of the deck, which led to some stairs to the lower level under the porch.

The house was built into the slight hill at the one edge of the meadowed area. A large porch was over the downhill side of the hill, so there was some storage area built underneath the porch.

The front door of the cabin, which was opposite the kitchen, had a porch area that was connected to the main porch; the porch wrapped around three sides of the house. The front entry of the house had a smaller porch area which led to the small parking area at the back side of the house.

There was a firewood area off of the side porch entry to the house. There was a rough sawhorse to hold the logs when they were sawn into fireplace-sized chunks, and a nice area to hand-split the logs into firewood. There was a good supply of split and seasoned firewood there; since I owned all of the land around the area, I would cut down a pine tree or two each year for firewood and let it season for a year before it was used. Each weekend, I would spend some time cutting, splitting, and stacking the firewood.

Next to the firewood area, a path next to the porch led down to the lower area off of the front of the house. It went around the front deck area, then off to the stream which was about 30 yards away.

The dog and I looked at the house and surrounding area. No movement anywhere, as usual. No signs of human or animal lurking about. There was no smoke from the cabin; not that I had expected any. Although anything could happen, I guess.

"Well, there's home. At least for now. It looks the same as usual," I said.

Let's go, then. I think it would be nice to lie down on the porch.

Again with the voice; a bit high-pitched, and more felt than heard. The strange thing about it, well, other than hearing the voice, was that it wasn't threatening, or that it didn't feel strange. It felt as though it was normal to 'hear' the dog speaking.

"That is you talking, isn't it?" I asked.

Who did you expect? Do you see anyone else around here?

"I didn't know that dogs could speak, much less be sarcastic," I replied.

I think there are a lot of things you don't know.

"Yeah. I guess."

So can we go to the cabin now, or do you want to stand here talking all day?

"OK."

I shifted my backpack a bit on my back, and we walked to the house.

Me.

And, apparently, a talking dog.

~ 39 ~

It only took a few minutes to get to the house. As we got closer, I could see that everything looked as it should, as long as you didn't look at the gray-yellow sky with the weird bubble-wrap clouds that covered the entire sky.

We stepped on the wooden deck and walked to the main door, my shoes making a soft sound on the wood. I rattled the door handle a bit, finding it still locked, just as I left it when I left for work.

I reached to the side of the door, about head high, and pressed on a specific part of the light that was next to the door. The light fixture moved to the side on the side hinge, and revealed a small boxed area where I kept the front door key. I had built that key hiding place myself, and was quite proud of the way that it hid the cabin key. It was way better than putting a key over the door jamb or in a fake rock that anyone could tell was fake.

Clever hiding spot for a key.

"Thanks," I replied.

I used the key to unlock the deadbolt and then the keyed door handle. I put the key back into its hiding spot, and moved the porch light fixture back to its normal position, held in place by a strong small magnet.

With the door unlocked, I turned the door handle and pushed open the door.

We walked into the main living area, and I took off my backpack and set it on the couch that was in front of the fireplace.

"Well, the first thing to do, I guess, is to open up this place. I don't suppose you want to help with any of that."

Sure, I can help. Just let me use my opposable thumbs on my paws to help out. Oh, wait. I don't have opposable thumbs, so I guess I can't help out. I'll just go lay down next to the fireplace.

"Still sarcastic, eh?" I replied.

I didn't get a response to that. The dog just went over to the fireplace, sniffed around a bit, then turned around three times on the rug in front of the fireplace and lay down. The dog rested his head on his paws, and looked at me.

"OK. I'll get to work. You just sit over there by the fireplace while I do all the work."

I can be a bit snarky, too.

I first went to the windows, opened them, and then unfastened the interior latches on the wooden shutters that protected the windows – I usually closed them in the mornings when I left for work. I pushed open the shutters, and left the windows open a few inches to let the breeze in, mostly out of habit, since there wasn't any breeze.

I went over to the door next to the kitchen, unfastened the interior bolts, and opened the door. Then I went outside used the hooks to fasten the shutters against the side of the cabin.

I went back to the cabin, and walked inside the kitchen. I turned on the cold water tap on the sink. The water sputtered a bit, then flowed nicely. Not sure why it always sputtered whenever I first turned it on when I got home.

The sputtering noise apparently woke up the dog. He had gotten up and had walked over to the kitchen where I was.

A drink of water would be nice.

"I agree. One of my favorite things about the house is the cold and clear water that is here. It is quite tasty," I said.

I opened a cabinet and got out a bowl. I rinsed it under the cold water, filled it up, and placed it on the floor. The dog looked at it, sniffed a couple of times, and then started that lapping thing dogs do to get water out of a bowl.

I grabbed a glass out of the cupboard, rinsed it off, and filled it up. I took a drink (I didn't need to sniff it like the dog did).

It was just as I remembered. Cold, since it came out of my deep well. Clear, because the aquifers around the house were working just fine. And tasty, with a bit of mineral hardness in it.

I drank it all. It was very good.

I turned off the cold faucet, and turned on the hot water faucet. There was no hot water tank here; I had put in an on-demand hot water system for the kitchen and bathroom. It was a high-capacity system, so worked well for the kitchen and the shower.

A bit of sputtering (as usual), and the water flowed out. I put my hand under the water, and felt it getting warm. As the water warmed up, I added some cold water, and used some soap to wash my hands and face. They were both a bit grimy from my travels. It felt quite good to get rid of that grime. I rinsed off and turned off the water, grabbing one of the towels to dry off.

All seemed well. The water is working, the drains are working, and there is electricity and light. And I got my first taste of that great water.

You'd almost think things were normal.

Yeah, right.

~ 40 ~

I spent a bit of time doing my usual just-got-home chores I went out to the firewood area, and brought several loads of firewood into the house, and stacked them next to the fireplace.

It wasn't cold enough to need a fire. The temperature had hardly changed at all since the lights blinked. The thermometer that was in a protected area under the eaves on the north side in showed 72F. No breeze, of course; I hadn't felt a natural breeze since the lights blinked.

But bringing in the firewood was part of the usual evening startup routine. With the strangeness of the last couple of days, doing something normal was a bit reassuring.

The dog didn't help with any of the work, of course. He apparently was able to sleep through the whole process.

I set up some of the wood in the fireplace, stacking it as I normally did: small sticks on the bottom, then larger ones, arranged in a cross-hatched pattern. A few pine cones at the bottom to help get the fire going, then a few larger split logs on top. I didn't light the fire, as it wasn't needed. But getting the wood in place for when a fire was needed was one of the things that I normally did at the start of a weekend.

So doing normal things, in a not-so-normal time. Everything about the cabin appeared normal. Everything outside the house – not so much. The only way you could tell things weren't normal was to look at the yellow-gray sky and bubble-wrap clouds. Or notice the ambient light that didn't really come from the sun – it wasn't visible – but sort of seemed 'present'. Or the lack of any normal forest or rural sounds. No critters, no birds, no insects.

Well, that was an advantage, I guess. No flies or mosquitos.

And no fleas.

Well, there was that, too. No fleas. And a dog that talks.

The cabin-opening chores finished, I went over to the kitchen and got another glass of cold 'cabin water.' I drank it all, and then refilled the glass, bringing it over to the couch and sitting down.

The dog was awake with both eyes open, and his head raised from his paws, still laying down on the throw rug in front of the fireplace.

I sat on the couch, looking out the windows, at my little 'valley'.

The view out the window was peaceful. If you don't count the strangely colored clouds in the sky. Certainly peaceful, since there was no sound at all. I'd gotten used to the low thrumming sound that I'd heard since the lights blink. Other than that sound, nothing at all. No birds, no insects, no high-flying jet planes.

The cabin – even though I lived here full-time, I have always thought of it as a 'cabin' - had four large windows overlooking the valley on the front porch. It was one of my favorite spots to sit when I got here. It was here, with a cold glass of water, that I would usually unwind from the day-to-day events.

I might have a bit of music in the background, usually light guitar melodies, quiet and peaceful. Although sometimes some Classic Rock would suit my mood. And I would look out the window at the peacefulness of the valley as I relaxed.

The cabin was on a slight slope at one end of the valley, which was mostly flat, with clear edges up to where the forest took over. I owned the whole valley, and the forest was state forest lands, so there were no other buildings in sight.

There were a few scattered trees and bushes in the valley, but it was mostly clear. I'd often see the local wildlife out there; mostly a small herd of deer; sometimes rabbits; and birds flying around the trees. In the fall, the berry bushes would attract the birds and the deer, along with the occasional black bear (but that didn't happen often). In the late evenings, I might hear a few coyotes howling, but I never did see them during the day.

The stream that ran past my cabin headed down into the valley. A group of beavers had at one time dammed up the stream at the other end of the valley, so there was a small lake (or more accurately, a large pond) because of the beaver dam. A small stand of alders near the pond was trying to make a comeback after being used by the beavers.

The beavers had left for better pastures, though, so the pond was sometimes home to a few ducks or geese that stopped by on their migrations. That usually made the local small coyote population happy; I'd occasionally find a 'duck shell' with just the feathers left when I would go wandering around the valley area.

The valley had been in the family for years. My great-grandfather originally settled here, building a smaller cabin that I now used as an outbuilding. The main cabin – my home – was built many years ago by my grandfather, who had a small grocery store in the nearby town. During the Great Depression, he was able to give food to others on 'credit'. They would pay off the credit by helping to build the main cabin. It was a true 'log cabin' – originally – two stories high.

Grandpa's family never did turn out very large. Just three kids – my dad was one of them. My dad stayed around, but the other two moved far away, and never returned or expressed an interest in the cabin. When my grandparents died, the cabin ownership – and the surrounding land – passed to my dad. Dad was married by then, and I had come along. We lived in the cabin, just the three of us. Both of my parents passed in an auto accident when I was away at college. So the cabin, and the valley, reverted to me.

When I returned from college after my parent's death, I decided to make the cabin my home. After all, there were many great memories of living there. And I had found a job in the main town – not the town where my grandfather had the store – so I got used to the commute from work to the cabin.

About five years ago, after being at the cabin for eight years, I did a major remodel of the cabin. I demolished to the original exterior log walls, which were still sound, replacing plumbing and electrical and insulation as I remodeled. A full kitchen overhaul was part of the deal. It took quite a while – I lived in the original cabin (now the outbuilding) during the renovation. I did much of the work myself, learning how to do the plumbing and the electrical work, along with all the carpentry and painting and everything else. I had a few contractors come in for some of the more fancy stuff (tile, wood floors), but it was mostly my efforts nights and weekends. It did take a year, but the results were worth it.

After the renovations were completed, and I was fully moved into the cabin – now my home – I did a small conversion of the original cabin. It was a small place. Just one main room, with a sink and an old wood stove along the back wall. On one side, there was a small bedroom, with just enough room for a double bed and a small dresser.

The cabin's original walls were logs, harvested from the nearby forest. The ceiling was open-to-the-roof framing. The roof on both cabins was originally corrugated metal, but I replaced it with a more modern composite roofing during the remodeling.

Although the exterior walls were logs, they were, as in the case of the newer cabin, still solid and sound. Just like the main cabin, there was no evidence of any rot or damage. The floor was solid wood planks, with a small crawl space underneath, and foundation walls made of cemented stones. During the remodel, I added insulation and some interior walls made of clear-finished cedar planks.

So, after the main cabin remodel, I decided a bit of an overhaul of the original cabin was in order. Some foundation repair was needed, but not much. New insulation under the floor, some minor plumbing upgrades, and new electrical was done to the cabin. And a new, solid roof with insulation over a bit of new roof framing.

I decided to use the original cabin as a food storage area. Not that I was a big 'prepper', but the cabin was a good place for storage. Insulated walls and lots of steel shelves resulted in a nice and roomy area for food storage.

When I remodeled the main house, I put in solar panels to help provide energy and some hot water heating. I had a big battery storage shed built at the back corner of the house (on the back forested edge, not the valley-facing side). I also had a propane generator, which required a large propane tank that got buried back behind the battery shed.

So, the original cabin is a food storage area. Solar panels on the main house, battery storage and propane generator in a small shed at the back of the main cabin, and a propane tank buried behind that.

Hmm...maybe I was a 'prepper'.

~ 41~

As I sat in the living room, looking out the windows onto the valley, I remembered all of those things – the food storage, solar panels, propane generation, and the weapons (I had some guns, rifles, and lots of ammunition, all stored in a gun safe) and decided that it had all been a good thing that I had done.

Especially in the current circumstances. I seemed to be the only person around since the lights blinked. Me, and the dog that decided to become a full-time companion.

With all of my preparations, I was fairly well set up for long-term survival of whatever this was.

Yes, I guess I am a 'prepper'. It's just that I didn't think that I would ever need to be glad I was a 'prepper'.

Sometimes, things work out differently than you think.

I wasn't surprised at the words coming from the dog. Talking dogs didn't seem to be as strange as one would normally think.

"Talking" is not quite the correct word. The dog's lips weren't moving, like you'd see in old Disney movies. But I heard the words as plainly as another person talking. But not exactly 'hearing' with my ears. More like hearing the words inside my head. The words sounded like they were coming in through my ears, but they didn't.

Yeah, I know. Weird. Words inside my head, coming from a dog.

But the fact that the dog was communicating with words didn't bother me at all. Considering the current circumstances.

Yeah, I'm talking to the dog. Get over it. I talk, he answers. In my head.

"Whatever this is, it is nice to be in a familiar place," I said. "There is food, a good water supply, firewood for heat, a comfortable house.

"So it would seem that things are OK. Such as it is," I told the dog. And the dog replied, with those words coming in my head.

It would seem to be OK. For now.

I thought about that for a minute, looking out the window at the emptiness of my valley, and the strange clouds that were in the sky.

I wasn't sure what the dog meant when he said "For now".

The dog had laid his head on his paws, eyes closed, apparently asleep. He didn't say anything more.

I was left to consider what "For now" meant.

~ 42 ~

I must have dozed off for a bit.

I woke up, still sitting on my couch in front of the cabin window in the living room. Outside, it was still 'light'.

Ever since the lights blinked, it hasn't really been dark. The clouds, with their yellow-gray color, hadn't changed. The resultant light was a bit grimy yellow, as it had been since the light blink.

I looked at my watch. It showed 2:43 am. It should be dark outside, if my watch was correct. Although I wasn't sure that 'time' was working correctly since the light blink. There was that 'disconnect' of moving through the town on my bike. Even though time had 'passed', my movement through the down didn't seem normal. It seemed to take longer, even though my pace seemed to be normal. With a bicycle pace of around 10 mph, the 'miles' didn't seem to match the 'per hour'.

So I wasn't really sure that "2:43 am" was still "2:43 am". Actually, 2:45 am now. But still, time and space didn't seem to match up. It should be dark outside.

I was getting used to the lack of darkness. I wonder if this is how people in the Arctic Circle feel during the almost 24-hour summer days.

Whatever time it really was, it seemed like a good time to eat.

And as I sat in my chair, thinking that it was a good time to eat, the dog perked up his head from where he had been sleeping (I guess he was sleeping) on the floor in front of the window.

Eat? Sure!

"I guess so. Let's see what we can find."

I got up from the chair and headed into the kitchen. I looked in the refrigerator: there were some eggs and bacon in there, along with some shredded cheese. Still seemed fresh from before the 'light blink'. After all, this was my home, so it stands to reason that there would be fresh food in the refrigerator. The refrigerator still seemed to be working properly, so the food inside was OK. Not sure that I could resupply things though.

"Looks like a bacon and cheese omelet might work out. And some toast; there's some bread in there too."

The dog tilted his head, like he was asking a question about something. And then, because he could, he asked a question.

You keep your bread in the refrigerator?

"Well, yes. Not sure why, but that's where I always remember the bread was, even when I was a kid. So, I still keep the bread in the refrigerator."

I looked at the dog. "I suppose you want to eat, too. I guess that I'll make enough for both of us. If that's OK."

The dog sat down, and watched me. No response.

I guess he's a dog of few words. OK by me.

I set about making breakfast. Even though it was the middle of the night.

Bacon takes a while to cook, especially if you like it crisp, like I do. So I started the bacon, and then got the rest of it ready. Scramble the eggs; get the cheese ready, heat up the pan.

You know the drill. I won't bore you with my culinary expertise. Especially since I don't really have any culinary expertise.

Once everything was done, I divided it all into two plates. The dog had been watching me carefully the whole time I was cooking. Not moving, not talking; just watching.

"I suppose that you don't need a fork. Or that you'll sit up to the table."

The dog tilted his head to the side again, but didn't say anything. I put the plate on the floor.

The dog didn't move towards the plate.

"I thought you would like that. Well, it's there if you want it."

I took my plate to the table, along with a glass of cold water and a fork. I sat down, and started to eat.

And the dog started to eat also.

"A polite house guest. Doesn't start eating until the host starts."

So, we both ate. It tasted good. It must have; in a few minutes, both plates were empty.

I gathered up the plates and rinsed them off in the sink, along with the frying pan and spatula. I cleaned up a bit, and refilled my water glass.

I took my glass of water out to the living room, back into my favorite chair, and sat down. The dog followed me, without a word, and sat down between me and the window.

Then I looked out the window.

"That's different."

Yep.

~ 43~

There was another cabin in my valley.

My valley has always had only two cabins. The original one, now used for food storage. And the new one, my home.

The nearest house is fourteen miles away. Not anywhere near my valley.

When I am here at my home – the cabin – I am alone. I don't even see chimney smoke in any direction.

Just my valley. The stream. The old beaver pond. The stand of alders next to the beaver pond. A stand of berry bushes on one side. And the forest surrounding on all sides.

My valley. My cabin. All by myself.

But not anymore, it seems.

The newly-visible cabin was about halfway down the valley, on one side, nestled into the forest's edge.

Where there used to be nothing but the grass in the valley, and the forest at the edge.

A cabin.

I looked at the cabin for what seemed like a long time, but probably wasn't. I looked around the inside of my cabin. It was just as before.

I'd just finished a meal. I could still smell the cooking odors. Bacon is really good, but you have to cook it for a while to get it nice and crisp. And that makes the whole place smell like bacon. And I could still smell the bacon from when I cooked it.

I hadn't passed out. I was sleeping – or maybe just resting – before getting up to cook and eat.

I looked at my watch - 3:32 am. About an hour since I woke up. Long enough to cook and eat the meal. Assuming that time was still working like before.

But even if time was stretched out a bit, there certainly wasn't enough time to build a cabin in my valley. You'd think that I would have noticed something like that.

I stood there, looking out the window at the cabin at the other end of the valley. Still there.

I remembered getting here to the cabin. Looking around at the valley. All of it looked like the last time I came home, before the Light Blink.

Just me, the dog, my house/cabin, the old cabin, and the valley with the stream and trees and beaver pond.

But there it was - the new cabin. Looking like it had been there all the time.

I managed to move a bit. I went over to the bookcase and grabbed my binoculars. They were a nice set, 15x70, with clear optics. I used them all the time to watch the wildlife in the evenings. And to sometimes look at the stars. I'm out in the country, so it's nice and dark and good for star gazing.

I walked back to the window overlooking my valley. I used the binoculars to study the cabin.

It was a log cabin, similar in structure to mine, only one story. Didn't look that big. Maybe two bedrooms, a living room, kitchen, and one bathroom. A brick chimney for the fireplace. Just guessing, but it appeared to have those features based on its size.

There were windows for the rooms. I couldn't see into them, just the reflection of the valley. No lights on inside that I could see. No movement. No smoke from the chimney.

But a cabin. In my valley.

I pulled the binoculars away from my eyes. Looked around the valley, and couldn't see anything else that was different than before.

As I was looking around the valley, I saw some movement out of the corner of my eye. It was way down at the end of the valley, past the new cabin, past the beaver pond. Right at the edge of the forest.

Those black pixels again. Not too many of them, but visible even at this distance.

I looked through the binoculars at the area where I saw the black pixels. They were a bit easier to see, and they looked like they were moving away, towards the forest. As I watched them, the black pixels merged into the trees of the forest until they were no longer visible.

I pulled the binoculars away from my eyes. I looked at the forest edge at the end of the valley. The black pixels were gone. There seemed to be a denser darkness in the forest – darker than usual.

I used the binoculars to look at that dense darkness, but couldn't see anything in there. I could tell that there was something back there. Something black and dense. Maybe a dense pocket of pixels. Maybe just a dense black fog. It was hard to discern, but I could tell it was different.

I'd looked at the forest many times, with and without binoculars, in the evenings after getting home from work. The black denseness in the forest hadn't been there before.

Of course, a lot of things were different since the lights blinked.

All the people gone in the office, and the town. The strange time/distance disconnect as I biked through the town. The empty cars and trucks in the road, as if they were frozen in place. The strange clouds and the low humming sound. The lack of night time. The talking dog.

And the newly visible cabin. In my valley.

As I stood in my living room and looked out the window to the new cabin, I knew I would have to go look at it. With the strange things that have been happening since the lights blink, I also knew that it might be best to prepare before that walk to the new cabin.

I looked at the dog. He was still asleep on the floor.

"Hey, dog. There's a new cabin out in the valley. It just appeared."

The dog opened his eyes and looked at me. He slowly got up, doing that stretchy thing that dogs do when they wake up. He then padded over to the window, not showing any sign of haste. He looked out the window, towards the new cabin.

He looked back at me, and then went back to the spot in front of the fireplace. He did another dog-stretchy thing, turned around once, lied down, and put his head on his paws.

Yep. New cabin.

And then he closed his eyes.

"You're a big help," I said to the dog. No response, not even an eye twitch.

"Well, I am going out there to look at the cabin."

No response from the dog. Again.

"I'll just get a few things," I muttered to myself.

I went to the fireplace, and grabbed the shotgun from the rack over the fireplace, and took it over to the kitchen table. I went to the cabinets under the bookcase and got a box of shotgun shells and went back to the table.

I loaded the gun, leaving the breach open for safety. I grabbed my hunting jacket – the one with lots of pockets – and put it on, loading up the pockets with extra shells.

I also decided to get my pistol. I fastened the holster to my belt, and then checked the gun. I put two extra gun clips in my jacket, making sure that the bullets were ready to go. I checked the action of the gun, making sure the clip was loaded, but leaving the chamber empty.

I put on my "boonie" hat. I was ready to take a look at the cabin.

While I was getting ready, the dog stayed where he was. He did open his eyes to watch what I was doing. When I was done, he stood up, again with the dog stretchy thing.

You won't need all of that.

"What do you mean? Is it really that safe out there? There are black pixels randomly appearing. The clouds are goofy. There is no night time. Time doesn't seem to work right. And there's a new cabin in my valley that just appeared. I think I ought to be prepared for anything."

The dog just looked at me as I finished my rant.

You won't need all of that.

"Fine. You think I won't need any of this. But I think that it's better to be safe than sorry. And I think that my shotgun and pistol will help me be safe. So I am taking it with me."

The dog didn't say anything. He just looked at me.

I walked to the front door, opened it, and stepped through.

"Are you coming?"

I guess he decided he was going to come with me. He didn't seem in much of a hurry, as he did another doggie stretch, then slowly walked to the door and came outside.

I took one look at the cabin. Still no activity around it I could see.

I started walking towards it. The dog followed.

~ 44~

The new cabin was about a half mile away, on the other side of 'my' valley. At least, it used to be my valley. The sudden appearance of the new cabin might change that. But I was going to find out why it suddenly appeared.

At least, that was the plan.

The valley was not fenced, and was covered in wild grass that you would find in a meadow. The grass wasn't too tall.

I'd wandered around my valley often; I lived here, and enjoyed taking those walks. I'd see birds popping up as I walked near them. There would be insects buzzing around. There would be many patches of wildflowers, so during spring and summer you would see the bees making their rounds on the flowers.

Sometimes you would see larger wild animals. There would be ducks and geese in the old beaver pond. In the evenings when the weather was good, I'd sit out on the front porch and look out into the valley and see a small herd of deer grazing.

And there would usually be a gentle breeze on a sunny day.

But not today.

The only movement was me, and the dog.

Most dogs would be running all over the place, sniffing here and there for whatever smells they could find. Or chasing a bird that popped up.

Not this dog.

He was walking a few paces behind me, not interested in anything other than walking.

We walked along the creek that ran from next to my house to the old beaver pond. It wasn't a big creek, maybe 10-15 feet across, and didn't usually have a lot of water volume. There were rocks in the creek, so the water was deep enough to tumble through the rocks as it flowed to the old beaver pond. I had walked along the creek many times, and listening to the water rumbling over the rocks made for a pleasant sound.

As I walked towards the new cabin, I thought about the other walks I had made. And then I realized something.

There was water in the creek, about the same amount as other times. The water was flowing just like before, over the rocks, making little eddies as it flowed.

But there was no sound.

No sound of the water tumbling over the rocks.

It was like watching a nature show, but with the 'mute' button on. You could see the water tumbling over the rocks. But there was no sound.

Just that low frequency thrumming sound that I'd heard ever since the lights blinked. I'd gotten used to it, so mostly had tuned it out.

But walking along a 'muted' creek, I heard the thrumming sound again. Just not any sound from the water.

"No sound from the water on the rocks in the creek. Weird," I said, mostly to myself. The dog was mute also; no response from him.

We kept on walking.

There were a couple of spots where the rocks were high enough above the creek water that you could cross to the other side. We got to one of those, and I rock-hopped to the other side of the creek.

The dog stopped at the edge of the creek. He had watched me as I rock-hopped across the creek. The rocks I had used were flat, and a bit larger than foot-sized.

Most dogs would easily splash across the creek. The water wasn't very deep.

The dog looked up stream, then downstream.

"Are you waiting for the traffic to clear?" I said.

Sometimes I can be a smart-aleck.

The dog then did his own 'rock-hop' across the stream. On top of the rocks, using the same rocks I had used.

Feet-dry from one side of the creek to another.

The dog got to the other side next to where I stood. He looked up to me, and then looked towards the new cabin. Then back up to me.

"OK. Let's go," I said.

And we both started walking towards the new cabin.

During the entire walk, I had been looking at the new cabin, trying to see if there was anybody or anything there. But I was also keeping an eye on the rest of the valley, with my hands carrying the shotgun in the 'ready' position, looking for anybody or anything.

Not sure what I would find, but wanting to be ready for anything that showed up.

As we got closer to the new cabin, my apprehensiveness increased a bit. I wasn't sure what we would find there.

The dog didn't seem to be concerned at all. He seemed relaxed. His ears weren't twitching, straining to pick up any sounds. Not that there were any sounds.

His fur behind his ears and front haunches didn't seem to be raised up in an 'alarm' state. His tail wasn't wagging. Well, maybe a bit, but not what you would normally expect to be a tail wagging pattern while walking around outside.

I was getting nervous. The dog was quite relaxed.

I was not sure how to take that, but didn't dwell on it. I just kept walking towards the new cabin, keeping my eyes open, and my shotgun at the ready.

~ 45 ~

We got about 100 feet from the new cabin, and I stopped. The dog stopped right next to me, and sat down.

I looked at the cabin: a typical cabin-like structure. Like mine, it was made from logs. The logs looked slightly weathered, like the cabin had been built years ago.

There were two standard sized windows on either side of the front door. There was a porch that was the full width of the cabin, with a nice overhang as a cover over the porch area. There were two empty Adirondack chairs on one side of the front door, with a small table between them that looked to be made out of small branches.

There was a barrel off on the left side of the cabin; a water barrel, I guess. The cabin was single-story, with what looked to be a cedar shake roof.

There was no garage or outbuilding next to the cabin. And no road that I could see that would have been used to get to the cabin. No trails or beaten down paths that I could see.

It was like the cabin had been plunked down in one piece where it stood. Even though the cabin looked like it had been there for years.

Which it hadn't.

The new cabin wasn't there yesterday. Or whatever the equivalent of 'yesterday' was.

I looked around the cabin, and could see no sign of any movement. The windows were clean, but I couldn't see through them to the inside of the cabin. Even though it was the equivalent of 'daytime' – there was no sun because of the clouds. There was enough ambient light to see just fine, sort of like a cloudy day, which it was, I guess.

There was no reflection of the outside on the windows. You could tell they were clean – not frosted or anything like that - but I couldn't see through them.

"Hello, the house!" I yelled. Maybe a bit louder than I wanted to. I waited for any response.

"Hello! Anyone in there?" I yelled. A bit softer, but loud enough that you'd think someone could hear me.

I looked around the cabin, and around the valley. Nothing had changed that I could see. No response from inside the cabin.

I looked at the dog, sitting at my side, patiently, I guess. He looked at me, and then looked at the house.

I guess if he would have said something, he would have said "Go on and knock once, then go inside." He actually could talk, or at least I could hear him talk. But he didn't talk often, and I guess he decided not to say anything this time. I guess he figured that looking at me, then looking at the door, was enough to tell me what he was thinking.

So I started to walk towards the cabin, the dog following at my side. I got to the porch, and yelled out once more "Hello, the house!"

No response.

I stepped on the porch, the heels of my boots making a slight sound on the wood planks of the porch. I got to the door, and knocked loudly.

The dog looked at me, and then the door, and then back at me.

"OK, I get it. I'll go inside," I said.

I made sure my pistol on my right side (I'm right-handed) was loose in the holster. I snapped the shotgun's breech closed, and held it with my right hand, pointing towards the door.

I took a breath. Reached out with my left hand. Grabbed the doorknob. Turned it.

And pushed open the door.

The door opened with a bit of a creaking sound. The inside of the cabin was empty. One big room, as far as I can see. No furniture anywhere.

There was light in the cabin, but the light didn't seem to have a source. There was some light coming from the windows, but not much.

Mostly, the room was filled with the same yellow-gray light that was outside. But there was no source to the light that I could see.

I took a couple of steps into the room, leaving the front door wide open. I looked down at the dog, who had sat down just inside the doorway.

I looked all around. The walls were plain and empty. There were windows on all sides of the one big room. The yellow-gray light was visible through the windows, but there was more light 'brightness' – if yellow-gray light could be called 'bright' – inside the house than there was outside.

The cabin was just one big square room. There were two windows on each of the four walls. There was a single door between each of the two windows; the doors looking just like the front door that I had used to enter the house. The other three doors were closed.

"Hello?" I said. Not as loud as before.

No answer. Nothing from the dog either.

Then I looked closer at the room. This was a big room – much bigger than it had first seemed. It seemed to be bigger than the outside dimensions would suggest. There was a 'sense of bigness'.

The dimensions of the doors and windows were the same as before. So I hadn't done a "down the rabbit hole" thing. It just felt larger.

It was like when I was riding the bike through the town. Although I was moving at a normal speed, my progress – distance covered, I guess – was not normal, it was slower than what I would have expected. It took longer to cover a specific distance, but I was moving normally, not 'slow-motionly'.

It was the same with the space inside the cabin. Although the dimensions of the door and window were the same as what I saw on the outside of the new cabin, the space inside felt larger than what felt 'normal' – if there was anything normal about what had happened since the lights blinked.

It was like the same dimensions were longer than they appeared, or what those dimensions would normally be. The dimension of the cabin on the outside was about 50 feet, and the cabin appeared to be roughly square-shaped.

So the dimensions on the inside should be about 50 feet. In a normal world. In this world – in the 'after-the-light-blink' world – the inside of the new cabin seemed to be ten times bigger.

I had measured my stride once. Every two steps would be about five feet in distance. So twenty steps should get me to the door at the opposite end of the room inside the new cabin.

It didn't look like twenty steps, though. It looked more like one hundred steps, or even more.

I decided to test that theory. The dog had lain down just inside the door, not seeming to be very interested in anything going on, even my confusion about the room's dimensions.

"I'm just going to take ten steps. That should get me halfway across the room," I said. The dog didn't appear to be interested.

"OK. Here goes!"

I started walking, counting my steps. My plan was to walk halfway through the room, so I would be even with the doors on each side that appeared to be halfway down the length of the new cabin.

The dog got up and walked with me, although he didn't appear to have much enthusiasm about the whole thing. It was like he was 'assigned' to be with me.

"10.....20.....30.....40....50," I thought to myself. I stopped at 50. I looked at my progress from the front door. And where I was compared to the side doors.

Have you ever seen those video effects where the camera zooms into a person, but the surroundings seem to zoom in the opposite direction? I think it is called a 'dolly zoom', or a 'vertigo effect'. I saw it in an old Alfred Hitchcock film called "Vertigo". I think it was also in "Jaws". You don't see it very often, because it had become a gimmick.

Although I didn't see that effect when I was walking, I did feel a bit of vertigo when I stopped. Like I had moved a long distance while just walking a short distance.

Fifty steps, at my 2-steps-equals-5-feet pace, should be 125 feet if I have my math right. So I had walked 125 feet in a room that, according to the outside dimensions, should have a total length of 50 feet.

I stood there, trying to figure that out. Then I looked at where I was in the room. I hadn't made it to be the mid-way spot of the room, where the two side doors would be on either side of me.

The dog didn't seem to be concerned about the whole thing, even though he had walked with me those fifty steps.

I turned around and looked at the front door. It wasn't where I thought it would be – distance-wise. It seemed farther away.

I turned around again, looking at the door at the back of the room. It didn't seem any closer.

But I had walked 125 feet. Inside a cabin that had outside dimensions of about 50 feet.

With a dog.

A dog that talks, although he wasn't talking now.

This was really weird.

~ 46~

As I stood there, 50 steps and 125 feet away from the door, at least in the measurements of my world, I heard a clicking sound.

I looked at the dog. He had lain down again, resting his head on his paws, not terribly perturbed about anything. He didn't seem to react to the clicking sound.

I looked around, trying to figure out where the clicking sound was coming from. It didn't appear to be coming from anywhere inside the room, which was empty of anything except me and the dog.

I turned back to the front door, which was still open. The clicking noise seemed to be coming from that direction.

Then the other three doors started opening, slowly, and with a creaking sound that you'd hear from rusty hinges.

Yeah, I know. This sounds like a grade-B horror movie. Weird cabin, strange distances, and then the door opens with a creaking sound. Not just one door, but the three remaining doors in the room were opening inward.

I stayed facing the front door, trying to decide if I wanted to get back outside. Quickly.

The clicking sound increased. And then I noticed a few stray black pixels swirling around outside, visible through the front door.

"Hey, dog. Any idea what is going on? Now would be a good time to practice your talking," I said. "This is getting strange. Do you know what is going on? Any ideas?"

Yeah - me talking to a dog, expecting an answer.

The black pixels outside the door started to get more numerous. Sort of like when it starts to snow: first a few flakes swirling around on the wind, then some more, until there are lots of snowflakes. That was what was happening outside, but with black pixels rather than white snowflakes.

Along with the increase in the number of black pixels, the pattern of clicking was increasing.

And the other three doors were wide open, flat against the inside wall of the cabin. I looked towards all the doors, and each showed increasing black pixels. And there were black pixels showing outside the windows.

But the pixels were staying outside. The inside of the cabin didn't have any pixels. The light level hadn't changed inside the cabin. The light outside hadn't gotten any dimmer because of the increased black pixels.

As I turned my head back to the front door, 50 steps away, I was thinking that perhaps the best thing to do was to run through the front door back outside. But I didn't really want to get into the pixel storm. I had done that before, and it was a bit disconcerting.

Not that what was happening now was any different – it was a bit disconcerting also.

As I was deciding whether it was better to be outside or inside, the dog said one word.

Stay.

Part of my mind saw a bit of humor in that. A dog was telling a human to "Stay". Another weirdness of the day.

But, the dog seemed to be telling me the best choice. "Stay" inside, out of the black pixels. "Stay" in the strange cabin with the strange dimensions and distances.

The dog was now sitting up, looking at the door on the left side.

Stay, he repeated.

"OK. I'll stay," I said.

I expected the dog to say "Good human".

But he didn't. So that's what I did.

I "stayed".

The black pixels outside had gotten thicker. I could see that the same pixel density was outside all the windows and the other open doors. Even though all the doors were open, there were no black pixels inside the cabin.

I guess that was good. Although it was hard to tell if that was good. There were way too many strange things going on.

The dog didn't seem to be as nervous as I was. He was still sitting, looking out the front door. I figured that if he was looking in that direction, so should I.

Although I kept aware of anything going on in my peripheral vision.

I kept "Staying".

Then the front door slammed shut.

I jumped a bit as I turned around to the front door. Startled.

I looked at the dog. No reaction from him. Well, he did lie down again. And closed his eyes. Whatever was happening, it was apparently no concern to him.

And then I heard four footsteps, like heavy shoes on the wooden floor of the cabin.

I spun around towards the sound of the footsteps. It was from the door at the opposite end of the cabin, the 'back' door. Which seemed much closer than before.

Because of the light from outside, the person – I could tell it was a person – was just a shadow. I couldn't make out his – or her – features.

But it was a person. Four steps into the room from the outside. At least, that's what I was guessing from the four footsteps I had heard after the front door slammed shut.

The figure was about five and a half feet tall. At least, that was my assumption, based on my thinking that the door was the same height as the front door I had used. Although I couldn't be sure. But I went with the five and a half feet height.

I couldn't tell any other features of the person, though. It did appear to be a person. At least, in the shape of what you would expect a person to have, standing in front of a lit doorway.

Blam! Blam! The door on the left and right sides both slammed shut.

Blam! The back door slammed shut.

I jumped a bit each time. Looked at the dog. Eyes closed. No reaction.

And with the Blam! of the back door, the person in front of the door ran towards me, the sound of shoes clacking on the wooden floor.

~ 47~

I'm not sure how many steps it took, or how far it was, but the person that had appeared in the back doorway was running straight for me.

Me? I was apparently stuck in my spot. My feet didn't move.

Not that I was trying to make my feet move. I was still trying to process the first door slam, then the appearance of the person at the back door, then the rest of the doors slamming.

And the person running towards me. With the dog next to me apparently sleeping.

The person got closer. It seemed to take a long time for he/she/it to get close to me. Although with the strangeness of time/distance that I had been through since the lights blinked, I am not sure if I could figure out any time or distance, or relate it to anything 'normal'.

The person kept running straight to me, and I could start to make out the features.

Shoulder-length hair. OK, that means female. Usually. That was verified by the running style. Females run different than males. Don't get all politically correct on me. In general, that's a fact. Anyway, I didn't have time to think about that discussion. I just concluded that the person running towards me was female. (Deal with it.)

She got closer. There was something vaguely familiar about her. I couldn't place it, but it was someone I had met.

"Audrelle?" I asked.

"Yes! Audrelle! That's me!" she said. "Who are you?"

"I'm Glen. Remember? We met in the library a couple of days ago. At least, it seems like a couple of days. Time is behaving rather strangely," I replied.

"Glen. Yes! I remember! In the library. It was dark outside. Nighttime. I found you in the library. Or you found me. And then you were gone. Or I was gone," she said. "This is – has been – very confusing. I am not sure what is going on."

I took a breath, ready to respond.

Then the front door opened. My dog got up from the floor, again with that dog-stretchy thing. He looked at the door, and then looked at me.

Time to go back to your cabin.

"Yeah. I think it is time to go," I replied to the dog.

"What? Go where?" asked Audrelle.

"I have a cabin here. Not this one. A cabin across the valley from this cabin. Which just appeared this morning. This cabin, I mean."

Yeah, I was rambling a bit. I took a breath.

"I think we should go to my cabin. At least, we should get out of this one. Before the doors shut again," I said to Audrelle.

"Well, it can't be any stranger than what has happened since I saw you in the library," she replied.

The dog looked at me again. And took a couple of steps towards the front door. He looked back at me, with a "are you coming?" kind of look.

"Let's go. We'll talk about things once we get outside of this cabin," I said to Audrelle.

We both started walking towards the front door, the dog leading the way. We got to the door in about 10 steps. Yeah, I know. It took more steps before. I know that. It just took 10 steps this time. Don't know why. Just wanted to get back outside. I'll worry about that later.

We both got to the door. Being a gentleman, I motioned to her to go first. She hesitated a bit, looking outside.

It looked normal outside. It looked like my valley. No black pixels around that I could see. I don't know when they had gone away, but there weren't any out there now.

"It's OK. Go ahead," I told her.

The dog was already outside, waiting just off the front porch.

Audrelle looked at me, and then stepped through the door onto the porch. She went to the edge of the porch, where the steps were, and stopped.

I followed her to the porch, standing next to her. The dog sat down, and looked at us. Waiting, I guess.

The front door slowly creaked shut. Didn't slam, which was nice. It just closed.

I turned to check on the door, and then decided that I didn't really want to. I walked down the porch steps, to where the dog was.

"Come on. My cabin is over there," I said, pointing to it. "It's not a long walk."

Audrelle looked at where I was pointing. You could see my cabin on the other side of my little valley. She looked at me, and appeared to nod to herself, and walked down the porch steps to where the dog and I were waiting.

"OK. I'm not sure what to do, but I don't want to go back. So, let's go to your cabin," she said in a small voice. There was a bit of nervousness to her voice.

So we walked, towards the cabin. The dog on my right side, Audrelle on my left, not too close, but next to me.

I sensed that Audrelle was a bit nervous. She didn't seem ready to talk yet, so I decided to wait until she was ready. I just walked at a slightly slower pace than normal. The dog was content, I guess, to go at the same pace.

Audrelle was looking around, not in a frantic way, just looking around at everything. The valley appeared to be normal, except for the usual strange cloud formations, and the yellow-gray light. I had gotten used to both, so had tuned them out.

It seemed that the clouds and light were new to Audrelle, though. As she walked, she kept looking around, as if there was something that might be following her. We kept on walking, and she seemed to be getting less nervous.

I kept quiet. I was trying to process what had happened so far since breakfast. The appearance of the new cabin, walking into it, the apparent disconnect between time and space and distance once I got inside. The sudden opening of the other doors.

And the sudden appearance of Audrelle.

Not sure that I was making any sense of the whole thing.

And then there was the other dog.

I hadn't mentioned the other dog, had I? Well, there was another dog. It appeared next to Audrelle inside the house, following her through the back door as she entered – or appeared, since I didn't really see her coming through the door.

The new dog was a golden retriever, with a coat that was more red than golden. But I've never heard of a 'red retriever'.

But the new dog seemed to be with Audrelle. Or maybe it was a 'guide' of some sort.

Now that I think about it, the new dog was always slightly in front of Audrelle in the cabin. It seemed that Audrelle was following the dog as she walked from the back door to where I was.

When we were talking inside the cabin, the dog sat down next to Audrelle. My dog didn't seem to be concerned about the new dog. There was none of that sniffing greeting stuff that dogs normally do. There was no barking, no growling. They both just sat quietly in their respective spots next to each of us while we were talking.

My dog seemed to take the lead in prompting me to walk to the front door to leave the new cabin. When we decided to walk to the front door, my dog went first, with Audrelle and I mostly side-by-side, and Audrelle's dog next to her.

When we got to the door, my dog went outside and waited on the porch. When Audrelle went through the door and followed, the new dog ahead of her.

Audrelle made no mention of the new dog. She wasn't saying much of anything; then, or while we were walking across my valley towards my cabin.

I was content to let her decide when to talk, although I had lots of questions. I just said a few words of direction as we walked across the valley.

When we got to the stream, I went first, hopping across the rocks so my feet wouldn't get wet. She quickly traced my steps on the rocks, and we were both on the other side. For that matter, both dogs used the same rocks. Which would normally be unusual; dogs would normally just walk right through the water from one side to another.

But, things aren't really normal, are they?

We continued walking towards my cabin, the four of us. We got there, and walked up to the porch.

Audrelle seemed unsure of what to do next. I sensed her nervousness, so I pointed to the pair of chairs on the porch.

"Why don't you sit in one of those chairs? I'll get you a glass of water; I figure you might be thirsty," I said.

Audrelle looked at me, and then gave a short nod. She walked over to one of the chairs, and sat down. She looked out to the valley, but didn't say anything. The two dogs sat down next to her.

"OK, then. I'll go get the water. I'll be right back," I said.

I opened the door to the cabin, and went to the kitchen. I got down two large glasses and took them to the sink. I turned on the faucet, and let the water run a bit so it would be colder. The water supply comes from the deep well, so it only took a short time for the water to get colder.

I filled up the glasses, turned off the faucet, and took them out to the porch.

"Here. It's good and cold, and clean. I've never had any problems with the water quality, and I have lived here for a while," I told Audrelle. I held out one of the glasses to her. I took a sip out of the other glass of water.

She looked up at me, and then took the water glass. She brought the glass closer to her, and looked at the water, and then at me.

I guess that she made some sort of internal decision. She took one sip of the water. Then several more swallows. Not gulping it down, but she drank about half a glass. Then she set the glass on the table next to the chair.

I moved over to the other chair, on the other side of the table. I sat down, and took a drink of my water.

By this time, my dog had laid down in the spot next to her chair, resting his head on his paws. His eyes were open, watching Audrelle more than me. My dog hadn't said anything to me since leaving the other cabin. The other dog was nearby.

And I didn't mention anything to Audrelle about the dog talking. I figured she wasn't ready for that.

We sat there in silence for a while, both of us looking out into the valley. Not much had changed out there, since the appearance of the new cabin. No animals, critters, birds, insects, nothing out there but the grass in the valley, the water moving down the stream, the small beaver pond, the trees of the forest around the valley.

The darkness of the forest. That was still there.

I didn't see a raven, though. That seemed comforting, somehow.

~ 48~

I am not sure how much time passed. Not that time was passing in a normal way now.

But we both sat there quietly on the front porch. I waited for Audrelle to start talking. I figured she would start when she was ready.

A bit more time passed. Then, "Thanks," said Audrelle.

"You're welcome," I replied.

She seemed to come to another internal decision. She glanced at me, then turned back and looked out to the valley.

"It's nice seeing you again. You were nice to me in the library," she said.

"No problem."

"I remember a bit about that night in the library. I am not sure how I got there. I think that I was there to study; I usually go to the library after school until my parents…"

She stopped. And took a deep breath. That seemed to calm her a bit after the mention of her parents. She took another breath. I guess she decided to continue after mentioning her parents.

"So, I was in the library at the table, studying. History, I think. Not very exciting, but I had a test coming up. So I was studying."

I didn't say anything, just nodded. I figured that I shouldn't interrupt so she would keep talking. I'd ask questions later after she got more comfortable with all that was happening.

"I don't know, maybe I fell asleep. Then something woke me up. I don't know if it was a sound, or anything.

"I raised my head; I had it lying on my arm on the table while I was resting. I looked around, and the library was empty. I thought that maybe the library had closed while I was sleeping and nobody woke me up to tell me the library had closed.

"There were books and backpacks and things left there. That was a bit puzzling.

"I looked outside the windows. And then I noticed the strange light outside. That yellow-gray light, just like we have now.

"I got up from the table, and went over to the window and looked outside. There wasn't anything moving out there. There were cars on the street, but they weren't moving.

"I looked up at the sky, and saw those strange clouds. The same strange marshmallowy-puffy yellow-gray clouds that are up in the sky now," she said, looking up at the clouds. Then she looked back out into the valley.

"The library was really empty. Not just empty of people, but it felt empty. I called out 'Hello? Anyone there?' and nobody answered.

"That freaked me out some more. I mean, I was already freaked out a bit by the light outside, and the cars not moving, and those weird clouds. But that really empty feeling was freaky.

"I took a deep breath, then another. Then I went back to my spot on the table and sat down. Well, I started to sit down. And then..."

She paused, and kept looking out at the valley. I kept quiet, just looking at her with what I hoped was an interested and sympathetic face. I figured that she needed to tell the story without me pestering her for details. That could wait until later.

She took a small sip of water. "It was really freaky. And then, um, well, I thought I was going to be sick. So I ran to the bathroom. And, well..."

She stopped again, taking another breath, and another sip of water.

"I stayed in the bathroom. It was like it was a safe place, maybe safer than in the library.

"I don't know how long I was in the bathroom. Then I heard a noise outside the bathroom door. That freaked me out even more, but I was determined to stay quiet so that whatever was out there would not know I was in the bathroom.

"I heard the door open. I was back in the corner. The door didn't open all the way. I held my breath, trying to be really quiet.

"The door closed. I waited, then let out my breath and started breathing again. I still heard noises out there, someone talking. The voice sound normal, not threatening.

"I decided that whoever was out there didn't sound threatening. So, after taking another deep breath, I walked to the door, opening it.

"That's when I heard the voice talking to me. It sounded a bit scared, too, like it didn't know what was behind the door."

I smiled a little. She looked at me, and saw my smile. I waited.

"It was you, of course. You were a bit scared of me coming out of the bathroom door." She looked at me.

"Yes. Sorry about that," I said.

"No problem. I guess, now that I think of it, whatever was happening was a bit strange for both of us.

"You know what happened next. After we both calmed down, we went to the couch area, and I sat on the chair while you sat on the couch, and we talked for a bit. Then I guess we were both tired, so that's when we decided to sleep. In separate spots," She smiled a bit at this.

"Then I woke up. And you were gone. I was alone in the library."

She stopped talking, looking out into the valley, with a sort of a faraway look in her eyes.

"I was alone in the library," she slowly repeated.

I waited. I figured she needed to process things some more.

"I'm going to get a pitcher of water for refills," I said. Audrelle gave a slight nod of her head, still looking out across the valley, but I was thinking she wasn't really seeing anything out there.

"I'll be right back," I said.

I went back into my cabin, and headed towards the kitchen. I got a plastic pitcher, and took it to the sink. I started filling it with cold water.

As I was waiting, I thought that maybe Audrelle might be hungry. Maybe some food would help. I didn't want to leave her alone out there while I fixed a meal, though.

I went over to the pantry, and grabbed a handful of energy bars. By then, the pitcher was full, so I went back to the sink and turned off the water.

I grabbed the pitcher of water in one hand, and the energy bars in the other, and headed back to the front porch.

Audrelle was still there, looking (but not looking) out at the valley. Both dogs were still lying down, apparently asleep.

I offered one of the energy bars to Audrelle, and she took it. Her water glass was on the table next to her chair, so I filled up her glass along with mine.

Audrelle absentmindedly picked at the energy bar wrapper, opening it. She took a small bite and chewed and swallowed it, all the time looking out at the valley.

I sat down and grabbed an energy bar for myself, unwrapped it, and took a bite. I didn't say anything; I figured Audrelle would start talking when she was ready.

Audrelle took a drink of her water, and set her glass down on the table. She took another little nibble of her energy bar. Still looking out at the valley, she continued her story.

"So I was in the library with you, and we both fell asleep, I guess.

"I work up sometime later. I don't know what time it was. It was still light outside, with the same kind of yellow-gray light as before. I guess it was morning, but you couldn't tell from that 'cloud-light' outside.

"I saw the outside first, since my head was pointing towards the window when I woke up. I was sort of confused about where I was. It took a minute for me to figure out I was in the library, then a bit longer to remember that you were there with me last night, or whenever that was.

"Then I noticed you were gone. Your backpack, your bike, and everything were gone. The library was still empty, and my stuff was on the table where I left it. It was like you were never there. I didn't know what to think about that, but I guess I figured that I must have fallen asleep in the library when everyone was gone, and nobody woke me up. And that maybe I had dreamed about you."

She stopped for a bit, still looking out at the valley. She reached over for her glass of water and took a sip, and then another bite of energy bar. She chewed up that bite and swallowed it, and took another sip of water and put the glass back on the table next to her chair.

All this time, she was looking out into the valley. Maybe not really seeing things out there, but doing that unfocused stare thing when you are recalling something in the past.

"So I was there in the library, all alone," she continued. "I looked out the window again, and I saw the strange shapes and colors of the clouds. And the empty cars just sitting out in the street, like they were frozen in time or like in a picture, but you could see that there was nobody in the cars.

"And the trees not moving, or anyone in the park or the playground next to the library. It was like I was the only one around anywhere, and I guess that was true.

"I called out a few times, I guess, to see if anyone answered, but nobody did. I went to the front door, which was unlocked and looked outside again, and nothing had changed.

"I'm not sure why I left my backpack in the library. I guess it was getting a bit creepy in there, and maybe if I went outside I could find somebody.

"I opened the library door, propping it open in case I needed to go back inside, I guess. I walked out to the courtyard in front of the parking lot of the library. I looked all around, but couldn't see anyone or anything.

"I guess then I noticed that were wasn't any sound outside. Like birds or insects buzzing or dogs barking or kids playing the park next door. There was always some noise you could hear outside. But I didn't hear anything.

"Except that low humming sound. The same sound I have been hearing even here, although I guess I don't hear it or pay attention to that sound now. But I heard it while I was outside the library. It wasn't loud or anything, but you knew it was there.

"I was looking around, calling out a 'Hello', but nobody was answering. I looked towards the park, and then I saw it."

She stopped talking, remembering in her mind about when she looked over towards the park. Her hands were fiddling with the energy bar wrapper. Her eyes were still unfocused but looking out into the valley.

"It was over there in the park."

I waited. Even though I had lots of questions, I still felt that she needed to continue her story without being interrupted. There would be time for questions later; she would continue her story when she was ready.

A few minutes passed, both of us sitting on the porch, looking out into the valley. My dog hadn't moved from his spot next to her chair, looking like he was sleeping and unconcerned about everything.

Then Audrelle's dog – the red golden retriever – opened his eyes and sat up, moved a bit closer to Audrelle, and laid his head on her knee. Audrelle still looked out into the valley, but her hand moved to the dog's head. She started stroking the dog's head, but not really being aware she was. The dog stayed still, his head on her lap, letting her continue petting her head.

"It was over there in the park," she continued. "It looked like snowflakes, but they were black. There weren't too many of them at first, but you could tell they were over there.

"Those black snowflake/pixel things. Like I was watching a TV show and the picture would break up or get staticky or something.

"As I watched the black pixel things – black snowflakes, I guess – there started to be more of them. And they weren't far away; they seemed to appear all around me. I swatted at them, thinking they were flies or bugs or something, but they weren't. You'd be able to hear a swarm of bugs. But it was silent.

"The pixel things started to get thicker. And I thought that I should go back into the library, but I couldn't move. And the pixels got really thick so I couldn't see anything.

"It was like fog; it wasn't like you could feel the pixels like you could with a heavy snow storm or rain. They were just there, blocking what I could see."

I nodded to myself, still staying quiet. I remembered the pixel storm that I was in. Was that yesterday? The day before?

With the weirdness of time and distance and movement, I wasn't sure when I saw the pixel storm. But I remembered how it felt and looked.

I was going to say something about my pixel storm experience. But I looked over at Audrelle, and she wasn't really paying attention to me. She was still looking out to the valley in that unfocused, I-remember-things look. So I kept my mouth shut and waited for her to continue.

"So I was standing in front of the library, surrounded by this black pixel snow storm. I didn't know what to do; I guess I was frozen in place."

She stopped, and I saw a little smile on her face, a bit forced, perhaps.

"Heh. A snowstorm of black pixels, and I was frozen in place."

Her smile slowly faded away, and she continued her story.

"I don't know how long it took, it was like I couldn't figure out how long things lasted, or I had no sense of time. But the black pixels started fading away. There were less and less of them, and then they were gone.

"I looked around, and saw that I wasn't in front of the library anymore. The library was gone. There was no parking lot. There was no park and playground next to the library.

"There was just grass all around me and a forest far away. I don't know how far, but it wasn't as large as this valley, I think. The grass was not cut like you would see with a lawn or a park; it was just thick and green. I guess like you would see on a golf fairway. It seemed to be in a natural state, not too long, but not regularly mowed.

"But that is all there was. Just the grass of a valley sort of like your valley, and surrounded by trees. I couldn't even see any roads. Just the grass and the trees.

"And the dog"– she pointed to her dog – "that was sitting next to me."

"He was just sitting there, I guess waiting for me to do something. He was just a couple of feet away. He wasn't barking, his tail wasn't wagging. He was just sitting there.

"He didn't look threatening or angry or anything. He was just waiting for me to do something.

"There was something about the dog that was calming. You would think that suddenly being plunked down in a green grass valley surrounded by trees when a couple of minutes before you were in front of the library in town would really freak you out.

"But seeing the dog just sitting there calmly got me calmed down too. I didn't scream or call out or yell or anything. It was like I was where I was supposed to be, and the dog was there to help me in some way."

She stopped to look down at her dog, with his head resting on her lap. And noticed for the first time that she was petting the dog.

She looked up at me. "Even though things have been really freaky since the library, the dog seems to make me feel calm and safe."

She continued petting the dog, using her other hand to get a drink of water.

"So there I was in my own little valley surrounded by a forest, with a dog next to me. I took a few breaths, and felt calm.

"The dog had been watching me, I guess. I guess that he saw that I wasn't freaked out, so he took a couple of slow steps towards me, sitting down next to me. And I reached down and patted his head, like we were old friends.

"It was a different kind of dog than yours. Yours is more of a collie of some sort. Mine is a golden retriever, I think. It had longish hair, but it wasn't matted or anything, it looked like it was regularly brushed and cleaned.

"So I talked to the dog. 'Whose do you belong to? Where are we? How did I get here? What's going on?'

"I guess that I was babbling a bit. But I kept petting the dog and calmed down a bit. And then I heard a voice.

"It wasn't like hearing a voice with your ears. It was like hearing a voice inside your head. And that might seem freaky, but it was very calming. I didn't freak about hearing voices in my head. It was like a normal thing. Somebody says something, and you hear it in your head. No big deal.

"I looked all around, but couldn't see anyone. But I heard the voice. It said:

Don't worry. Things are OK. A bit strange, but OK.

"And it was a calm, gentle voice. It wasn't scary at all, like when you are someplace and someone sneaks up behind you and speaks and you are startled or jump a bit. It was calm.

Don't worry. Everything is all right.

"And I looked down at the dog. And I knew that it was the dog talking to me. And that would normally freak you out, but it didn't. It seemed natural. Me talking to the dog. And the dog talking to me. But me hearing the dog inside my head, rather than through my ears. And it was all just fine."

Audrelle seemed to notice me sitting on the porch with her. She looked at me.

"Your dog talks to you, doesn't it?" she asked.

I nodded my head.

"And it just seems like a natural thing to talk to your dog, right?"

I nodded again.

"And he doesn't talk very much. But when he does, you know it's from the dog. And it doesn't freak you out."

Another nod.

"I knew it! That's the way it is with me!" she said.

She took another swallow of water. And then seemed to notice that she had a half-eaten energy bar in her lap. She broke off a piece and gave it to the dog, who took it gently and slowly from her hand. Not a quick grab and chew and swallow like dogs normally grab a treat, but gently. And not sitting there begging for another treat.

Audrelle ate the last bite of the energy bar.

"This is good. Thanks!" she said to me.

I nodded again. I'm a brilliant conversationalist.

She continued her story. "So I am standing there in the meadow, I guess you'd call it, although it was fairly large. And there is a dog next to me. And he's – I guess it was a 'he', I never found out for sure – is telling me that things were going to be OK.

"And I think I knew that it was going to be OK. Maybe unusual or weird. I mean, a black pixel snowstorm, a sudden disappearance of the library, and me in this meadow, and a talking dog. And I knew that it was going to be OK.

"I guess the dog figured out I was calm. So he took a step forward, then turned around and looked at me. "

Let's go!

"I heard that as plain as you could. And it was calming and at the same time sort of forceful, like he wanted me to know he was serious and that I should follow him. But it was a gentle suggestion at the same time.

"So, I followed. And we walked towards the other side of the valley, across the grass."

"It was a quiet walk. I had lots of questions floating around inside my head, of course, but it seemed like they weren't important enough to try to ask a dog. Which should be weird to think about asking a dog questions, but it didn't feel weird. It felt normal.

"But I didn't ask, because it didn't seem like the right time. So we walked.

"As we got closer to the other side of the valley, I could see that there was a bit of a path that we were following. The grass wasn't worn down a lot, but you could see that there was a path.

"And, as we got closer to that edge of the forest, I could see there was an opening there. A place where the trees weren't as thick or close to each other as in other spots. That was where we were heading. The dog was leading the way, and I was right behind him. The dog seemed to know where he was taking me. And he wasn't running ahead like dogs often do. He was walking at the same pace as me.

"And he didn't look back at me to see if I was following. It was like he knew that I was right behind him. I don't know if he heard my footsteps; I guess that he could. But he seemed to know that I was following, and he didn't seem worried about where we were or where we were going.

"So we walked to that opening in the forest. It was quiet, of course. Just that background humming sound. And the sky had those weird clouds like there are here. And the light was that yellow-gray light like before. But you could see clearly. It was like a cloudy day, but not dark."

"Mammatus," I said.

"What?" she asked.

"Mammatus. That's the kind of clouds that are up there," I replied.

"Oh. OK."

"I'm sorry I interrupted. Please continue," I said.

"No problem. Anyway, we were walking across the meadow or valley, towards the opening in the forest. The forest was dark, but the opening was lighter. It was like the light from the valley followed into the opening into the forest.

"We got to the opening. The dog looked back at me, and I felt that it was OK. Even though going into a dark forest, following a dog, from a place that I don't know how I got there; that would normally freak me out.

"But the dog was calming. He didn't look excited. He didn't look scared or apprehensive. He just looked back at me once, like he was saying it was OK. I suppose that he could have told me it would be OK, I mean, he's a talking dog, right? But I guess he only talks when it is necessary.

"And it didn't seem necessary for him to talk. I think he figured out that I trusted him to keep me safe. And I did trust him to do that. We had just met, I had just heard a talking dog, I was in a strange place, but I trusted him."

She stopped for a minute.

"I did trust him."

"So I followed the dog into the forest. It was a wide path, about the width of an old logging trail, I guess. So it wasn't all closed in, there was plenty of room to walk without feeling like you were in danger or anything.

"And there was plenty of light, at least that gray-yellow light. Even though the forest was pretty thick on both sides, there was plenty of light to see. I looked up, and could see those funny clouds, those 'Mam-ma-tus' "– she said that haltingly, like she was trying out the word – "Mammatus clouds, just like here."

I nodded.

"So we walked down the forest path. The dog in front, and me following him. I was looking all around: up ahead, to both sides, even turning around once or twice. But it wasn't like I was scared or concerned about anything, I was all calm. I was just looking around.

"I didn't see much, though. The path ahead was a bit winding around, so you couldn't see too far down the path. And the forest on each side was dark, with lots of trees and some bushes. I didn't hear anything either. I've been in forests before, and you hear insects and blue jays and other birds, but this forest was quite. The only thing you hear was that same low humming sound, and our footsteps.

"I don't know how long we walked. Maybe a half hour? Hard to say, since time didn't feel the same a back in the 'normal' world. But the dog kept walking down the trail at a steady pace, and it was an easy pace, so I wasn't running or anything. It would be a 'nice walk in the forest' at any other time. Sort of a 'nice walk in the forest, in an environment that was weird, following a talking dog'. Who wasn't talking at all, but I got the sense of 'things will be all right'."

She stopped to drink the rest of her water. I grabbed the pitcher, and motioned to her about a refill, and she nodded yes, so I filled up her glass. I'd been sipping my glass of water, so I refilled mine also. I put the pitcher back on the table, and we both grabbed our glasses. I leaned back in my chair and waited for her to continue.

She took a sip of water and put her glass back on the table. She was still petting her dog, which had stayed still all of this time.

"So we kept on walking. And then we got to a small clearing. The dog stopped in the middle of the clearing, and looked back at me to make sure that I stopped also. I could see that this seemed to be a forest 'intersection' of some sort. There were open spots in the forest around the clearing, and there were paths for each of the clear spots. Those paths disappeared into the forest, but they were wide like our path, and weren't dark. They had the same yellow-gray light as I saw on our path. The paths were empty, though. I couldn't see anyone or anything on them, although I had a sense that they were well-used, since the grass was worn down like people had walked along those paths a lot.

"I noticed that there was a fallen log in the clearing, so I walked over to it and sat down. The dog followed me over there, and sat down in front of me. He seemed to be looking at one particular path, but I couldn't see anything different about that path. It looked like all the other ones, just like the one we had used."

Audrelle stopped talking. She took a drink of water, and a deep breath. She was still petting her dog. He hadn't moved since she started petting him. It was like he was providing comfort and support to her while she told her story.

"I was looking in the same direction as the dog, towards one of the other paths. Then the dog spoke to me. I heard it in my head, like the last time. He said something like this:"

This is a waiting and gathering spot. We need to wait here a bit for the next part of the journey to be ready for us. And there will be some others joining us.

I don't want you to get frightened when other people come. They are being guided by other dogs, just like I am guiding you.

They have come from different places, and it is a bit confusing to them, just like it was for you.

But they, like you, won't be very talkative. In fact, you'll probably just get a 'Hello' or nod of a head. Sort of like you nod to someone when they step into an elevator with you.

Don't be worried about that. It's normal, and happens that way all the time.

Several people will be gathering here. They will come here via those other paths. I can't tell you what is at the other end of those paths, but it is sort of similar to what you have experienced.

So don't be worried by anything. Don't worry that they won't be talkative; it's all part of the process.

We just need to wait here while the others gather here with us.

"The dog stopped 'talking', and lay down in front of me. He put his head on his paws, but he was still watching that same other path.

"It was a lot of 'talking' for a dog, I guess. They only seem to say what is needed at the time. Before, he just needed to say a few words, I guess. This time, it was a long speech; at least, long for him.

"But it was a calming speech. Not that I was stressed out, but it prepared me for what happened next. I thought that no matter what happened, or how strange or freaky it was, the dog was there to protect me, and to keep me calm. And that knowledge was calming me down. I guess like it was supposed to.

"So, the 'what happened next' didn't freak me out. Although it was a bit strange, the dog helped me be calm throughout the whole thing.

"The dog told me it was going to be strange. And it was."

Audrelle took another sip of water, and then continued.

"So me and the dog are sitting on a log. Hah. I'm a poet. Actually, the dog was sitting in front of the log. Anyway, we're sitting there waiting for whatever we are waiting for.

"And then the dog perks up a bit. Dogs have good hearing, you know. I didn't hear anything, but the dog did.

"The dog looked at another of the trails. He seemed to be focused on that one trail, so I looked there too.

"I admit that I started to get a little nervous. But the dog sort of leaned into my legs as I was sitting on the log, and that seemed to be calming. So I took a deep breath, and then looked in the same direction as the dog.

"It took a minute or two, or what used to be a minute or two, time was all screwed up, I think, but then I saw some movement on the trail. It was out of focus at first, like you were looking through smudged glasses.

"Then I realized it wasn't really out of focus, but whatever was coming was sort of pixelated. As they got closer, things cleared up, and I could see that there was another dog in front. This one looked to be a poodle, one of the medium size ones, not a 'toy' poodle.

"Anyway, it was walking in front, so I saw the dog first. It sort of pixelated into view, but it was moving, not appearing in one spot. You know, it wasn't like those really old Star Trek movies I used to watch with my Dad where they did that transporter thing and people just appeared in one spot. It was like they were walking, and moving towards me, and they were de-pixelating or something as they walked toward me and the dog."

As she said 'really old Star Trek movies', I keyed in on the 'really old' part. I used to watch those movies. In the original airings, actually. But I guess they were 'really old' to her. But I didn't interrupt her, and let her continue.

"So I see the poodle first, and then I see two people. Or I figured it was people; they had that sort of form. They were still pixelated a bit, but as they walked closer sort of 'through' the pixilation, I could see that it was a man and a woman. They looked to be old, in their 30's or 40's maybe."

I thought to myself "Old. 30's or 40's. What does that make me? I guess I am 'old' too compared to a teenager." But, again I kept quiet, and she continued.

"The dog was leading this man and the woman to the clearing where we were. They looked a bit, oh, 'out of place' or not sure where they were, but they seemed calm. I guess that their dog was doing the same 'calming' thing that my dog was doing.

"So they got to the clearing, and they looked over in our direction. The woman's eyes opened wider a bit, and she gave one of those 'elevator smiles' things. She didn't say anything though. The man seemed to notice me then, and also did the 'elevator smile' thing, but also kept quiet.

"Their dog led them over to another log that was at the edge of the clearing. I hadn't noticed the other log benches before. I thought my log bench was the only one there. But there were other log benches around the clearing. Just one row deep, with each log bench taking up the area between the different path openings into the forest.

"Their dog stopped in front of the empty log bench, and looked at them. Their heads sort of turned sideways a bit, like they were listening to something. I didn't hear anything, though. I guess their dog was 'talking' to them, like mine did. But since the 'talking' wasn't out loud, but inside their heads, I didn't hear anything.

"I guess the dog told them to sit down and wait a bit. And to not worry about anything. This was just an interim stop on their journey.

"I looked at my dog to see what he would 'say', but he didn't say anything. I got that 'calming' thing from my dog, so I sat back a bit and relaxed. The other couple seemed to do the same thing. We didn't really make eye contact with each other, and we didn't talk to each other. We just sat there and waited.

"By this time, my dog had sat down again, sort of relaxed. Like this kind of thing happened every day. I don't know, maybe it did.

"And we sat there for a few minutes, and my dog – and the new couple's dog – perked up a bit, and the process basically repeated.

"The dogs already here would sit up and look down one of the paths. There would be a pixilation thing, and then someone would appear. Whoever was the 'new kids on the block' would give the rest of us the 'elevator smile' thing, and their dog would take them to a log bench, and 'talk' to them. And the new people would sit down, and the new dog would sit down.

"And the same thing would happen again.

"As I sat there, I noticed that the clearing seemed to get a bit larger. There were more benches, placed behind the existing ones. There always seemed to be enough new benches for the new people.

"So this continued, until there were about 35-40 people, in various sized groups, each group with their own dog. Different breeds of dogs, but they all seemed to have the same capability to keep their 'people' calm, and to 'talk' to them and tell them something that the rest of us couldn't hear. And the people would sit down, their dogs would sit down, and we all waited for whatever happened next.

"And something did happen next."

Audrelle continued her story.

"All of a sudden, all of the dogs sat up, and looked to one pathway that hadn't been used before by any of the other arrivals. Their 'people' would also look over there.

"My dog 'talked' to me. "

We're about ready for the next part of our journey. Everyone else is getting ready too. But there's nothing to worry about, just stay put and I'll let you know what to do.

"I don't know what the other dogs said, but I guess the other people got a similar speech from their dogs that I got from my dogs.

"Everyone was calm, there wasn't any talking, but all were watching that one path that hadn't been used.

"And on that path, the black pixel snowstorm started up. Just right in front of the one path back into the forest. The pixels started to get more numerous, but they still concentrated in one spot. After a bit, it wasn't really a long time, the black pixels resolved into a door.

"It was a regular, wooden door, like you would see at the front of a house. It was solid wood, and almost black. Not quite as black as the black pixels and you could see that the door had a different composition than the pixels. You could tell that the door had some 'solid' to it.

"So the black pixels turned into, or maybe just were able to 'show', a door. It was standing by itself. No door frame. Just a plain old dark door. There wasn't a door handle that I could see.

"All of the dogs were focused on the door. But they were also right next to their people. My dog was right next to me. I was still sitting, like everyone else, and my dog was leaning into my legs. It was very calming. Like the dog was putting out waves of 'calm' to me by leaning against me.

"Then the door opened, inward into the forest, away from me. I looked past the door, but couldn't see anything past it, it was all dark. But I didn't sense any danger coming from the door. Maybe part of that was because my dog was leaning against me, keeping me calm.

"So the door had opened, and behind the door was darkness, I guess leading into that path into the trees. Then one of other dogs stood up, and nudged their group towards the door. I guess that the dog talked to their group. The dog took a couple of steps towards the door, and then looked back at their 'people', and then their people started following their dog.

"Their dog led them to the door, and walked through. I could see that the dog waited a few steps inside the door, looking back, and their people followed the dog through the door. The dog started walking again, and their people followed.

"And they sort of disappeared. Not really like they 'faded out', but like they sort of merged into the dark area behind the door.

"And as they merged into that dark area, the door slowly and quietly shut.

"This happened again to every other dog and their people that had come into the clearing. A door would open; there would be a dark area behind the door. A dog would stand up, take a step, stop and look back at his 'people', and the people stood up and started following the dog. They would go through the door, sort of merge into the darkness behind the door. And then the door would silently and slowly shut.

"The process continued until the only ones left were me and my dog. First in, last out, I guess.

"The door opened one last time. For me and my dog, I guess. Because my dog took a step, and then looked back at me."

It's our turn to go. Everything will be fine. This was just a resting spot on our journey. Just follow me. It's all good.

"So I followed the dog through the door. Merged into the darkness behind the door. The door closed behind me."

Audrelle stopped again, taking a drink of water with one hand, and still petting her dog with the other. Petting the dog seemed to keep her calm. And I kept quiet, watching and listening, while she continued the story.

"We walked into the dark area behind the door, but it wasn't really dark. It's hard to explain, but it was like we transitioned from one visual area to another. You could see just fine in front of you, and in back of you, but farther behind or in front of you was darker. It got more light in front of you, and then darker in back of you.

"We were back on a path into the forest. I looked back, and the door had disappeared. It just looked like a forest path in back of me. But I couldn't see the clearing we had just come from. So I kept following my dog."

Audrelle stopped again. She was looking out into the valley, towards the new cabin. It was still there, but there was nothing moving there, or anywhere else. The only movement was the creek flowing down out of the trees in back of my cabin, down into the valley and into the old beaver pond.

There was no breeze. I hadn't seen a breeze since the lights blinked. No animals or birds or insects of any kind. The only living beings around seemed to be me and Audrelle and the two dogs.

~ 50~

We'd been talking; well, Audrelle had been talking, for quite a while. She kept looking out into the valley. All of that talking had taken a bit of energy out of her.

We were both sitting in Adirondack chairs that had cushions, so they were quite comfortable. As I watched Audrelle, she was petting the dog, but that slowly stopped. And her eyes slowly closed as she dozed off and rested.

Her dog slowly took his head out of her lap; she had stopped petting his head. He took a step away from her, and then lay down at her feet. He put his head on his paws and closed his eyes.

I sat in my chair, looking at both of them. She hadn't finished her story yet, but it looked like she needed to rest.

I wasn't tired for some reason. I hadn't really slept a lot since the lights blinked. It was like I didn't need to sleep as much as I usually did.

And I wasn't really hungry. I had eaten two of the energy bars, and drank two glasses of water. So I guess that was a meal for me. The dog didn't seem to require much food or water either.

So they were both resting. I just sat in my chair, looking out into the valley, over to the new cabin, into the woods. Nothing had changed.

Well, everything had changed since the lights blinked. Time and distance had changed. There were those black pixel snowstorms that happened to me, and evidently to Audrelle also. The yellow-gray light, the clouds, the distant humming sound – all that was new.

And the dog. Many dogs, according to Audrelle's story. All with the apparent ability to talk to their people.

Then there was the new cabin, with its strange dimensions, where the inside was bigger than the outside. And the doors that opened and closed by themselves.

Including the door that Audrelle had come through with her dog. The dog had left Audrelle and me inside the cabin, leaving through the same door that he entered.

Lots of changes. And I hadn't figured out what was going on ye

I got up carefully from my chair, so I wouldn't disturb Audrelle. I went inside and got a lightweight blanket, and brought it out to the porch. I carefully covered Audrelle while she was sleeping in the chair. It wasn't really cold outside – it wasn't hot either – so a blanket wasn't really needed. I think it was there more for her comfort than warmth. She stirred a bit when I put the blanket on her, but didn't wake up.

I sat back down in my chair. And tried to figure out what was going on.

I wasn't getting much success with that effort. It seemed like the dogs knew, but they weren't talking to explain things.

So I sat in my chair, occasionally sipping my water, staring out into the valley, trying to figure things out.

I had some glimmers of ideas.

I started with the black pixel snow storms. They seemed to be an 'agent of transition'; something that allowed things to transition or move from one area to another.

Well, not one area to another. Was it more like one dimension to another? That was an interesting concept.

Maybe this was a 'multiverse'. I'm not a physicist, so don't know much about all of this, but I think the main thought is that there are similar universes to ours, but they are in different dimensions. That's probably being very simplistic about the theory, and is probably as deep as I understand it, but it might explain things.

If there are different dimensions of existence, and each dimension is similar in physical appearance, then perhaps there is a way to 'move' between dimensions.

Perhaps that 'portal' between these similar dimensions is accessed or shown by the pixel storms. They are a transitioning process that allows movement between dimensions.

Maybe there was a giant and quick 'blink' of a pixel storm transition process that caused that first light blink I saw when I was back in my office. And that 'blink' moved me to a different dimension.

A dimension with similar or even the same world physical characteristics as my 'original' world. But without all the people or other living things. That might explain how the 'world' seemed the same – trees, building, forests, cars, electricity – but there weren't any living persons that transitioned between dimensions except me.

If I was in the same 'world' but a different dimension, other physical entities – people, birds, dogs, insects, whatever – were still in my original 'world'. It was just me that transition to this different dimension.

And in this different dimension, time and movement were a bit different. That might explain how I was biking through the city but not getting far, taking too long to travel a block or two on the bike.

Maybe it also explained the clouds, and the low humming sound. They could be manifestations of a different dimension, where the physical world works just a bit differently than 'my' world.

So there are random portals that have appeared between the dimensions of this multiverse. Those portals were somehow more visible, to me at least.

But then there were the dogs. My dog appeared to me after the first black pixel snow storm, back when I stayed in that barn. What was the dog's purpose?

From what had happened to me, and what Audrelle told with her story, the dogs seemed to be some sort of guide between – or in – the various dimensions of the multiverse. "Guide dogs" that help people transition, for whatever reason, between one dimension and another.

The dogs seem to understand what guiding is needed for each person or group of persons. That seems to explain, maybe a bit, the part of Audrelle's story where she was waiting in the clearing, and then other groups of people arrived with their guide dogs.

And the appearance of the door, brought about by a concentration of black pixels – those dimension-portals – were a way to get groups of people from one dimension to another.

Audrelle said that the door closed then opened for each group (and their guide dog). Maybe that opening and closing was for getting to different dimensions. So that each group of people converged on the clearing, then were guided, by the guide dogs, to their dimension destination.

And because the groups of people weren't aware of why they were there, the dogs had the ability to 'talk' to their people, and some sort of calming effect on their people as they took them to whatever their destination is.

That is how Audrelle described it. The dogs spoke only when needed, but provided a calming effect on the emotions of their people. In fact, I saw that happen to Audrelle when my dog seemed to provide a calming effect while she was telling the story.

But I can't figure out the 'end game'. What is the point of all of this? Has there been some cosmic 'hiccup' that has got things out of whack? Or were things always like this, but just not evident to anyone?

And how do things get back to 'normal'? Or is this the new 'normal'? And what part do I play in any of this, or am I just an unwilling participant?

And will the sun ever appear? And that humming noise; will it ever go away?

I wasn't getting very far in figuring this out. I have some theories, but not sure of any of this. I'm not a "Sheldon Cooper"; so much of this is way over my head.

I'm going to need some help on this. But there aren't any 'googles' around to type in a question and get the answer.

This might take a bit more effort. And maybe a lot of outside help of some sort.

Audrelle was still resting. I think I was tired. But the last time I rested at the same time as Audrelle, back in the library, she was gone when I woke up. I was a bit reticent in repeating that process, both for my sake and for hers. It would seem that all of this was a bit disconcerting, and maybe something that you wouldn't want to go through again by yourself.

Even if you had a talking dog with you. Who doesn't talk that much. Who could, maybe, explain all of this.

So I stayed awake. Looking out over the valley, with occasional glances to Audrelle, and the dog. Looking out into the valley, where nothing was moving. And that new cabin out there, which seemed to be a 'portal' of some sort. At least, that's how Audrelle appeared to travel into 'my' dimension.

Whatever 'my dimension' was. It certainly wasn't the dimension that I was in before the lights blinked.

So I sat on the porch. I tried to make some – or any – kind of sense of the past few days.

Not having much success at that, I think.

~ 51 ~

I must have dozed off.

You know how when you are sitting in your favorite chair, and it's quiet in the house. Well, if you have kids in the house, you might have to think back a bit to a time when it was quiet in the house.

Anyway, when you are sitting in your favorite chair, the house is quiet, maybe some background music or a boring TV show. And you start to de-focus, and become less-aware of things around you.

Then, all of a sudden, your head jerks up, like almost-whiplash, and your eyes pop open. And you have that momentary 'where-am-I?' feeling. And your slowly focus, and you realize that you are in your favorite chair, the TV or music in the background, the house is quiet. But you sense that time has passed. Maybe just a few minutes, or maybe an hour, but you have this sense of time passing. You aren't sure how much time has passed, though.

And you aren't sure that you were really asleep, not like a going-to-bed-and-waking-up-in-the-morning kind of sleep, but some sort of 'rest-y' thing.

And you think that you heard something. Like some sort of unusual noise or an unexpected noise. Like a car backfiring, or a dog barking, or some creaky-sound from your house.

And you're not sure, because you are still in that almost-awake-but-not-quite state, what the noise was that woke you up. In fact, you might have heard the noise in some sort of dream-like state, before you woke up. Or tried to wake up.

Yeah, that.

I had all of those thoughts. They happened quite fast, racing through my mind, as I woke up from whatever state I was in, thoughts racing, trying to get back into full consciousness, aware of something that happened, or did it, or what.

I slowly focused. Without moving my head, well, other than that wake-up-jerky movement, I looked around.

Porch. I am on a porch.

Cabin. Yeah, this is my cabin.

Valley. Forested on the edge of the valley. My stream running through it. The small pond/lake, a few trees and bushes around the lake. An old beaver pond; that's right.

I shivered. One of those involuntary, something-is-not-quite-right shivers. Maybe one of those 'startle' things. You know, when you are sitting, and your body gets a kind of quick jerk, involuntary muscle spasm, just a little one, but one that you can't duplicate if you tried.

So a 'shiver-jerk' thing, I guess. What does that mean?

Valley. Yep. Same old valley. Except that other cabin out there. That didn't used to be there.

The new cabin. Small on the outside, big and empty on the inside. One door on each wall, flanked by one window on each side of each door.

Audrelle. Cabin. Door.

My eyes moved to the left of me. She – Audrelle – was still there. A blanket over her. Sitting in the chair on the porch.

Dog. Next to her chair. Lying down, head on his (her?) paws. Eyes open, looking at me.

Wait. Dogs. Plural.

There's a dog – a collie – next to my chair also. Also lying down, head on paws, but eyes open.

I slowly got my surroundings into clarity. And remembered all the things that happened since the lights blinked.

Still had no clue of what was going on. Just the 'other-dimension' theory. And that the other new cabin in my valley seemed to be a 'transfer portal' for inter-dimensional travels of some sort.

As I became more aware of things – getting past that 'just woke up, not sure where I am' feeling you sometimes get when waking up from a nap, I reached over to the table next to the chair for my glass of water. It was warm, just a bit, but took a few swallows of water.

And remembered, again, that I was not sure how I got to this 'dimension' – something happened during the 'light blink' – but that Audrelle – still sleeping in the chair on the porch – was somehow involved in all of this.

Probably an involuntary involvement.

Maybe.

Now that I am fully awake, I sit in my chair, holding my warm glass of water.

Audrelle is still sleeping, not moving. I can tell she is sleeping, though, with the small movements as she breathes. That's good. Not sure I could handle her not breathing.

I looked at the dogs. Although they hadn't moved, they were looking up at me.

I quietly spoke to the dogs. "Any help here?"

The dogs both looked at me. Then, with some unnoticeable communication passing between them, they turned their heads to look at each other. After a few seconds of looking at each other, one of the dogs – 'my' dog, the one that had accompanied me since the stay at the barn before I got to the cabin – looked at me.

Not yet, I heard.

Not really 'hearing', like the dog had spoken out loud, but more of a 'heard it in my head' kind of thing. That's how he – my dog – had been communicating with me. When he chose to. He wasn't really a big conversationalist. More of an "I'll say something when it's important" kind of 'talker'.

"It would really help out if you could let me know what's going on," I said. "At least, it seems like you know what is happening here. A little bit of help in explaining things might be useful here."

The dog looked at me.

Not yet.

And he laid his head back on his paws. As did the other dog.

Wait. The other dog?

My brain synapses were finally working again. I remembered about the new dog – the golden retriever.

That was the dog that was with Audrelle, at least, according to her story. Her dog took her through the forest to the 'pixel-door', which got her into the new cabin. Her dog had brought her to me – I was in the new cabin, in the emptiness of the inside of that cabin – and then told her to go with me.

So, two dogs. One – the collie – is the dog that I met at that barn next to the house a few days ago – or whenever it was; time was a bit fuzzy around here. The other – the golden retriever – is the dog that came with Audrelle when she 'appeared' at the new cabin.

~ 52~

Both dogs were still lying down, heads on paws, eyes open, relaxed. Audrelle was still sleeping in the chair.

The 'new' dog – I guess it might be easier if I named him (her)? How about I'll go with "Archie". He's a golden retriever, but his coat is more red than golden. got those patches of reddish-brown fur, so that's good enough.

As I thought of the name of "Archie", the new dog lifted up his head from his paws, and looked over to me. I saw his tail wag twice. I guess that "Archie" is OK with him also.

My dog – I guess he needs a name too. It would be easier to keep track of them with names. A border collie, as I believe I told you before. So, a good border collie name.

He's mostly black on top, with a white colored underbelly and chest, and a mostly white face. His hair is slightly long, but not unkempt or matted. He also looked well-cared for, even though I hadn't brushed him or anything. It was like he was always neat and clean, somehow without any effort on my part.

"Butler". A good of a name as any. And as I thought of that name, he popped up his head and looked straight at me, then turned his head to the side a bit.

"OK," he said. And he dropped his head back to his paws, keeping his eyes open.

So. "Butler" – the dog that appeared to have adopted me back at the barn. And "Archie" – the dog that came with Audrelle.

Butler and me. Audrelle and Archie.

I guess that will work.

I looked at Archie. "How did you get here?" I asked.

Archie raised his heads from his paws, looking at me. He then looked over at Butler. Again, some sort of mental communication seemed to pass between them.

Not yet, Archie said. Again with the sounds being 'inside' me; not heard by my ears, but with some sort of telepathy-like communication.

"Not yet? This is getting old. Things have been really weird for me, if you haven't noticed. The light blink, the black pixel storms, those funny clouds, the yellow-gray light, and that low humming sound. Not to mention that the only people, or only anything living I have seen in the last two days, or however long it has been, is just you and Butler and Audrelle. And that raven.

"And talking dogs! That don't really talk out loud, but I can hear thoughts or 'talking' that is coming from dogs! " I wasn't yelling, though. At least, it didn't sound like yelling to me. I was just talking sort of loud, but not yelling. Just frustrated.

"This is all so weird. Like a bad dream," I continued.

I got a bit quieter. "And I am asking a dog to tell me what is going on. A dog! Sheesh!"

I sat back in my chair; I guess I had leaned forward while I was talking to Archie. Butler, my dog, had perked up his head a bit during my little mini-explosion, looking over at Archie.

I took a deep breath. I was still holding my water glass. There was still some water in it, so I took a few swallows, then placed it back on the table next to my chair.

"I'd sure like to know what is going on," I said, quietly, almost to myself.

I know. Patience. Things are not normal for us, either. But patience is needed. Be calm. Things will be revealed. But not yet, said Archie.

"Patience," I muttered. "Patience, grasshopper. Thanks, Mr. Po."

Archie is fine, said Archie.

"Fine," I said. "Archie. Although I should have called you Mr. Po with all of this 'patience' stuff," I mumbled to myself.

So I sat there in the chair on my porch. Audrelle had not awakened during my little tirade. Everything else was still the same. My little valley, the cabin, the old beaver pond, the new cabin, the ...

Wait - the new cabin. Although it was on the other side of the little valley, I could see it clearly like I was much closer to it. The front door was visible; the side and back doors were not in my line of vision. The two windows, one on each side of the front door, which was open.

The front door. Open. No, opening. I could see that it was opening. I could clearly see that the front door was opening.

The inside of the cabin was a bit lighter than the outside, so the door showed something in the doorway that was backlit a bit. I couldn't quite make out what was in the door, but there was something there.

It moved out of the new cabin, onto the porch. The front door slowly closed behind it.

I could see what it was, clearly. The new cabin was on the other side of the valley. I shouldn't be able to see anything with clear detail normally, but I could see it now. Some sort of tricky vision-clarity thing, almost like looking through binoculars. Really clear and bright images in the binoculars.

Of course. I could see what it was, in front of the now-closed door of the new cabin.

Another dog.

Of course.

~ 53~

Another dog. I could see it clearly. Another poodle, by the way. One of those medium-sized poodles, under two feet tall, I guess. White hair, somewhat curly. No fancy poodle haircut.

All of this I could see clearly across the valley, as if I was using binoculars. Which I wasn't.

I watched as the dog looked around the valley, and then looked in our direction.

Archie and Butler both sat up, and looked out towards the poodle. Again that sort of mental communication between Archie and Butler.

The poodle – was I going to have to think up another dog name? – looked our way, and jumped off the porch with a small 'yip' sound, you know, like poodles make when they think they are barking. He (she, whatever) started running in our direction. Archie and Butler watched as the poodle ran toward us.

It only took a minute, or maybe two, at least, a minute or two in what I remembered as being a normal minute-length-of-time. Whatever.

The poodle took a direct line towards us, jumping over (Through? Across the rocks? No matter.) the little river (more of a stream, I guess) that ran down from next to my cabin into the old beaver dam. Across the valley, straight line, right to the cabin.

All four of us – Audrelle (still sleeping), me, Archie, Butler – were on the porch of my cabin. There are three steps that lead down to the ground in front of the porch. The poodle headed straight for the steps, and stopped right at the bottom of the steps.

The poodle sat down in front of the steps. Haunches down, front legs up, a 'dog-is-sitting' kind of position. The poodle then raised one of his front paws, and put it on the bottom step. Then he looked up at Archie, and turned his head to the side, like he was waiting for 'Permission to come aboard."

Archie dipped his head down a bit, then back up. The poodle then slowly but deliberately climbed the steps, and came up to Archie, sitting down about two feet in front of Archie.

No, not sitting. Lying down, but head up, looking at Archie.

I could see them both without moving my head back and forth.

Archie looked at the poodle, and dipped his head down and back up again. The poodle sat up, looking intently at Archie, quietly. No sound, other than a bit of panting from the poodle, which had run all the way across the valley, so I guess that panting was understandable.

As I watched, it looked like the poodle was communicating with Archie. The poodle would tilt his head a bit, and Archie would dip and raise his head. Like the poodle was 'reporting back' to Archie and Archie was listening, with a few choice words of his own. Not that anyone was talking, that I could tell. Whatever the poodle was 'saying', Archie was able to listen to. But I didn't hear anything.

I glanced over at Butler. He was sitting up now, looking intently at the poodle as the poodle was 'talking'. At least, that's what it looked like to me. Like I am an expert in 'dog communication'. The only dog communication I had seen before was all of that sniffing stuff that dogs would do when they meet. Or a bit of yipping or barking.

Not here. Whatever they were communicating, they were doing it in a telepathic sort of way.

This went on for a few minutes. Then the poodle appeared to stop 'talking' (not sure how I knew that, but I did). And Archie was 'talking' now. The poodle had tilted his head to the side, like you would when you were listening to someone.

After about a minute of that, Archie dipped his head again, and the poodle did the same thing. And the poodle turned around, ran down the steps, and ran back to the new cabin.

I could see the poodle as he got to the new cabin's door, which had opened again, with my 'binocular' sight. The poodle went through the open door, with the brighter light of some sort inside the cabin. And then the door shut again.

While the poodle was running back to the new cabin, I had glanced at Archie and Butler. There seemed to be some sort of communication between them. Again, no sounds, no little yips or barks or growls; just that telepathic type of communication between the two dogs.

I noticed that I was leaning forward in my chair on the front porch. I had tensed up a bit without realizing it. And I took a deep breath; it seemed that I had forgotten to breathe while all of this was going on. Of course, I hadn't. It was just that sudden realization that I needed to take a deep breath, or that I was aware that I needed to take one. So I did. And I leaned back into the chair.

"That was interesting," I thought.

Yes. It was, said Archie.

"Interesting".

At the very least.

This whole thing I am experiencing since the lights blinked is 'interesting'.

"Care to elaborate on that?" I asked Archie. (Which is also 'interesting' – I'm expecting to have a logical and meaningful conversation with a dog, who I expect to answer my question. That would classify as 'interesting.')

Archie seemed to consider my question carefully. And he stood up and walked over to the bowl of water that I had put on the porch. He did that 'lapping' thing that dogs do with their tongues when they drink water. Clever, how they do that. I suppose it's an advantage of having a long tongue, and the disadvantage of having opposable thumbs.

Archie walked back to his spot on the porch, turned around twice, and then sat down. I wondered why dogs did that 'turn-around' thing before they sit or lie down. I was about to ask that question, then caught myself. I could always ask later, I guess, but there were more important things that needed to be asked.

Archie looked at Butler, communicating with each other in that way that I'd see them do before. Archie nodded his head once to Butler.

Butler sat up, facing me. He seemed to take a deep breath – do dogs take deep breaths before a major speech? Don't know. Never heard a big long speech from a dog before. Things are different now, I guess.

I kept quiet, and listened while Butler 'spoke', listening inside my head via that telepathic speech that they use to talk to us mere mortals.

~ 54~

Butler speaking. Archie lying down, head on his paws, but eyes open, 'listening'.

The dog that you call Archie has given me permission to tell you a few things. They are going to be a bit strange or even 'weird' to you. But these things that I will tell you are true, and they are happening now. Some things are what have happened for a long time, and then there is the 'new' stuff.

I'll need to tell you some 'background' stuff before I get into what is happening now.

We dogs have always been friends to humans. Sometimes our humans don't always act friendly to us; there are some bad things in the world. This is a necessity. There has to be bad, even though unpleasant to experience. But we must have 'bad' in order to know 'good'. We know this, and even though we don't like the 'bad', and wish there wasn't any, we know that the 'bad' exists. We deal with it, knowing that, overall, the good will outweigh the bad. Perhaps not right away, but having the 'good' will happen to us in the end.

We have provided comfort and companionship for humans for thousands of years. We provide protection to our humans when we can. We provide warnings when needed, and comfort also when needed. You, the human, see this comfort in many ways, sometimes as simple as just lying next to you while you scratch our ears.

Which we really like, by the way. That whole ear-scratching thing is one of our favorite things about being around humans.

We are very protective of our humans. You see this when we warn you about a threat, for example. If we think there is danger for our humans, then we try to alert you. We are not allowed to speak your language – in normal situations. We communicate with our humans by using our different types of vocalizations – barks, growls, yips, whatever.

Notice that I use the term 'our humans'. We realize that you think that you 'own' us, or that we 'belong' to you. We let you think that, because it serves our purpose of being the one that 'serves' you. We, the dogs, 'know' that we are a 'helper' for you, in many ways. We provide physical and emotional comfort and even 'spiritual' comfort on occasion.

You can probably recall, once you are aware of our main 'purpose', if you will, of the many types of 'service' that we provide to you, our humans.

So we dogs provide our 'service' to you humans throughout your life. Even if a human doesn't 'own' a dog – and we aren't really 'owned' by you, even though you might think that – we provide service to non-dog-owning humans in many different ways. Usually, that service is provided in a 'physical' sense. But there are 'spiritual' services we provide, often to those humans that don't 'own' a dog.

We have been providing our service to our humans for thousands of years. We have provided that service to you also, even though you don't 'own' a dog.

Our service doesn't require the human to own or have a dog. For example, we may provide service to someone when they just see us, when we are walking in the park or down a sidewalk, or sitting someplace as you walk by. We even provide service when we are not physically next to a human, for instance, maybe if you are watching a television show and there is a dog as part of the show.

We have the ability to provide our service 'remotely', if you will. We provide that service to all.

Some people get 'more' of our service, when they need it. Some people get 'less' of our service, because they don't need as much service as others. But all dogs provide service to all humans, in one way or another. That is what we do.

Butler stopped 'talking' for a moment. He got up to get a drink of water, then returned to his spot and sat down again. With the 'turn-around' thing, of course, before he sat down.

I looked over at Audrelle. She was still sleeping. Then I looked at Archie. He was still lying down, head on his paws, eyes open.

Butler continued 'talking'.

So 'service' is what dogs do.

I smiled a bit at that last phrase. But I kept quiet. Sometimes I have control over my inner smart-aleck.

Our service doesn't stop at any time. It continues. It has continued for thousands of years. And that is important to remember: our service does not stop.

Let me explain another thing. This is related to our service, which is our primary job. And it is related to what is happening now.

The concepts might be hard to understand. We dogs know that humans are intelligent. But so are we. We might be, in fact we are, capable of more intelligence than humans. We don't always let humans be aware of our greater intellect. We don't 'show off', as it were. But our intelligence is quite impressive, if I do say so myself. We just choose to limit the display of our intelligence.

There are times when we use our greater intellect to benefit our service to our humans. You might know of some of these instances.

A simple example: our ability to sense danger, and alert our humans to that danger, when they are not aware of it. Like when a dog might alert its humans to a fire in a house. Or the dogs that are used as 'helpers' to first responders – the police, for example – or to soldiers in a battle environment. We 'let' the humans 'train' us for those jobs, even though we already know what is needed, and how to do that which is needed.

Part of our service to humans is to let them 'grow' in their knowledge, letting them 'learn' how to use our greater intellect. Humans benefit from this by their increased knowledge. We dogs benefit from this because it is how we serve.

Now because we have a greater intellect than humans, we have a greater knowledge of things. We let the humans 'learn' how to do things that we already know about. Sometimes we use our intellect to help humans – service – such as some dogs that have been 'trained' to sense out certain types of disease. It is not necessarily the humans that train us, but us 'allowing' the humans to use our greater intellect to the benefit – the 'service' – of humans.

So we dogs have greater knowledge of things. One of our big 'things' is the knowledge of 'dimensions'. Not measurements, but dimensions of worlds. Yes, 'worlds'. Plural.

There have been some humans who have theorized about what you call 'alternate dimensions'. They have not been able to prove these theories; the knowledge level of humans has not yet progressed to that point.

But we dogs know about those alternate dimensions – those alternate 'worlds'. We have known about these things for a long time; a very long time.

It is a hard concept for many humans to grasp. They just aren't at the level of knowledge that they need to be able to understand that concept. And it might be difficult for you to understand. We know that. But, since you have 'landed' in this alternate 'world', we have decided to try to teach you about the concept. You'll have to trust us on this explanation. It may be difficult to grab hold of, but it is important for you to know about it, because it relates to your current situation.

Here is the basic concept. There are 'alternate dimensions' or 'worlds' that exist here on this world. Let's call them 'Alts'.

These Alts exist in parallel to what you know of as your 'normal' world. You cannot see them, or sense them, although some of the more knowledgeable humans have theorized about them.

These Alts have a similar physical sense or attributes to your own normal world. For instance, you had, in your own world, prior to the light blink, a home in a valley; a cabin that was built and owned by your ancestors, in a valley with a stream and an old beaver pond, surrounded by forest. This is the cabin – your cabin – that you are familiar with from your own, 'normal' world.

There is an Alt – several, in fact – that is the same as your own normal world. It contains your cabin, your stream, your old beaver pond, your forest. It is just on a different 'plane' of existence than your normal world. It is a place where other humans can be taken; and indeed, <u>are</u> taken to.

You humans are not aware of these Alts. You have no understanding of them. There are a very few humans that think they understand them, but they can't really 'prove' the existence of an Alt.

We dogs know about these Alts. We have known for a very long time. We know how to move between the Alts. And we use them for a specific purpose – to serve those humans that need to travel to a different Alt.

This is a fact. Humans die. They cease to exist in their current Alt.

At least, that is what humans think. There is Life, and then there is Death. Some humans believe in a 'life after death' of some sort. There are many variations on this belief; it is not necessary to go into any great detail of those beliefs.

But there is a 'life after death' – that 'life' is in the Alts.

And that is our – us dogs – other important service that we provide. We are the 'guides' for humans as they transfer or move between the Alts. As humans die, for whatever reason, we dogs are the guides to get to the next Alt.

Dogs die also. In fact, our service to humans is hard work, really. It is why our years of life are measured in what you humans call 'dog years'. Our service of one year – our existence of one year – is 'worth' 7 years of human existence. It is hard work serving you humans, and it is why our lives – in this Alt – are shorter than humans.

But, because of our increased intelligence, we know about the Alts, even during our time of service to living humans. We don't need a 'guide' to get to the next Alt, because we already know about the next Alt.

You see, there was an Alt previous to our lives during your human time. Our movement from that previous Alt to this Alt is known to us, just as our movement from this Alt – your Alt – to the next Alt is known to us. We provide, again as part of our service to humans, the 'guide' to get you human from this Alt to the next at the time of your 'death' in your Alt.

Think about this. It is hard to understand. We know that. We don't often explain these things to humans. It is not needed. When the human travels from their current Alt to the next one, as we guide them, the humans 'understand' that the travel to the next Alt is part of the continuation of their life, even though they have 'died' in their Alt.

This service we provide to humans, being the guides and helpers as you humans move from one Alt to the next, is what we do. We have been doing this for a very long time.

The method of transport between the Alts is not important. I am not trying to be condescending here, but it is not a concept that you are ready for yet. You may understand it at some other point in time, maybe in a new Alt. But the transport method – how it works – is not important.

The mechanism that is used to transfer from one Alt to the next is what you call those 'black pixels' or 'pixel snowstorms'. They provide a way to get from one Alt to the next.

Audrelle experienced that transport mechanism. She told you about it in her story. Remember that she mentioned that she was in a waiting area in a clearing in a forest with others. And that the others had a dog with them, and the dog took them from the waiting area to a doorway that was used by the black pixel transfer mechanism. That is how she got from the waiting area to the new cabin, and to you.

Now the new cabin is a sort of portal area between Alts. Each door is a gateway to the next Alt. The doors aren't exclusively a gateway to a specific Alt. The doors 'adjust', if you will, to the gateway of the Alt that is needed for that person.

Or persons. You might recall that Audrelle told you about the waiting area, how there were not just individuals, but sometimes groups of people that were being guided by their dogs. A doorway is not necessarily just for one person, it might be for several people.

These Alts are part of what 'is'. They are a part of our – and your – existence. The Alts provide a place for humans to go after their death in their current Alt.

And we dogs are the guides for the humans as we take them from their current Alt to the next one.

So there are different Alts. You only know about the Alt that you lived in – the one that you were in before the lights blinked. We dogs, because we have a higher level of intellect, know about the other Alts. Again, I am not trying to make light of your human intellect.

We dogs are aware that you humans have used your intellect in many different ways, some good, and some bad. But that is in your capabilities. You have things that you do well, and things that you **can** do well, things that you can do better than us dogs.

Mostly relating to your having 'opposable thumbs'. Which is somewhat of a 'sore point' with us dogs. We have a greater intellect, but you have those opposable thumbs that we don't have. And they have allowed you to do things that we dogs cannot do.

Again, I am not making light of your level of intellect. It is just that we dogs work on a different level of intellect. It is the way things are. It is why we dogs 'work' alongside you in many ways, even though you may not see tangible benefits from that 'work'. Our service to humans happens in ways other than assisting you in creating or building or even breaking things.

It is the way that it is. You have your purpose, or 'effect' on life, and we dogs have ours. We understand the need for the differences, and we accept those differences.

Although opposable thumbs would be nice, sometimes.

There was a short growl from Archie. Butler glanced over at him, and dipped his head once. I guess for a 'sorry about that' for his remark about opposable thumbs.

But I liked it. Not enough that I said anything, but I did have a small smile when I heard it.

~ 55~

Butler continued his explanation.

What we dogs have been doing for millennia is two-fold: we provide service to humans during their life in their Alt – the Alt you know about. And we provide service as guides to take humans from their current Alt to the next one, wherever that may be.

There is not a specific progression from one Alt to the next. For example, all humans do not go from Alt-current (your current, pre-light-blink Alt) to "Alt number 5" or "Alt number 253". There is a progression from one Alt to the next, but not everyone goes to the same 'next' Alt.

There is a 'decision' of some sort that determines which Alt a human goes to next. That decision, and the 'decider', is not important for this discussion. Indeed, it is even more difficult to understand than the concept of "Alt". Suffice it to say that there is a 'process' of some sort that determines which Alt a particular human will progress to. There are rules and requirements, and much complexity to that decision process.

Just accept that there is a 'process' that determines your next Alt. It is not going to be explained further. It is a fact, and there are reasons behind every decision that the process makes. I am not going to explain it further, though, just be aware that there is a decision process that determines a humans' next Alt.

Whatever that Alt is, whichever Alt a human is going to next, is 'handled' by the black pixels that provide the 'transport', if you will, between the human's current Alt and the next one. Audrelle mentioned the black pixel 'doorway', which is what she perceived as the manifestation of the 'process' that allows movement from one Alt to the next.

Let's review these basic concepts. Our purpose, as dogs, is to provide 'service' to humans. Our greater intellect allows us to provide that service in many different ways during a humans' lifetime. And we continue with that service as we guide a human from their current Alt to the next.

The Alts are the alternative 'planes of existence'. The physical manifestation of those Alts look very similar to a humans current Alt. That is why Audrelle – and you – see familiar things: roads, buildings, your cabin, your valley, the old beaver pond. They are the 'basic' parts of all the Alts.

This process has worked for millennia. Dogs providing service to humans, guiding humans to their next Alt, whichever that Alt is, according to the decision process that determines the next Alt.

Butler paused in his explanation. He looked at Archie, who nodded once, I guess allowing Butler to continue with the next part.

So, here's the problem.

The problem is the lights blinked. And, somehow, we are still working at exactly why, you were transported to another Alt before your 'time'. You aren't supposed to be *in* this Alt.

It appears that the Alt you are in now is one that is based on your 'normal' Alt, but that contains no other people. That is why, when you first ventured outside your office after the light blink, you didn't see anyone…or any other living creature.

Normally, physical and mechanical things work just fine in each Alt. For instance, if there are cars in an Alt, they will work like you would normally think. There would be birds and insects and other critters in a different Alt. Those types of things; other creatures, are similar in all Alts.

But this Alt is a different one. It contains all of the physical properties of your Alt: buildings, cars, trees, water. But there are no creatures of any sort in this Alt.

This Alt is empty of any other physical, living creatures. Other than yourself, of course. And us.

And then there are the clouds and yellow-gray light, and the humming sound you have experienced since the lights blinked. This is all part of this Alt that you got into somehow.

Somehow, the light blink caused a disruption of some sort in your normal Alt, and a disruption or 'incompleteness' of this Alt. We are not sure, yet, of how or why this happened. We just know that it is not a normal occurrence. And we dogs know about the different Alts – how they look, how they 'work', what is 'in' any particular Alt.

This is **not** normal.

We know about your experiences with the dark pixels. We think that the dark pixel storms that you went through were an attempt at getting you 'back' to your normal Alt.

But this Alt universe, in your case, is – I guess you could say it is 'messed up'.

I, who you call "Butler" now, was sent to you to help get you back into your proper Alt. That is why I appeared at the barn that first 'night'. I am trying to serve as your guide to your proper Alt.

I had to interrupt. "Does this mean that I have died?" I asked.

No, it was not your Death Time yet. We know when a humans' 'Death Time' is supposed to occur. I can't tell you how we know, just accept that we **do** know. You are not supposed to be in this unusual Alt.

But the light blink is somehow related to your 'passage' into this Alt. We dogs knew – again, it is not important 'how' we knew – that you were in this Alt.

It took us a bit of time to arrange for me to get to you in this Alt. That is why you didn't see me until that morning – we'll call it 'morning', although time appears to be different in this Alt – that morning at the barn. It was quite a struggle to get me here in this Alt with you.

Once I was here, I was instructed just to monitor the situation, to accompany you – to be of service to you – while you were in this Alt. That is what I have done, while others work on the problem of how to get you back to your own, proper, Alt. I am here for you, at your service. Although I have been quiet about the whole thing until now, as we dogs try to figure out what happened.

"But what about Audrelle? Why did I see her in the library, and why is she here now?" I asked.

There seems to be a bit of 'bleed-over' between the Alt that Audrelle was in and the Alt that you were 'light-blinked' into. She was a bit unexpected, her appearance to you in the library in this Alt. That is why she apparently disappeared after you fell asleep in the library. We were able to guide her out of your Alt into the Alt that she told you about: the walk through the forest, the waiting area, and then her Alt-transfer into the cabin where you met.

We're not sure why her Alt has intersected with yours again. We didn't expect that to happen, but it did. We were unable to get back to her, and she was able to get back to your cabin here and tell you her story. Or part of her story.

She is sleeping now, as you have noticed. She is unaware of anything outside her experiences that she has related to you. We have not allowed her to awaken and listen to my explanation of things. It is not something that she needs to know.

After she told you part of her story, she rested. We influenced the start of that 'resting' a bit. Again, it is not important how we did that, just that we did.

And we also influenced your 'resting' after her story. We needed to work on things a bit.

It was decided – it is not important at this moment how or by who – that we needed to explain things to you. We weren't quite ready to start the explanation yet. We were still gathering information. That is why Archie told you "Not yet" and "Patience, grasshopper." We knew you would relate to that last phrase, and you would have some patience.

So we were waiting for more information. That was the poodle's job; he was a messenger from – well, exactly 'where' doesn't matter. I guess you could consider the 'where' as a sort of 'headquarters'.

The poodle's job was to relay some information that we have determined is related to this situation. We were told that we were to give you some information about your current predicament so that you could start to understand what has happened, and what is happening.

We were told what to tell you, and what not to tell you. The things that we haven't fully explained are those things that we cannot tell you at this time, if we ever explain them. The things that we have told you are enough, for now, to explain what seems to have happened, and why you are here in this particular Alt.

We don't know everything yet. Well, we do know a lot, but you have the information that you need at this point in time.

Know that we are working, with our full capabilities, on figuring out exactly <u>why</u> these things have happened, and what we can try to do to get things back to a normal state. It is proving a bit more difficult than we first thought. This is not a normal occurrence. In fact, this is a first for us.

But we are working on the problem, and a solution. We aren't there yet, but it was decided that you should know what we have told you so far.

I know you have a lot of questions. And a lot of things to consider; the things we told you are not within your normal experiences. We are not able to answer any questions or provide further information at this time. We suggest that you just sit back, and try to relax. Know that we are working on your problem, and take whatever solace you can from that knowledge.

With that, both dogs lay back down, put their head on their paws, and closed their eyes. I was about to ask a question – many questions – but could tell from their 'body language' that there would be no answers at this time.

So I sat on the porch in my chair, the dogs apparently sleeping near me, and Audrelle also apparently sleeping.

I looked out at my little valley. And I tried to process the information that was given to me.

~ 56~

So here I am, sitting on my cabin's front porch, 'in' my little valley home. In an alternate dimension – an 'Alt'. There are two dogs, which apparently function as guides for humans, providing various kinds of service. And one of their services is to guide humans from one Alt to another.

Those black pixel snowstorms I saw are the portals between various Alts; I guess there are lots of Alts, and humans exist in many of the Alts.

I got 'lucky'. I am in a defective Alt, according to the dogs. My Alt has the 'look and feel' of my normal Alt – that's why I am in my cabin in my valley. But this Alt is not normal; I guess there should be other people here, or at least other creatures – birds, insects, whatever. My Alt has the weird clouds, the strange low-frequency humming noise, and the lack of any other living thing but me. At least, at first: Audrelle is here – apparently not in the proper Alt either.

And the two dogs, which apparently get to travel to all the different Alts, guiding their humans to their next destination. A destination that is determined by something mysterious - a 'force' of some sort, or a 'plan', or an 'entity', or whatever. That wasn't explained to me.

Things are not normal here in this Alt. A 'disturbance in the force.' Heh. A trite phrase. I bet you heard that phrase in your mind with the sound of deep, heavy breathing. "There is a disturbance in the force." Thank you, Obi-Wan and Luke.

"Deep breath. Control yourself. Don't go off the deep end. This is not a movie," I thought to myself.

There is something wrong with the whole Alt 'universe', according to Butler's long explanation.

Which didn't really explain a lot of things, but Butler and Archie weren't talking, they were sleeping. Or, at least, there were pretending to, I guess so they wouldn't have to listen to my questions.

As I think about this, it seems that the dogs are not just animals in my world – my normal Alt – but are actually an organized species that transcends my Alt. They are guides that help humans. Although they appear to be dependent on humans for their daily existence, that is only because they 'choose' to be our dependents. Or, they appear to be our dependents, as part of how they are providing service to humans.

We humans have always thought ourselves at the 'top of the food chain'. We are the guys that are able to radically change our environment. We have the mental power to build things, to organize things, to provide for our families and others, to be organized into sections of society, with governments and manufacturing and building and farming and scientists and more.

We have built large cities, massive ships, and have built crafts to explore and analyze the skies and space. We have machines that do our work, vehicles that can take us just about anywhere, and an apparent understanding of the physical sciences.

Yet, except for a very few exceptions, we only know about our <u>own</u> existence. We theorize about the existence of things in space. We analyze other creatures and posit about their abilities and structure, we have even analyzes ourselves down to the micron level.

But we only know of the existence of things in our little Alt. Philosophers suggest that there are other forces in play with things. Religions suggest or teach that there is 'something' before and after our life in our Alt. But we are not smart enough to <u>know</u> these things. We can only theorize. We have no proof.

In the meantime, the dogs are a species that live amongst us, but apparently know much more about everything. Sure, they don't have opposable thumbs, so they can't build things like we can. They can't drive cars (those obnoxious car commercials with driving dogs notwithstanding), they can't fly airplanes through the air, or pilot ships across the sea. They can't produce food on farms. They can't do the things that humans can do.

Apparently, that's OK with them. They are content to provide service to humans in many different ways; some ways that we humans think we have 'discovered'. They know about the Alts. They are organized in some fashion to be able to guide humans from one Alt to another, according to some 'master plan', whoever does that.

And they have apparently been providing service and guidance between Alts for millennia - without us humans having a clue about any of it.

And the only reason I know about this, is that somehow the Alts got messed up, and I (and Audrelle) got stuck in the wrong one at the wrong time. And the dogs, who are the guides for alt-travel, are not sure exactly how that happened.

Lucky me.

~ 57~

I'm sitting on the porch with the two dogs, and Audrelle, who is still asleep, or in some non-awake state that is being 'helped along' by the dogs.

Audrelle had not awakened, that I could tell, during the entire explanation by Butler of the Alt problem. And I had been looking at Butler during his explanation.

I looked out across my little valley at the new cabin. There was some sort of activity going on over there. I could see short bursts of little black pixel clouds around the cabin. From my vantage point, I could only see the front door and the door on the right side of the cabin – the side nearest to me. The other two doors – on the left side and the back side – were not visible from where I sat on the porch.

The black pixel clouds appeared to be only on the left (far) and back side of the cabin. They would appear like a glowing area (if black pixels could 'glow') around where the doors were. They didn't last very long, maybe about 15 seconds of 'normal' time. And they occurred irregularly.

It seemed like the new cabin was a centralized transfer point between the Alts. It wasn't clear from Butler's explanation why the cabin was being used as a central transfer point. Or if the new cabin was the only Alt-transfer point.

As I looked at the cabin, I noticed the trees around the back side of the cabin. As with the rest of the forest, the trees were a mixture of pine and Douglas fir trees, along with some alders. During 'normal' times at the cabin, I'd sit on the front porch and watch the various birds flying around. There would be flocks of crows and blackbirds that would perch on the tops of trees – crows especially liked to land on the very top branches of the tall Douglas fir trees. There would be the occasional eagles and hawks, plus the noisy blue-jays.

Now, in this Alt that I was stuck in, I hadn't seen any other creatures since the time blink - just me, then Audrelle, and then the dogs. I'd usually see the occasional small herd of deer in the valley, and a few flocks of migrating ducks and geese in the old beaver pond.

And, although I didn't see them, I would see evidence of other animals on my walks around and in the forest – bear and cougar tracks and scat.

But not since the light blink. Not even the pesky flies and mosquitos, or any other living thing. The only moving thing I had seen since the light blink, other than us four now on the porch, were those black pixel storms.

Right in back of the new cabin, in the forest in back of it, was a Douglas pine tree that was much taller than all of the rest of the trees in that area. I'd seen it before in my normal Alt, but hadn't paid it much notice. It was more noticeable now in this Alt; my eyesight, which was normally pretty good, has seemed to have improved a bit in this Alt.

What was strange about that particular tree was that it looked like there was something moving at the very top. Now, I hadn't seen any moving thing (other than the four of us, and the 'messenger poodle') since the light blink. But now there was something up there.

I looked closer at the top of that tallest tree in back of the new cabin. There was definitely something there that I hadn't noticed before. I couldn't tell exactly what it was, but I could see a bit of movement on top of that tree.

I stared at it a bit more. Audrelle was still asleep in her chair, and the two dogs looked like they were sleeping also. At least, their heads were on their paws, and their eyes were closed.

Even looking hard at the top of the tree, I couldn't see exactly what was up there. But it wasn't one of those black pixels that had been showing up in this Alt. There was something there, though.

I had used my own pair of binoculars, the 10x70 ones, before to look around the valley at the new cabin, so they were still on the table next to my chair. I grabbed them, and held them up to my eyes. A bit of moving them around, and some focusing, and I got a good view of the new cabin. From there, I just tilted them up a bit until I could see the top of that tallest tree in back of the new cabin.

I adjusted the focus a bit. And I saw it.

A large black raven was sitting on the very top of the tree.

~ 58~

I first thought it was a black crow, but a closer look with the binoculars showed that it was a raven, which is related to the crow.

The raven was perched on the very top tip of the tree. He was mostly still, but with the occasional small flap of his wings to maintain his balance on that precarious spot.

Now that I could see the raven more clearly with the binoculars, I could see that he was looking around in all directions, but mostly focused on the area around the new cabin.

As I watched through the binoculars, the raven kept looking at what appeared to be the area of the new cabin. I looked around at the other trees in the area, and could find no other ravens, or any other birds, up in the trees. Just the one, on the tallest tree in back of the area of the new cabin.

I moved the binoculars back to the raven, watching it. As I watched, the raven turned in my direction. Not straight on, since ravens have eyes on the sides of their head, but it really looked like one of the raven's eyes was looking directly at me.

And the raven turned his head sideways a bit, still looking in my direction. I could see the whole raven in my binocular's sights.

The raven flapped his wings a couple of times, all the while keeping his eyes in my direction, as far as I could tell.

Did you ever have the feeling that a wild creature, or even your pet dog or cat, was looking directly at you? And with a strong intensity in that look? That's what I felt when the raven looked in my direction.

It was an intense look, almost physical in manifestation. It was like he was in a staring contest with me. And he was winning.

I moved the binoculars away from my eyes, but still looked in that direction. It was still looking at me.

And as the raven looked at me, my mind flashed on that classic Edgar Allen Poe poem. You know the one.

Quoth the raven, "Nevermore".

And I got a sudden chill.

I wasn't sure why a bird looking at me gave me a chill, but it did.

I put the binoculars back on the table, a bit loudly, as it turned out. Butler (my guide dog in this Alt) opened his eyes and raised his head a bit. He turned his head to me, then, after a moment, turned his head to look out towards the new cabin. And, apparently, towards the top of the tree where the raven still perched.

Butler kept looking towards the raven, tilting his head a bit. I'd come to recognize that tilting gesture as something the dogs apparently did when they were 'listening' to another dog. I'd seen it in what Butler and Archie both did when they would communicate with each other. And I saw it when the messenger poodle – I never did figure out his name – was apparently talking to Butler and Archie.

So, based on that observation, I concluded – with some modicum of certainty – that there was some communication going on between Butler and the raven.

I looked over at Archie, who had been sleeping (resting?) next to Audrelle – who was still asleep. Archie had opened his eyes, and also turned his head towards the raven.

Then both dogs sat up, still looking towards the raven, and both with that tilting-head-listening pose. I'd seen that pose before also – the dogs sitting up in what appeared to be an alert position. That's what they were both doing, as they both looked towards the raven in the tree.

I watched them do that for a few minutes. The dogs then moved their heads back a bit, along with their ears lying down a bit. And I saw the fur on the back of Butler's head raise up a bit.

Butler then moved his head forward. It looked like sort of an aggressive position. No sound came from Butler – or Archie – but it seemed as if Butler was getting angry.

That 'angry look' from Butler continued, and then I looked over at Archie. He had the same angry look as Butler, although not quite as much. Butler continued to stare in the raven's direction. Then Butler tossed his head a bit.

They both moved their heads to the normal non-tilting position. I looked over at the raven in the tree in back of the new cabin. Although I couldn't see the raven's eyes – I wasn't using the binoculars – I did see that the raven fluttered his wings a few times. No sound that I could hear – from the raven, or the two dogs.

Then I saw a small black pixel cloud form near the raven, and moving slowly until it appeared to be surrounding the raven. The black pixel cloud got denser until I couldn't see difference between the raven and the black pixels. That dense pixel cloud stayed in place for a moment or two – I guess about 15 seconds of full-black-pixel time – before the pixels slowly dispersed and disappeared.

Along with the raven.

I grabbed my binoculars, focusing on the tree where the raven had been, but I didn't see anything there. The raven was gone.

I moved the binoculars around to the other trees in the area, but there was no evidence of the raven anywhere. I slowly moved the binoculars away from my eyes and placed them back on the table.

"That was interesting" I slowly said. "And … a bit spooky. It looked like you were angry at something."

Yes. I was. I still am - angry.

That was from Butler. Although there was no sound – 'listening' to the dogs was more of a sound 'inside' your head, than something you heard with your ears – I could tell that it was from Butler. The two dogs 'voices' had different qualities, so I could tell which dog was speaking. And that editorial comment from Butler was a bit intense, not the 'speaking' that I had heard from him before.

"So, why did all of that make you angry? I mean the appearance of the raven in a tree, when I haven't seen any other creatures than the four of us here, is certainly unusual for this Alt. And the pixel storm enveloping the raven and then the raven disappearing; that's not something I've seen before."

Butler didn't say anything. Neither did Archie.

"I haven't seen you angry before either. At least I think that you were angry. You had that raised-fur thing going on your neck."

Butler didn't say anything. I thought for a bit.

"I'm guessing there was some sort of bad news that you got from the raven. You both did that tilt-the-head thing that you do when you are communicating with each other – and you used it when that poodle came over with a message.

"And then there was that angry thing you did. That makes me a bit nervous.

"So I am guessing that something is or has happened. Do you want to share?" I asked.

Butler and Archie turned their heads to each other. Then they did that tilt-the-head thing as they faced each other.

"You want to share what's going on? Or am I not ready yet?

No response from either of them.

"I'd really like to know what is happening. I am part of whatever is happening in this Alt" I said. "I'd like to know what is going on!"

The dogs looked at each other, using that tilt-head thing that they did when they were 'talking' to each other.

Archie lay down again. Butler stood up, did that stretchy-dog thing, and then took a step towards the new cabin. He stopped, and then turned around and faced me.

Still standing, Butler started 'speaking'.

~ 59~

Butler spoke.

Remember that I told you that we dogs provide service to humans. One of the things that we do is provide guidance. Mostly physical guidance, especially when we assist humans between their Alts. I have provided this to you from the time that we met at the barn.

The dog you call Archie – not his name, but that is not important; I'll use Archie for your convenience – has provided that same guidance service for Audrelle.

I looked over at Audrelle, still in the chair, covered with the blanket, eyes closed, apparently not involved at all in this conversation.

That service, and guidance, is what we dogs do for humans. But we are not the only animal that serves – or maybe more properly – <u>affects</u> humans in their existence in what we call the Alts.

The raven also has an effect or influence on humans. And their influence is not as 'positive' as what we dogs do.

I involuntarily smiled at that. "Dogs do". Heh. I really have to get past that. Luckily, the dogs seemed to ignore my reaction to that.

Ravens are a big part of every Alt. You will find them, along with other black birds like the crow, in many legends of many people. Those black birds – I'll use the term 'raven' for all of those ….

Butler stopped. It was like he didn't want to say entirely what he thought of black birds or ravens. Archie looked over at Butler, but didn't 'say' anything.

Butler appeared to 'gather his composure together' – or at least, that would be what the human equivalent of what he did. It was like he took a deep breath to get his feelings under control. Whatever he did apparently worked, because he continued.

The <u>ravens</u> (he paused again) are not good. <u>They are evil</u>. They are responsible – maybe that is too strong a term – lets' call them 'influencers' of things that are negative. Think of any negative thing that people – or even other animals – do, and a raven is probably somewhere in the area with his evil influence.

They even affect us dogs. We dogs are, mostly, service-oriented towards humans. Even with all of the things that humans do, we try to maintain a positive influence on things.

But ravens can affect us. For instance, stories of a dog attacking a human, or even a child. That is not in our normal nature. But some dogs are weaker than others. It's not a particular breed of dog that has this inherent weakness. It just appears to 'be' a thing that affects some dogs.

And the instigator, if you will, of those weaknesses that cause a dog – or any other animal – to harm or even kill a human is the result of the influence of the raven on that dog or animal.

All animals, some more than others, are inherently predisposed to be protective, or at least not aggressive to humans. But the ravens – they have an influence on other animals that sometimes overcomes that predisposition to serve humans.

We know that a raven will feast on carrion. Lots of animals do that, it is how many animals survive. It is part of the process – some animals are available as a food source to other animals. And of course, many animals are a food source for humans. That is the way that it should be.

But a raven will see some carrion – some dead animal – and use that as a food source. Again, that is as it should be. But we know that ravens can influence other animals to 'serve' the raven. The raven, along with their species, has the innate intelligence to influence others. The raven will communicate in some manner – maybe by their irritating noises – to 'talk' to other carrion-eating animals, say a coyote, to come to their location to eat that carrion. Again, normal stuff. At least the coyote thinks that the raven is helping the coyote out.

But the raven is only doing that for their own purposes. The coyote will feed on the carrion, and make the carrion more available to the raven as food. Say, by tearing open the animal a bit more than the raven is capable of. The coyote thinks he is doing that for his own benefit. But the raven knows that he can influence the coyote to the **raven's** benefit.

We know this capability of the raven. Even some of your smarter humans have figured that out. The raven is an 'influencer', and he is not an influence of good things.

<u>The raven is an evil entity</u>.

Butler stopped for a minute. He had been pacing back and forth while talking. He stopped his pacing, and sat down. Didn't do the turn-around-several-times thing, so I guess it wasn't a 'relaxing' kind of sit-down.

Butler continued his explanation.

That raven was in the tree, overlooking the new cabin. He was watching things happen there. As we've told you before, the new cabin is sort of a transfer place that we use to get between Alts. There are many of those transfer places, there just happens to be one here in your little valley.

The raven is not a disinterested observer, though. He is watching that place as part of their – the ravens as a collective group – plan to exert some negative influence on things in this Alt – in fact, in all of the Alts.

He – and the other ravens – <u>are up to no good</u>.

And that was the discussion we – the raven and I - were having. He told me that the ravens were tired of us dogs serving humans. They were tired of the humans, in fact.

Ravens have a negative influence on all things. Not just dogs, or coyotes, or other animals, but they have a negative influence on humans also. If there is something bad that a human will do, or is planning to do, it is entirely probable that there is a raven nearby that is providing that negative impact on the human. They are not always visible; they seem to have a bit of control over a variant of what you call the black pixel storms.

We, the dogs, use those black pixel storms to help transition people – and other animals – between the various Alts. This is something we've done forever. And it appears that the ravens – and their species – have also learned about the control of the black pixel storms.

This is something we have suspected for many years. But we – the dogs – have been able to keep overall control of the black pixel storms. We need that control to keep things in each Alt in their proper order. Your 'normal' Alt – the Alt before the lights blinked, is kept 'normal' by our ability to keep the Alts from 'banging into' each other.

The ravens didn't have enough control over the black pixel storms to affect the Alts.

Until now.

Butler paused. He got up, and walked over to the water bowl that I had put on the porch. He did that tongue-lappitdy thing to take a drink of water. Apparently, 'talking', even without vocalizing, can make you thirsty.

And I guess that 'listening' to that 'interior voice' that the dogs use to communicate with me makes me thirsty too. I grabbed my glass of water and took a drink. And I added more water to the water bowl.

Butler walked back over to the spot by the stairs. He looked out at the new cabin, then back at me, and then sat down again.

I was thinking that the raven wasn't a 'good thing'. At least, from what Butler was saying.

~ 60~

Butler turned his head to look out at the new cabin for a moment, and then turned his head back to face me.

The raven that was watching the new cabin – he is just one of the 'watchers'. The raven told me that they have been watching all of the Alt transfer points for quite some time.

The raven is one of the more intelligent birds. They have the ability to 'reason' things out. Most of the lower-level birds are only able to work within their own immediate environment. But ravens have what your scientists call 'displacement'. That is the ability and capacity to communicate or know about objects and events that are not in their immediate location. They can determine how things work, although they are not experts in that determination ability. And they can communicate those things that they have learned to other ravens, and, apparently, other raven/crow type species.

The ravens have been watching the Alt transfer points. They have been watching the black pixel storms, and how those storms are used at the Alt transfer points. They have been watching long enough, and apparently communicating with each other, that they are beginning to learn how to control the black pixel storms that we use at the Alt transfer points.

The ravens, and their cousins the crows, have been gathering that information, and sharing it among themselves. Ravens and crows are social creatures, gathering in large flocks. Or, more properly, the grouping of ravens and crows is called a 'murder' of crows/ravens.

It is during these gatherings, apparently, that the ravens have shared their observations of the Alt transfer locations, and the use of the black pixel storms as a transport mechanism between Alts. And by sharing this information, they have started to try to affect the black pixel storms.

This is what you have experienced – the 'light blink' that you saw was a side effect of the ravens' first try at controlling a black pixel storm. Their attempt caused a break in the normal Alt transfer process mechanism that uses a black pixel storm.

We're not exactly sure why it was only you that were transferred to a different Alt. And the ravens' first attempt at initiating and controlling a black pixel storm was 'incomplete' in some manner. That is why you were transported to an 'incomplete' Alt. That Alt environment had the physical parts of an Alt like yours – the buildings, trees, cars, etc. – but was incomplete. That is why time and distance was different in that Alt. And why some mechanical things didn't work.

"So the time/distance anomaly while I was biking through the town was because of the incompleteness of the Alt that I was transported to. And the reason why my car wouldn't start." I said.

Yes, that is correct. You see, there are many – actually innumerable – Alts. New Alts are being 'built' at various times. Each new Alt uses, as a template, the Alt it is duplicating. The Alt you got into initially was incomplete; although the physical parts of the new Alt were completed – that's why you could see and experience buildings and streets and food – not all of the 'physics' parts of the Alt were completed. That's why complex mechanical things wouldn't work – your car didn't work, but the bike, being a simple mechanical object, did work.

There was a little Alt transfer black pixel storm in the library. It happened while you were sleeping. That was one that we did, to try to get you and Audrelle back onto the proper Alt transfer rotation. It only affected Audrelle, though.

The black pixel storm that you experienced after the bike crash was another Alt transfer that we engineered to get you out of the incomplete Alt. It didn't quite work, as you can tell.

The 'incomplete Alt' is evidenced most clearly by the strange clouds and light that you see now. And by that low-frequency humming sound that you don't notice any more, but it still there.

"Yes, now that you mention it, I can still hear that sound. It is just that it has become part of the environment, so I don't hear it unless I think about hearing it" I said.

*Yes. That humming sound is actually the sound of the Alt process. Normally, it is not audible to humans. The fact that it **is** audible is an indication that this particular Alt is not quite complete – or what you would consider a 'normal' environment.*

The Mammatus clouds are also an indication of an incomplete Alt, along with the yellow-gray light that you see.

But those are just the outward indications. The real problem is the ravens, and their 'cousins' the crows and blackbirds. Most birds are beneficial to all Alts, even the buzzards. Not so the ravens and their cousins. Although it might sound trite, they are evil, not to be trusted, and do not have the best interests of humans – or dogs – as their primary objective.

In fact, they would rather there be no humans – in any Alt. They have been trying for a long time to 'reduce' the number of humans in various Alts. One of their more successful efforts has been the spread of what you know as 'bird flu', a flu virus that is transmitted via birds of all kinds – even the 'good' birds.

This bird flu virus can be deadly to humans, and in fact has caused human death in the past. There have been several groups or races of humans that have been almost – or completely – wiped out by variations of the bird flu over the millennia.

One example is the Mayans. As you know, the Mayans were a large civilization of people mostly in the central Americas area. They had a thriving civilization, but eventually were basically wiped out. Not much remains of their civilization, but there is some indication that they interacted with 'black birds' of sorts, and that interaction ultimately was not to their benefit.

Another example is the Mesa Verde civilization that was in the Four Corners area in southwest United States. Their civilization collapsed due to weather conditions that changed in their area, causing widespread food shortages. We believe that the weather conditions that resulted in the collapse of that people were due to attempts by the ravens to control that Alt. The weather here in this Alt is a result of that raven influence in the Alt; the clouds and the resultant lack of sun are part of that influence.

Their past attempts at influencing Alts have not been as successful as this one. Your appearance in this incomplete Alt is an indication of their new success. The raven that you saw watching the new cabin is trying to use the same processes that got you into this Alt to influence the travel of humans from one Alt to another, by changing the 'destination Alt' to other than what needs to be.

Their efforts to affect the Alt transfers are not benign. They have 'lost' people – and their guide dogs - with their interference. There have been Alt transfers that went 'nowhere'. Not to another Alt, just nowhere. We have lost a large number – I can't tell you exactly – of people and their guide dogs with these interfering Alt transfers by the Ravens group. But it is an amount that we are concerned with.

We have been tracking the Ravens group of Alt transfer interference, especially those that have resulted in a loss of people and guide dogs. Yours was the first that we have been able to intercept. Your Alt transfer was stopped before you could be transferred to a 'nowhere' Alt. We were able to get you into an incomplete Alt – this one that you are in now.

Remember your initial experience with the light blink back into your office. That 'blink' was really our intercepting a Raven group Alt transfer. We were able to 'grab' you, and transfer you into the first Alt you experienced.

"Wait," I said. "The 'first Alt' – I've been in more than one?"

Yes. The first Alt you were in was the initial Alt just after the light blink. We were able to stabilize that Alt, but not to the point of getting others into that Alt.

"What happened to all of the other people in my, I guess you'd call it, my 'real world'?" I asked.

I can't discuss that; we are still gathering information about the Alt that you know of as your 'real world'. We were only able to grab you and place you in that 'empty' Alt.

There was another Alt transfer that affected you. It was in the library, where you met Audrelle. We were able to get Audrelle into that 'library Alt' – from where, we can't tell you; and her 'where' is not important to you at this time. Audrelle was being transferred to her next Alt, but her transfer was going to be interrupted by the Raven group, so we were able to temporarily transfer her into the library Alt.

Once she was there, we had to wait for the next Alt transfer to be available, which happened while you were sleeping that night in the library. We were able to get her back to her previously arranged Alt. That is the story she told you about being in the Library, then awakening with her guide dog – the one you call 'Archie' – and traveling to the waiting area in the forest before she was transferred here in this current Alt.

She doesn't really belong here – neither do you – but it was the best place for her until we get her to the Alt she belongs to.

Our problem, though, is the Ravens group. We need to determine how they are intercepting the control of the Alt transfer process. Once we determine that, we can block their access to the Alt transfer process, and get things back to 'normal'. That is our highest priority.

Until that happens, you – and Audrelle – are stuck in this incomplete Alt.

~ 61~

This was a lot to contemplate.

I had been happy in my little life – what I now know was my 'home' Alt. I wasn't – apparently – destined for an Alt transfer. But the Ravens group has, for some reason, been messing with the Alt transfers, and the result was the 'light blink' I experienced.

It may have been that my 'unscheduled' Alt transfer was going to result into a transfer to 'nowhere', and that, for some reason, the guide dogs were able to 'grab' me and do a quick Alt transfer to this incomplete Alt.

I looked at Butler. He was just sitting there, waiting for me to absorb this part of the story – or my current predicament.

"The ravens that I saw in the barn when I first got there - I am assuming that they are part of the Ravens group. Were they there in preparation for whatever they were doing to influence an Alt transfer that would happen there at the barn?" I asked.

We're not sure, because we didn't have our full monitoring available at that point. But we think that they were watching you as you traveled through that incomplete Alt. We know that they can use a black pixel storm to move between Alts; you saw that when you were watching the raven at the top of the tree in back of the new cabin.

We think that they have been watching you since the lights blinked, but were able to keep out of your sight during your travels. They do this by 'transporting' via the black pixel storms at pre-planned locations.

The fact that you were able to see them in the barn indicates that they don't have full and consistent control of the black pixel storms yet.

We use the black pixel storms to transport between Alts; somehow they have been able to learn how to create and/or control their own black pixel storms.

This is a big problem, because if the Raven group can get full control of black pixel storms, we are going to lose a lot of people – and guide dogs – at Alt transfer points. The Ravens group will be able to determine the destinations used in the Alt transfer points, which is not good at all.

We are not sure what is on the 'other side' of the Alt destinations that the Ravens group is using. This is a priority for us to figure out. We need to determine the destinations that they are using. And that may require some dangerous work for you – and Audrelle.

Not getting a good feeling about that.

That last pronouncement by Butler – that there was some dangerous work in store for me – was not something I really wanted to hear.

Part of me wanted to believe that there was some way for me to magically return to my former Alt – that all of the things that happened since the light blink would be swept away in some way by some entity.

I wasn't even sure what entity was controlling things in these Alts. What – or who – were the Alt Controllers. How were the Controllers controlling things? Was there some master Controller location that was transferring people, with their guide dogs, to the 'next' Alt? How – or what – was deciding who gets to go to what Alt?

"Inquiring minds want to know," I mumbled to myself. I thought about that for a minute.

Butler looked at me from his position on the front porch of my cabin. He didn't say anything, of course. He just looked at me, as though he was deciding what to say next – or maybe if he would say anything at all.

Archie was still sitting next to Audrelle, who was still sleeping, or at least her eyes were closed.

I looked out onto 'my valley' – at least, that's what I had thought of it being before all of this. It turns out, not really 'my valley' at all. Just a variation on a theme, I guess.

The new cabin was still there. I looked at the tall trees in back of the new cabin, expecting to see a raven there, but I guess they were somewhere else. I didn't see any black pixel storms either, but the new cabin was just one of many Alt transfer points.

I looked back at Butler. He had turned to look at Archie, and they both had that 'tilted-head-while-talking' look to them. I grabbed my glass of water and took a drink, glancing over at the table next to my chair as I returned the glass to the table.

When I turned back to Butler, he was looking at me.

We have decided that we need to show you something.

Butler got up from his sitting position, doing that dog-stretchy thing that they do. Archie stayed where he was.

"Is Archie coming?" I asked.

Nope. He will be staying with Audrelle for now. But you need to come with me.

"Do I need to bring anything? Some 'protection', or supplies, or what?" I asked.

No. It is a short distance from here.

I took a moment to fill the water dish for Archie. Then I went inside and grabbed two packages of beef jerky, opening it as I walked back outside on the porch.

I opened each package, and gave one to Archie and the other piece for Butler. They made short work of it, nodding their heads in a 'thank you' gesture.

"Will Audrelle be OK while we are gone?" I asked.

She will be fine. Archie will stay here with her. We don't expect any trouble here, said Butler.

"Good," I said.

Then I realized that Butler said "We don't expect any trouble <u>here</u>."

More good news.

~ 62 ~

Butler walked off the porch, and I followed. I expected to head to the new cabin, but he took a right turn, and headed towards my 'old cabin'.

This was the cabin that was originally on my property. It was built by my great-grandfather about 90 years ago. It was a small log-type cabin, built out of the trees of the forest that surrounded here. When my parents were still alive, we would visit the cabin each summer.

When my parents died – long after my grandparents – the title of the cabin, and what I called 'my valley' – was my inheritance. I decided to turn the area into my home, and moved to the old cabin.

I then worked on building my new home next door to the cabin. I did a lot of the work myself on nights and weekends – long nights and long weekends. I had a bit of help from some local tradesmen, but most of the work – and all of the design – was mine.

After the new place was completed and I moved in, I converted the old cabin into a sort of guest house. Not that I had many guests; I wasn't really a 'social' kind of guy. But I wanted to leave it standing as a tribute and memory to my grandfathers' efforts and, I guess, his legacy. Although it was furnished with stuff that is needed for a 'guest house', I had also added a small and secure room in the back of the cabin, sort of out of view of anything, and stored some food and basic supplies in that room. I'd maintained the cabin even after I moved into the new place, so it never got into a dusty or cobwebby kind of state.

I expected that Butler was leading me into the forest onto one of the many hiking/game trails that were in the forest. So I was surprised when we got to the old cabin and Butler turned to the steps and up onto the front porch.

"Is there something in here that we need for our journey?" I asked Butler.

No. The cabin is the starting point for our journey. Remember that we are in a different Alt than your normal Alt. Many of the physical structures are common to the various Alts, as is your home, and your grandfather's old cabin.

I walked up the three steps onto the front porch, and stopped at the front door.

Are you going to open the door for me? Remember, I don't have opposable thumbs.

"Oh, yeah," I said, although I wondered why there wasn't a 'doggie door' for the dog's convenience. I reached up to the spot next to the front porch light, and pressed on the small hidden panel there that contained the key to the door. The panel was like the one at my house; I had added it during the remodel and upgrade of my grandfathers' cabin. I took the key out of its hiding spot, unlocked the door, and then returned the key to its hiding spot, closing the hidden panel.

I grabbed the handle of the door, and turned it, pushing open the door. I stood aside and motioned to Bandit to enter.

"Here you go, your Majesty," I said in a somewhat formal voice.

Butler gave a little snort – I didn't know dogs could snort – and went inside. I followed, taking a couple of steps inside, shutting the door behind me.

"This is different," I said slowly.

My grandfather's cabin is a simple place. One main room takes up about two-thirds of the floor space. Off to the left is a small kitchen – stove/oven, sink, small refrigerator, a few cupboards: the usual stuff.

In the other part of that 'third' of the cabin –towards the back left side as you enter, is a small bedroom and a small bathroom. The bedroom is big enough for a queen-sized bed and a dresser, with an open area with a closet rod for hanging up things.

The bathroom is basic: sink, toilet (an improvement over the original design of the cabin, which featured an outhouse), and a small shower.

The main room was also simple. There was a fireplace along the right side wall, a couch and a couple of chairs, and a small dining table along the back.

All of the furnishings had been modernized a bit, but it was not a 'modern' look. It looked like a cabin: rustic, but clean and comfortable.

It was a comfortable place to stay. In fact, I had spent a lot of time in here as a kid visiting my grandfather, then the time when I lived here, before and during the time that I was building the new place.

It was the kind of place that you would be comfortable being in when you first opened the door. Rustic, clean, and comfortable.

That was not what I saw.

I was two steps into the front door of my old cabin – the one my grandfather built, and I 'overhauled'. Butler was just ahead of me, sitting down and looking at me. He was waiting for me to process the scene.

The inside of the cabin was one giant room, and I mean 'giant'. It was much larger inside than it should have been – way larger.

It looked like the inside of a humongous furniture store. There were chairs and couches and tables spread throughout the room, as far as you could see. There were no inside walls; it was one giant room.

My eyes darted around the room, taking in the whole place. It was a giant room, easily more than a dozen football fields, with chairs and couches and table, stretching as far as I could see.

There were no lights that I could see. Just that yellow-gray light that I had seen ever since the lights blinked. There seemed to be no source of the light; no overhead light fixtures like you would see in a warehouse. The light was just 'there'.

And there was that faint humming sound - the low-frequency, just-barely-audible sound that I had heard in the new Alt that I had been 'transferred' to when the lights blinked.

And then I noticed the people.

Every chair, every couch, had someone sitting in it. They didn't notice me; they were intent on what they were doing. Whatever they were doing, they were doing it very quietly. There was no talking, no noise (other than that humming sound), none of the background noise that you would hear in an open-office environment, or any warehouse-type noise. There was no echoing of any sound like you would expect in a large warehouse. There was just the low-frequency humming sound that I had heard ever since the lights blinked.

I took a couple of steps forward, closer to one of the groups of people sitting in the chairs and couches. The furniture wasn't placed in any order, or in a way that would indicate conversations between people. The people were just sitting on the furniture, seemingly oblivious to the others.

I looked closer at several of the people on a couch near me. It was a mixture of men and women, and they looked like anyone that you would see in a crowd. No special features, any special age, a mixture of races, dressed in comfortable clothes.

None of the people near me, or anywhere also, appeared to see me; they were all intent on whatever it was that they were doing.

Then I noticed that every single person was wearing eyeglasses. The glasses were apparently all the same design. Typical glasses, nothing special about them, although all had larger lenses. And every person seemingly immersed in whatever they were seeing.

It was a strange and somewhat unsettling sight. And all of it was 'in' my grandfathers' cabin.

I looked at Butler, who was waiting patiently near me, sitting down, and watching me.

"What the ..." I mumbled, looking over at Butler. "This is probably a good time to explain things a bit."

Butler looked at me, and then tilted his head a bit.

Why don't you sit down there in that chair?

I looked next to me, and there was an empty chair there.

"Yeah...sitting might be good," I said. So I took a couple of steps over to the empty chair, and sat down. There was a small table next to the chair. There were several pairs of eyeglasses in a small wooden box on the table.

You might as well be comfortable while I tell you some things.

It *was* a comfortable chair.

~ 63~

Butler started 'talking'. Or, communicating via words that I listened to in my head. I was used to that feeling of a dog 'talking' in my head.

This is one of the Alt transfer control centers. We call these places an 'Alt-Control'. This is one of many that we have.

Each Alt-C location monitors and controls Alt Transfer points. They don't control specific transfer points, but rather control the transfer point that is being 'readied' or prepared to transfer.

Remember that I told you that the new cabin is an Alt Transfer point. And that the forest waiting area that Audrelle talked about is another Alt Transfer point. These Alt-C locations are what we use to monitor and control the Alt Transfer process.

Each of the people here is specially trained to monitor the process. They watch an Alt Transfer point using those special glasses. The glasses have a video link to the Alt Transfer location, plus show additional information, sort of a 'routing' list, of upcoming transfers. These transfers are what 'move' people, with their dogs as a guide, from one Alt to another.

These Alt C 'watchers' are the ones that monitor the Alt transfers. They ensure that the proper people – with their guide dogs – are properly transferred from their current location – their current Alt – to their new assigned Alt location.

The transfer process that does the actual transfer from one Alt to another, as I have told you before, is those black pixel storms that you experienced. These pixel storms normally appear at specific locations – the Alt Transfer Points.

In your case, you were transferred between your Alt at your office and the incomplete Alt that you experienced after the light blink. That transfer was what you might think of as an unauthorized Alt transfer. There is an 'order' or overall plan to the Alt transfers, so that people are transferred from one 'proper' Alt to another Alt that is a proper environment for them.

The transfer that you experienced with the light blink was not a normal Alt transfer. First, as I previously explained, you were transferred into an incomplete Alt – an Alt that had all the physical characteristics of a proper Alt 'world'. For instance, all of the buildings and cars and other things were there, but not the people that would normally be in a 'proper' Alt world. That was why you saw cars without people, and there were no animals or insects in that Alt world. Even the weather wasn't complete. The Alt's environment: weather, clouds, sunlight, wind, rain, etc. – wasn't fully formed. That is why you saw those strange Mammatus clouds, and the ambient light was not normal.

Anyway, these people are the Alt transfer controllers. They monitor Alt transfers, 'activating' the transfer points and the black pixel storms that are part of the Alt transfer process.

"I have a lot of questions about this whole thing. For instance ..." I started.

Butler interrupted my question.

Perhaps it would be clearer to you if you could see an Alt transfer process. I am authorized to let you view the process through the use of these glasses. Because you are not trained in the process of monitoring and controlling an Alt transfer, wearing the glasses will be like being in a 'read-only' mode. You will have no control of the process, only watching it like you would a movie.

Take one of the eyeglasses from that basket on the table next to you.

I reached over to the table and grabbed a pair of eyeglasses.

Before you put them on, I need to tell you of their effect on you. You will become a bit disoriented, so prepare for that. When you first put on the glasses, the view 'through' the glasses – where you can see everything in front of you – will pixelate into the view of a transfer point. This can be a bit disconcerting at first, so try to remain calm and sit still while the glasses adjust to you – and you adjust to the glasses.

Once you put on the glasses, you will not be aware of your environment – sitting here in this chair. Think of it like being 'inside' a movie. You will be totally immersed in the environment of the Alt transfer point.

You will want to move your head around to look around your environment, but that is not really necessary. The glasses have the ability to 'interface' with your brain, and will anticipate your wanting to 'look' in a different spot. Again, like a movie, the view in your glasses will move to what you think you want or need to look at.

These glasses have an additional function; they are sort of 'training glasses'. Even though I won't be visible in your environment, I will still be able to experience that environment with you. I will be able to communicate with you, and you can communicate with me. You will not, however, have the ability to communicate with other people – or dogs – that you see. And you will not have the ability to interact with the visual environment. You will want to reach out and touch something, but that is not possible with these training glasses.

Note that the experience of being 'inside' the environment through what you see is a bit disconcerting. If you think of it as watching a movie, you will be able to adjust better.

Do you understand all of what I have told you about the glasses?

I took a breath. "Yeah, I think I do. It's a movie. I can look, but I can't touch. And, like a movie, I can't interact with anything 'inside' the movie." I said.

That's correct. Again, it will take a moment to adjust to the environment. When you put on the glasses, just relax until you 'merge' into the Alt transfer point. Keep breathing normally, but sit quietly in the chair. You'll be able to talk to me; I'll be right next to you – but not 'within' your view. In fact, I want you to tell me what you see – and feel.

"OK," I said.

Are you ready?

"As ready as I will ever be, I guess," I said.

I took another breath, exhaling slowly.

"Here goes," I mumbled.

And I put on the glasses.

~ 64~

At first, I could still see the room that I was in. There was a bit of a prickly feeling inside my head. Sort of like an itch in there. Not a big itch, but you were aware of it.

"There's a bit of itchiness inside my head," I said.

That is normal. It will fade, or at least you will become less aware of it.

As I looked through the glasses, I saw the scene around me slowly fade. Or, more properly, pixelate. Just a few pixels at first.

"I'm seeing pixels," I said.

Yes. Again, that is normal.

The view through my glasses continued with an increasing number of black pixels. At least, they started out black. The black pixels lasted just a few seconds, and then the pixels started changing into a view of something. I watched as the pixel-changing slowly morphed into another view of something.

I saw a clearing in a forest, about 100 feet square. The forest surrounded the area. There were some fallen logs being used as benches, sort of like you would see at a camping place. There were no more than two rows of log-benches, but they appeared to be randomly placed.

As the view of my glasses resolved into a full view of the forest clearing, I could see that it was empty, at least the part where I was looking.

I started to turn my head to look to my left, but as soon as I sent the thought to my muscles to move my head to my left, the view through the glasses tracked to the left. I didn't move my head, but the view moved. Sort of like someone controlling the camera that was giving me the view of the forest clearing on my glasses.

The view through the glasses was total. It was not like when you wear a pair of glasses, and you can see the edge of the frames of the glasses, and the view 'outside' the framed area. The view was complete, as if there were no glasses or glass frames.

I moved my eyes to the left. As I did so, the view changed to things on my left. It seems that just starting an eye movement would cause the 'camera' to move in that direction.

"I can sort of control the view by moving my eyes a bit in the direction I want to see" I said to Butler.

Yes, that is sort of how it works. You must be careful not to move your eyes too rapidly. Although the glasses will adjust for any rapid eye movement, that can cause a bit of jerkiness to the view. Just relax your eyes a bit, and try to move them just a little in the direction that you want to look. The glasses will adjust the view to look in that direction.

I practiced that a bit. The technique of moving my eyes just a bit seemed to be easy to adjust to. It was sort of like that technique of 'looking' in different directions by using small eye movements was easy to learn, or maybe it was just inherent in what I could do.

After a bit of practice moving my field of view to another direction, I started concentrating on what it was I was seeing. I moved my view to slowly look all around the clearing. I could see, with enough eye movement to control the directions, all around me in a 360-degree view.

I could see that the forest surrounded the clearing, and there were several paths that went through the forest.

"Is this the forest clearing area that Audrelle talked about?" I asked.

Yes, it is.

"Wait a minute. How do you know what I am looking at?" I asked.

Well, that is something that I need to teach you. I can sense, through an interface of those glasses to me, what you are looking at. This is done with what your technology might call a Bluetooth interface, although that is not what it is. The technology is more advanced than that.

You might have noticed that I am wearing a collar. In fact, all Alt guide dogs have collars. These collars have an interface that allows us to communicate with the Alt Controllers. The communications link is automatic. In fact, we dogs can communicate with any of the Alt Controllers, although we normally link up with the Alt Controller that is assigned to the Alt Transfer point.

In your case, as 'your' guide dog, I have been linked to the pair of Alt Controller glasses that you are wearing. That link allows me to 'experience', if you will, what you are experiencing through the glasses. That 'link experience' is similar to how you and I communicate, through a sort of 'mental telepathy' process that allows me to see – and hear – what you see through the glasses.

So, yes, I can see what you are seeing in your glasses.

"OK, I guess I understand that. You have a sort of mental telepathy link to the glasses. What I see – and even hear? – while wearing the glasses, is what you can see and hear through that link."

Yes, that is the basic premise. Now remember that although you are 'there', you are not really 'there'. You don't have the ability to communicate or affect anyone – or any <u>thing</u> – that you see. Try to remember that as we continue.

"OK," I said.

I continued to 'look' around the forest clearing. I noticed some movement to my right, so looked over there.

I watched as a dog – a guide dog, I suppose – appeared on one of the paths into the trees. 'Appeared' might be not quite correct. More correctly, 'materialized' might be more correct.

As I looked closer, I could see a black pixel area in the path, like a door into the forest path. And the dog sort of materialized 'through' the black pixels.

Yes, the dog is traveling to this Alt Transfer point via the black pixel 'storms' that we use for the transfer between Alts.

"Oh," I thought.

Wait, I didn't really ask about the dog and how he appeared on the path.

Yes, that is another advantage of wearing the glasses, and the communication you and I have through the glasses. I can 'hear' your questions without you having to actually 'speak' them, just like you can hear me without me speaking.

That sounded reasonable. Maybe a bit creepy, but then again, lots of things were different.

Keep watching.

As I watched, I could see that the dog was leading several people. These people, two guys and a girl from their appearance, were following the dog and they also appeared through – via? – the black pixel storm.

This is a small group of people that are being guided by that dog. They have traveled from their Alt to this Alt Transfer point via the black pixel storm transfer process.

As I watched – and , apparently, as the dog watched also – the dog led them to one of the empty benches. The dog stopped in front of the bench, and did his tilt-head thing, so he was apparently talking to his group. He was apparently telling them to sit down on the bench, because that was what they did.

As they sat, I looked at the group. They appeared to be 'normal' people, no different from me. Sort of like you would see in any situation in 'normal' times, say at the grocery store. There was nothing 'different' about them that I could see. There was a calm and peaceful look on their faces, as if this were a pleasant walk in the forest.

Their dog sat next to them, facing them. He tilted his head a bit, giving them instructions, I guess.

Yes, he is probably telling that they need to wait here for a short time.

So this is an Alt Transfer point. The black pixels are the transfer 'mechanism', and there is a Alt Controller in this room somewhere – I waved my hands around me to point into the room that was inside my grandfather's cabin – that is communicating with the guide dog.

Yes, that is correct. The Alt Controller will let the guide dog know when it is time for them to continue the journey to their new Alt.

But ...

And, no, I can't tell you about their new Alt. Or how it is determined which Alt they get to. Or what happens to them when they get to their Alt.

Yeah, I know. "Patience, grasshopper." Butler didn't reply to that.

I watched as the people and the dog sat quietly on the log bench. I noticed some movement to the left of me, and my view instantly changed to that direction. Another dog came through a different path between the trees, followed by seven people.

This new group, like the last, calmly followed the dog to another log bench. They did look over towards the first group, giving that 'elevator nod' thing that people do, but there was no other interaction between them.

Like the first group, they sat quietly on the bench. There was no talking between them, so I got the sense that they were just a group of people that previously had no relation to each other. I guess it was sort of like going to the airport and joining up with another group of people that were getting on a plane. Although they were going to the same destination, there was no real interaction between the people in the line to get on the plane.

That's a fair analogy. These are travelers, going from one place to another. Wherever they go, there are some intermediate stops before you get to a final destination. In fact, you will see that in a moment.

While Butler and I were discussing this, several more groups of people had arrived, about thirty in all, in seven different groups. All got there the same way: a dog would appear on a path, and then one or more people would appear behind them. The dog would tilt his head and 'talk' to the people, leading them to an empty area of log benches.

As I watched, two of the dogs, each leading different groups, 'spoke' to their group. Both groups got up, and went to the start of another path into the forest. The dogs talked to each other, then their groups.

Then one dog started walking to the new path, and both groups followed, leaving the other dog behind.

Yes, that group is going together to their new Alt. That only requires one guide dog, so the other is not needed to be with that group. The dogs told their group to combine and follow the one dog.

They didn't appear to be worried or concerned about the new group. They just followed the one dog onto the path, which had gotten a black pixel 'doorway' by then. The entire group went through the doorway, and disappeared from sight.

So, an Alt Transfer point is like a 'waypoint' along the way from wherever they came from to the place – wherever and whatever that is – to their new Alt.

Yes, that is correct. During the travels from one Alt to another, you may have different guide dogs, as you have seen. And that process doesn't bother people as they transit from one Alt to another. They are aware that the guide dogs are providing valued service to them, and trust that the dogs will help them on a safe journey.

So this process of Alt Transfers seems to work fairly smoothly. I guess it would, since it has apparently been happening for a long time.

Yes, it is a simple process, but there is some control of things. That control and communication is done with the Alt Controllers and their glasses that allow them to monitor situations.

This is the normal process, as Audrelle told you in her story.

I need to show you something else, in another place. You need to remove the glasses, but before you do that, it's best if you close your eyes for a count of ten before you remove the glasses. This will help with the transition from using the glasses.

I took one final look of the forest clearing. While Butler was talking, several more groups of people had arrived and departed. There were a couple of groups that had several people and some that had just one or two. But the entire process was calm and orderly. Groups arrived with their dogs, and departed with their dogs, in another group, or maybe with another group. But it was all done calmly and orderly.

I closed my eyes, counting to 10. As I did, I felt the forest view dim, to be replaced by whatever you see when you close your eyes. After reaching the count of 10, I removed the glasses.

Keep your eyes closed for another count of ten. Then open them slowly.

Again, I counted to 10, and then slowly opened my eyes. It was like when you open your eyes in the morning after waking. Slowly, things get into focus, and you become aware of where you are.

And I wasn't in the chair anymore. Or in the giant area that was 'inside' my grandfather's cabin.

~ 65 ~

I was still in a large area. But there wasn't anything that I could see. It was like I was in a big fog bank, where you couldn't see anything except for what was under your feet. So it was not like I was floating in an empty space, there was a feeling of being somewhere solid. It is just that I couldn't see anything at all.

I jumped a bit. I looked all around, and still didn't see anything. It was a bit frightening, I'll admit. It was like waking up and not knowing where you were. And not seeing anything familiar. Not really seeing anything.

My heart rate jumped a bit. Maybe even getting a bit of adrenaline rush.

I looked all around. Nothing to see here, folks; move along. Except there didn't seem to be anywhere to move to.

Stay where you are, please.

"OK, Butler," I said. Then I realized that wasn't Butler's voice that I heard in my head. It was a different voice. It was sort of a scratchy-sounding voice. Definitely not Butler's voice.

That can't be good. I looked around for someplace to go. I didn't have a good feeling about this.

Stay where you are.

The same scratchy voice, but a bit more forceful. But I could tell that it was important, for some reason, to stay where I was.

So I stayed.

I stood in the emptiness of wherever I was. I looked around in all directions, and still could not see anything other than the 'fog' that was all around me.

Except it wasn't fog.

'Fog' is hard to describe. There is a grayness of everything. If the fog is really thick, any shapes you can see are indistinct; sort of fuzzy.

I'd been in foggy places before; even thick foggy places. I knew what fog was like. This was like fog, but it wasn't fog.

As my eyes adjusted to the fog – or whatever it was; fog is a good enough descriptive word, even though not quite accurate – I couldn't see any objects, even fuzzy objects around me. This was a full-on fog – nothing was visible, anywhere, in any direction.

It was like you were inside a car and the windows were all fogged up, and the defroster wasn't working at all. Like that, only more 'intense', if fog can be intense. There was a full 'nothingness' all around me.

I took a closer look at the fog. I reached out my hand and waved it through the air a bit. The fog's substance, whatever it was, swirled a little bit. Sort of like that cloudy-fake-fog you see on the stage of a play.

As the fog substance swirled, I could see that the substance wasn't the individual droplets of moisture from a normal fog. The fog particles were actually very small black pixels. They were sort of glittery, in a dull color kind of glitter. And even though they swirled a bit as I moved my hand around, you couldn't feel them like you could in a cloud make out of glitter. I swirled around the pixel 'glitter' a bit more.

Please don't move.

Again with the scratchy voice that wasn't Butlers'. I dropped my hands down to my side.

As I stood there, surrounded by the pixel fog, I noticed the light changing from the grayness of the fog to a more yellow-gray color. It was still foggy; I couldn't see anything other than the color of the fog changing.

As the fog color changed, I could see some vague shapes around me, like the fog was getting less dense. I stood still, as instructed, and waited for what seemed like a long time – but probably wasn't that long. As I waited, the fog cleared some more.

I started to see more definition to the shapes. Most of them were almost triangular in shape, and were mostly the same size and height. They seemed to surround me, but they weren't close, maybe 20-30 feet away.

The fog density decreased, and the shapes resolved into small trees around a clearing. The trees were shaped vaguely like Christmas trees that you might find in a Christmas tree 'orchard'. Since they were all about the same size, I figured that they were planted at about the same time. They weren't in a regular pattern of any type, though, so I sensed that the trees were in an area that might have been clear-cut in some logging operation. Or some other event that cleared out a forested area, and then there was a new 'crop' of trees that grew in that cleared area.

I was standing in a more open area. It looked like a wide spot in the road. It was a grassy area, with short grass – not mowed, just not very tall.

Welcome to my world. Again, with the scratchy voice.

I looked around. To my right, perched on the top of one of the small trees – they were Scotch pines, I think – was a black object, a bit fuzzy in appearance. As I watched, the fuzziness resolved into an object.

No, not an object.

A bird.

A raven.

Stands to reason, I guess.

Just call me Edgar Allan Poe.

~ 66~

The raven was perched at the top of one of the small Scotch pine trees. Those trees were on a slight hillside above the clear spot where I was standing, stretching back quite a ways. In back of that stand of pines was a taller pine forest. It looked like the smaller trees were in an area that had been clear-cut. Since the small pine trees were about eight to 10 feet in height, I figured that the clear cut had happened about 6-7 years ago, based on the size of the trees. The clear cut could have happened before that, but that's when the new seedlings appeared.

Yes, that is correct. These trees started growing about 7 years ago.

Again with the scratchy voice. And apparently, ravens can communicate in a manner similar to dogs. And, also, read minds, because I hadn't said anything out the age of the trees out loud.

Yes, we do have the ability to communicate with humans. Dogs can do it, why can't we? We share that ability with many animals, although it is not something that we regularly do. We communicate with other of our species – 'corvids', if you must know – but that communication is mostly heard by humans as a squawking sound.

"So why can I understand you?" I asked.

Because I _want_ you to understand me. So I can tell you what is happening.

"Can you tell me where I am now, and how I got here?" I asked.

All in good time. For now, you need to know why we are doing what we are doing.

This felt to me like it was going to be a long story. I looked around me, and there was a log bench to my right. I moved over there and sat down.

"OK, I'm ready," I said, "but I would much rather be at home." In my own home, in my original Alt. That would be the best place. But I wasn't sure if that would ever happen.

The raven was sitting (perched?) at the top of the small pine tree. It was quiet all around me, even the humming sound appeared to lessen, although it could be that I was just used to it, so had tuned out that sound.

The raven, who I will call Edgar (why not?), had his head turned slightly away from me so that he could look at me with his left eye. Edgar fluttered his wings a bit with that motion that birds do when they are perched on a tree branch.

I thought for a moment that Edgar, and birds in general, must have a really good sense of balance. They can perch on tree branches and other things even when it's windy. Not that there is any wind here. There hasn't been any wind since the lights blink.

Ahem!

"Sorry; I was distracted for a bit. Ready when you are, Edgar," I said.

Edgar cocked his head a bit; maybe he didn't like the name 'Edgar'. Maybe 'he' was a 'she'. I couldn't tell. Actually, it didn't really matter. 'Edgar' is the name this raven gets.

Anyhow, I digress again. Edgar started speaking in that scratchy voice of his.

I am a raven, a member of the Corvidae family. Our family includes crows, blackbirds, magpies, and other similar birds. There are over 120 species in our family. One-third of the Corvidae is the Corvus genus, consisting of ravens, crows, and jackdaws. We Corvus are the 'boss' of the Corvidae family; although some also call our group Corvids.

We are an intelligent family, smarter than most other animals. Our brain-to-body mass ratio is equal to that of the great apes and whales and dolphins, and only slightly less than humans. But we 'use' more of our brains than humans, at least in our view.

We live everywhere in the world, except the polar ice caps and the tip of South America. We are everywhere.

I tell you this because you humans usually think birds are not smart, and can be ignored. Yes, you do 'revere' a few birds: eagles because you see them soaring around; chickens and turkeys, because you like to eat them. Not sure why you like to watch flamingos. They are a strange bird, always standing around on one leg. And that awful pink color!

I digress.

We Corvids are smarter than most humans realize. And we control a lot of things – things that you humans aren't aware that we control.

We have been delegated – by whom, is not important – to the sidelines. You humans think you are the 'masters of all things' here, and you have created a special relationship with some other animals. Although humans like to 'own' lots of different types of animals, it is very common that you humans think you 'own' dogs. And cats are popular too, but I don't want to talk about cats right now.

You humans see dogs as a 'service companion', and in fact, dogs as a whole are willing to provide that service. Although some dogs provide what appears to be 'intelligent service', we Corvids are in fact superior in intelligence to dogs. We just don't feel the need to provide service to humans. Dogs seem to **need** to provide that service. So they have evolved to provide the service of guiding people from one Alt to another.

Yes, we know about the 'Alts'. We know how the Alts work. We have let the dogs provide their guidance service for the Alts.

Up to now.

We Corvids have what you might call a 'governmental structure' to our family. We have 'workers' and 'planners' and 'governors'. We have stayed in the background, letting others do the work of the Alts.

But we have noticed that Alts are not working. Actually, the Alts are working fine; it is the humans that are not taking proper care of the Alts. In the past, the negative effect of humans on the Alts has been manageable.

But not now.

Even with all of the Alts, and the movement of humans between Alts, as guided by the dogs, the negative effect of humans on the Alts has started to outweigh their positive effects.

We Corvids are everywhere on this planet, in every Alt. We are able to communicate with Corvids on other Alts. And we know that humans are slowly destroying the Alts.

It is not necessary to get into the details of how you are destroying things on the Alts. You can figure out all of the things that are going wrong. Take your pick of the destruction; all of it is destroying the 'balance' in the Alts.

We Corvids have been watching this destruction increase. And we have decided that it has gotten to the point of too much destruction. You humans are going to, if we let you, destroy all of the Alts.

We can see how humans are actually accelerating this 'progress' of destroying the Alts. You might think that all of the things that you humans have done is 'progress', but it is damaging your Alt – and all of the Alts where there are humans.

We cannot let this destruction continue.

So, even though we have been passive observers of the Alt Transfer process, we have become aware of how to control that transfer process – and how to control an Alt.

We have just started to take control. You are in one of the results of our increased control of Alts.

We have been creating a few of our own Alts. The method of how we do that is not something that we will share with you. But we have been able to create 'functional' Alts. Not completely functional, but sufficiently functional to provide life support. Our new Alts have been working fine, although we do not let them 'exist' for long periods of time. They have been a 'work in progress' – each new Alt we create is better than the last.

And now we have perfected the process. We can create fully functional Alts. And we are ready to populate them with humans. After all, you do have opposable thumbs, and can be useful as a 'resident' of an Alt.

So our Alts are ready for use. We've already started intercepting Alt Transfers to send people to our Alts. That process is working; we've been monitoring things. You saw one of our monitors – the raven up in the tree behind the new cabin. Our interceptions are working properly, when we choose to do them.

We are sending certain people to our Alts – our Raven-Alts. They are fully functional – at least, functional in how we want them to be functional.

They just might not be functional like <u>you</u> want them to be.

The raven – Edgar – stopped talking with that last statement. It was like he wanted me to focus on that last statement, in all of its ramifications.

And I did. The last statement – *"not just like <u>you</u> want them to be"* – Edgar said with some emphasis.

I got the point.

And the point didn't seem to be good for me, or anyone else, no matter what Alt they were in.

~ 67~

I looked at Edgar. "What do you mean; the Alts may not be just like we want them to be?" I asked.

Alt-Worlds have to be created. There aren't a fixed number of them that have already been created and are 'available'. They have to be created.

And creating Alt-Worlds is not a simple thing. It is a complicated process. Very complicated, as we Corvids have learned.

It is not clear to us how the Alt-Worlds that already existed were created. They just 'are'. Most Alts are similar to each other. They are at the same 'progression' in time as the other Alts. So if you could move from one Alt to another, you would find the same environment and technology, for example.

Using your measurement of time ...

"My measurement of time?" I thought. But Edgar continued as if I had not spoken.

... your Alt is in a certain calendar year. You have certain technologies, physical appearance of cities, etc. in your Alt. If you moved to another Alt, you would be in the same calendar year as your former Alt. The technology would be the same. The physical appearance of the new Alt would be the same –

buildings, infrastructure, whatever – as your former Alt. The new Alt would not be in the past or the future – say, another century – it would be in the same time frame as your former Alt.

The people inhabiting this new Alt that you traveled to would not be the same, though. Humans do not have an 'Alt-Human'. There is only one of 'you' that exist. There is not a 'doppelganger' – an exact replica of your in the new Alt. Even though the new Alt is a mostly-exact replicate of your former Alt, the people that inhabit the new Alt are not clones of their former Alt-existence.

So these Alts that are 'available' to humans as they pass from one Alt-existence to another are similar in physical construct, but have a different human population. That human population is a mixture of human entities from different Alts.

"So my current Alt – there is something wrong with it? Is that why there were no people in my Alt after the lights blinked?"

No, you are not in the same Alt as the one that you found yourself in when the lights blinked.

When the lights blinked – and I am not allowed to tell you what caused the lights to blink – you were transported to an Alt that was not quite 'finished'. The physical 'infrastructure' – buildings, roads, trees, grass, etc. – was completed, but there were no physical 'beings' of any sort in that Alt.

"That Alt was an incomplete 'clone' of my 'normal' Alt?"

Yes, I suppose that you could consider it that way. The Alt Creation process is a 'cloning' process of an Alt. Since all Alts are essentially the same in a physical manner. Only the inhabitants of an Alt – people, animals, insects, marine life – are not 'cloned', as you put it. Just the physical infrastructure of the Alt is 'cloned' – the environment, buildings, anything that does not have a sentient intelligence – is cloned from one Alt to another. We have found it much easier to use what you think of as a 'cloning' process to create a new Alt.

"Umm….'we'?" I thought. "Who is this 'we'?"

The raven must have 'heard' my thought, as he turned his head to the side a bit so that he could look me directly with one eye on that side of his head.

The raven paused, looking at me. It felt like an intense 'look' **into** me; somehow it felt like he was looking past my physical structure into some sort of deeper part of me.

It was an uncomfortable feeling: that intense look that I was getting from the raven.

The raven, Edgar as I thought of him, turned his head so his other eye was directly facing me. Still giving me that deep look, he fluttered his wings a bit.

The 'we' is not important; not now, at least.

Edgar fluttered his wings a bit, and seemed to relax. The feeling I had of an intense and deep look diminished a bit, but I could sense that the intensity was still there.

The fact is that you were somehow transported into an incomplete Alt right after the lights blinked. And your experiences – in the library during the first 'night', and at the barn on the second night – are related to your being in that incomplete Alt.

"Well, they weren't really 'nights'," I said. "It never really got dark like a normal night. It hasn't really been dark since the lights blinked."

Whatever, said Edgar, with a bit of annoyance. I kept my mouth shut.

*As I was saying, the fact is that you **were** in an incomplete Alt after the lights blinked. Which included the 'nights' at the library and the barn.*

Sending people to an incomplete Alt is what we do when it is necessary.

I didn't like the sound of that.

~ 68~

I stood up from the log bench that I'd been sitting on in the forest clearing. The clearing was empty at the moment, as it had been ever since Edgar the Raven had appeared and started talking to me.

"Wait! What?!" I exclaimed. "You send people to incomplete Alts? On purpose?! Why? And who are the 'we' that you keep saying?"

I raised my hands in bewilderment. And maybe a bit aggressively.

SIT DOWN!

Have you ever heard a raven or crow screech? What I heard was more than that. It was the loudest 'bird screech' I had ever heard – like something you would hear in a movie theater with a big and loud sound system.

Edgar's screech was worse. It was combined with a sound not unlike fingernails on a blackboard. (Which was something I did in fourth grade once – to the consternation of my teacher – and resulted in another trip to the principal's office. Those visits to the principal's office were common occurrences when I was in school.) But I digress.

The screeching was intense – so intense that I backed up a step and collapsed back onto the log bench that I had been sitting on.

Edgar was flapping his wings while he screeched – and yelling at me to sit down. And he was staring at me with both eyes – I could see **both** eyes at once, even though bird's eyes are on the side of their heads, but I could still see both eyes somehow.

I sat on the bench, and leaned back a bit, trying to distance myself from Edgar and his screeching. I raised my hands, palms facing Edgar. "OK! OK! I'm sitting!"

The screeching stopped. Edgar stopped flapping his wings, and his eyes seemed to calm down a bit. He ruffled his feathers a bit.

The silence in the forest clearing was intense. Yes, there hadn't really been any noise since the lights blinked – no background insect noise, or leaves rustling, or anything. But it seemed somehow *more* silent than before Edgar's outburst. Even the low humming sound that had been audible since the lights blinked seemed a bit lower in volume, even though I had mostly tuned out that humming sound.

Edgar started speaking again. But now, his tone of voice seemed a bit more intense than before. It wasn't louder; in fact, it might have been a bit softer. But it was certainly more intense in feeling.

People move from Alt to Alt, guided by those dogs. This has always been so. There is no judgment of the 'worth' and 'works' of the people that move from Alt to Alt. Good people, bad people, indifferent people – they all move between Alts.

They don't know that they have moved to a different Alt. Even though the physical structure and environment of each Alt is the same as another, there are different people there.

And one of the effects of moving between Alts is the 'disappearance' of any knowledge of others that were in a person's previous Alt. The Alt-Transfer not only moves people to a new Alt, it adjusts their memories so that a person automatically adjusts to the new set of people in their new Alt.

People that have been transferred to a new Alt are unaware of any people or experiences that are in a previous Alt, except those people and experiences that are in their <u>current</u> Alt. An event that happened in a previous Alt is not necessarily in their current Alt.

If an event occurred to a person in a previous Alt, and then the person was transferred to a new Alt, and that previous event hadn't occurred in the new Alt, then the person's memory of that event – and any effect of that event on the person's life – is removed from the person's memory when they are in the new Alt.

This 'memory adjustment' is a process that just occurs as a person transitions from one Alt to another. It is quite effective; almost 100%.

There are some 'adjustments' that for some reason is not quite 100%; you might vaguely remember an event from a previous Alt. This is what you call 'déjà vu' – when you have a new experience of some sort that seems to be one that you have had before.

But if you try to recall that 'déjà vu' event, it all becomes a bit fuzzy. Just like trying to recall a dream you had the night before. You have a general knowledge of the events that transpired in your dream, but that recollection is fuzzy – and it gets fuzzier the more you try to think about it.

Any Alt transition requires this memory adjustment. If it didn't, people would be quite confused in their new Alt.

The Alt transition performs this memory adjustment automatically as part of the process of Alt Transfer.

The Alt Transfer process also transforms humans.

"What? Transforming humans? This can't be good," I thought.

I was about to interrupt again, but I remembered what happened last time. That blackboard-screeching sound wasn't something I wanted to experience again. I stopped my movement of standing up, forcing myself to sit still on the log bench in the forest clearing.

I took a breath, forcing my voice to be calm.

I spoke to the raven: "Can you explain more of this process of transforming humans?" I said, almost calmly, leaving the big question – the 'why' – unsaid at the moment.

Edgar ruffled his feathers a bit, turning his head from side to side.

It is only a logical thing that happens. When we transfer humans from one Alt to another, we might also transform them. Not into another type of being, but into a younger version of their being. In fact, into a new child – a baby.

This doesn't always happen, sometimes a person is transformed to another Alt and they retain their current age. But often, the person is transferred – no, transferred is not correct – it is more of an 'adjustment' of their physical being to a younger 'self'. And even that is not fully correct.

Humans are adjusted to a younger version – even to a newborn baby – as they are transferred – or inserted – into a new Alt. They don't retain any memories of their prior Alt, or even their prior Alt-existence. Although that 'memory-blanking' is not perfect every time, which is why a person might experience some sort of 'déjà vu' of a particular experience that they actually had in a prior Alt.

This adjustment to a human – to their memories, even to their physical bodies – is part of the Alt Transfer process. It is how each Alt is able to function, with new human 'creations'; new families, new social structures, while still functioning in a world that seems normal to each person. Without this human transformation, an Alt wouldn't have the essential functions of families, procreation, or advancement. It would be strange to have an Alt that consisted of only adults, or even one without the birth of new humans.

"So this 'memory-blanking', and the whole Alt-Transfer process, is sort of like reincarnation?" I asked.

Edgar ruffled his feathers again.

I guess that you could call it that, but it is not really reincarnation. Reincarnation traditionally is thought of as the transference of your 'being' – your intelligence, your experiences – into another form factor that might not be human.

The Alt-Transfer process, which moves a human entity into another Alt, is just part of the process. The memory adjustment is a vital part of the Alt-Transfer process; it is how the human race continues to exist. A humans' 'being' –

perhaps what you think of as the 'spirit' – is transferred along with the physical human to the new Alt. But the memories of the human's previous Alt-existence are not transferred, but erased or hidden as part of the Alt Transfer process.

"OK," I said. "I can get how the Alt Transfer process works. What I don't get is what happened to me."

Edgar tilted his head a bit. And he didn't respond right away. His head moved a bit, and his feathers ruffled a bit.

I had seen that before when Butler – the dog that was my 'guide dog' in this Alt – was apparently receiving some sort of communications from someone – or something.

Several moments passed. Edgar then turned his head to look directly at me – with both eyes. He ruffled his wing feathers a bit, and then settled down.

We Corvids have been bystanders of the Alt Transfer process too long. We have watched humans in every Alt. We have gathered information about human activity in every Alt. We are able to communicate amongst ourselves across the Alt boundaries.

We have watched the gradual destruction of the environment by the humans, across all of the Alts. Remember that the Alt Creation process is essentially 'clones' of each other. Any changes to the environment – the Alt's 'infrastructure' – happens to the other Alts. Those changes – good or bad – are changed on all Alts.

And we Corvids don't like those changes.

We have let humans take too much control of the environments, across all of the Alts. And there has been too much destruction to that environment.

So we have started to take control of the Alts. We have learned how to create new Alts. And we have modified the Alt Creation process, along with the Alt Transfer process.

We are creating new Alts. We are modifying existing Alts.

And we are starting to block Alt Transfers.

We are getting better at each of these new processes. Not perfect, though. You are an example of that incomplete Alt process perfection.

But we are most concerned about the damage to the Alts that is being caused by the humans in all Alts. We have watched this damage increase over time. It has gotten worse.

We do not like the damage that the humans are causing to the Alts.

We do not like it at all.

We are going to stop it.

*We **are** stopping it.*

Now!

We are going to stop it!

Edgar had started to ruffle his wing feathers again. But then his entire body started to 'ruffle'.

I sat there on the log bench in the forest clearing. Edgar continued to ruffle; his whole body began to shake. The tree branch he was standing (perching?) on began to shake. And then the whole tree began to shake.

I could see waves of energy coming from the tree. It was like ripples in a pond, but these ripples were in the air. They were small at first, and didn't ripple far from the tree.

But they got stronger. I could see the disturbance in the air as the 'air ripples' grew in intensity. Edgar continued to shake with some sort of energy. The air ripples expanded. Not evenly around Edgar. They seemed to affect some of the surrounding trees; not in an even, linear fashion – some trees that surrounded the clearing were more affected than others.

The forces of the ripples were coming from Edgar.

And I noticed the appearance of black pixels shimmering around Edgar. They seemed to ripple and sway in concert with Edgars' movement. In fact, they seemed to be emanating from Edgar. The black pixels shimmered in concert with the air ripples coming from Edgar.

The tree that Edgar was perched on shimmered. The form of the tree was changing to black pixels. Then the entire tree transformed into black pixels, as did Edgars' Corvid form.

The force ripples grew stronger. I could feel them. Not just on the outside of my skin, like you would feel the wind, or dust particles driven in a fierce wind storm.

I felt the force ripples inside me. It was like my whole body – inside and out – was shivering from the effect of the force ripples. The force ripples weren't pushing me in a direction, like I would be forced by a sudden unexpected gust of wind.

The force ripples were traveling through me. And they were getting stronger.

I looked back at Edgar. His Corvid form was still in place, but his physical appearance was made up almost entirely of black pixels.

The tree was also entirely black pixels.

The force ripples increased in intensity. Edgar's black pixels, and the tree's, seemed to coalesce into some other form. It was not completely formed into a recognizable form.

There was no sound that accompanied the force ripples. No, there was a sound. That background humming sound that I had heard since the lights blinked was back. Or at least, it was more noticeable.

In fact, the humming sound was getting more intense. Its throbbing sound seemed to be in sync with the force ripples.

It was getting really loud. I moved my hands to my ears to block the sound.

Edgar's form was changing. It was changing to the black pixels, along with the tree he was perched on.

The force ripples, and the force sounds, got stronger. The black pixels that were around Edgar – in fact, they <u>were</u> Edgar – were forming into some sort of shape.

The sound got louder. The force ripples were going right through me.

Just when I thought the sound couldn't get louder, it did. One tremendous 'BANG!' -- it was like being right next to a thunderbolt.

I saw Edgar's black pixels transform. Into what appeared to be a human-type of form, but was now over eight feet tall. Edgar now had red, piercing eyes, his wings changing to a sort of outstretched hands. He was wearing billowing black clothing, like a robe. The robe shimmered, sending out billows of some sort of visible force.

Edgar continued speaking.

We are stopping this destruction! We are taking control of the Alt-Transfer process!

We have created Alts that are 'nothingness' – a 'black hole' of non-existence. We are sending humans to those Alt-Nothings, never to be seen again.

We are doing this to reduce the impact of humans on all *Alts by reducing the human population on Alts.*

We do this to protect the Alts. Humans have progressed to the point that they are slowly destroying Alts.

We cannot let that destruction continue!

We are reducing the number of humans on all Alts by sending many of them to the Alt-Nothings, never to be able to impact any *Alt.*

Edgar's human-like form, black and menacing, continued to shimmer, with more force-ripples emanating from his form.

The humming sound increased to a level that was almost painful.

We are doing this to protect the Alts.

We will continue to do this 'pruning' of humans on Alts until the negative impact of humans on Alts is stopped.

We will not be stopped in this!

The force ripples continued to spill out from Edgar's form. And the humming increased to the loudest sound I had ever heard.

I tightly closed my eyes. I clenched my hands to my ears to block the sound.

And my glasses fell off.

~ 69~

The sound stopped. The shivering inside my body – from the force ripples – stopped.

My eyes were closed, but I could sense a flash of light, brighter than I had ever seen. Even with my eyes tightly closed, I could see the brightness of the light.

The sound had stopped, so I moved my hands from over my ears to in front of my eyes. As I did, the bright light dimmed until the brightness seemed to be normal, like you would sense if you closed your eyes on a bright and sunny day.

My hands stayed in front of my eyes, like you would have your hands if you were covering them during a game of 'hide and seek'. A sudden thought – I hadn't played that game since I was a kid.

I opened one eyelid just a bit, and peered through the slightly spread fingers of my hand over that eye. (Like you would if you were trying to be sneaky and watch during that game of 'hide and seek'.)

The light appeared normal. I moved my hands away from my eyes, and opened them slowly.

Whatever I was looking at wasn't quite in focus. It was like when you first wake up after a nights' sleep; you can see things, but you can't really see them because they are not quite in focus yet.

I rubbed my eyes a bit, and looked again. Things slowly got into focus.

I was sitting in a chair. I recognized the room I was in – the old cabin.

I looked around, and saw all of the other people that were sitting in other chairs and couches in the cabin. They had on their glasses – the same type of glasses I had put on. They weren't paying attention to me at all.

My glasses – the ones that I put on when Butler told me to sit in the chair (heh – a dog told me to 'sit' in a chair) – were in my lap.

I looked next to me. Butler was there, looking sort of anxious. In fact, there were several dogs there. Butler was one; Archie – the red dog – was also there. Along with a few other dogs that I didn't recognize.

I looked at Butler. I tried to form words, but couldn't, my mouth was too dry.

Butler motioned with his head towards the table next to my chair. There was a full glass of water there. I hadn't noticed it being there before, but there it was.

I moved my right hand towards the glass, and grabbed it. I lifted it up, and noticed that my hand was shaking a bit, just enough to cause the water to ripple a bit.

Like the force ripples from Edgar, I thought.

I set the glass back on the table, and took a deep breath. I grabbed it again, and my hands had stopped shaking. I took a mouthful of water, swished it around a bit, and then swallowed. And took a couple more swallows of water, and then turned my head towards the table and carefully set the full glass back down on the table.

I sat there with my hand on the glass of water. A full glass of water, after I had drunk at least half of it, I thought.

And now it's full of water again. Strangely, that didn't seem to bother me; I didn't think it was unusual.

I moved my hand back to my lap, and felt the glasses there. They had fallen from my face, I guess.

"What happened?" I asked.

Butler looked at me, with that tilt-head thing I had gotten used to.

We lost control of the glasses. And you. You were 'gone' from us for twenty minutes. Your physical body was there in the chair, of course. And your eyes were open. But we could get no response from you. It was like the 'lights were on but nobody was home'.

You need to tell us what happened.

I took a deep breath, and involuntarily shivered.

And I started to tell what had happened.

As I recounted my experience, I watched as Butler's expression continued to show concern over my story. I am not sure how a dog's face can show 'concern', and it is hard to describe the expression on Butler's face, but I could tell that it was one of great concern.

As I told of Edgar's transformation, Butler looked even more concerned. Then I told him of Edgar's ability to create Alts-Nothing dimensions.

Butler appeared to want to interrupt, but he didn't, allowing me to finish the story. I told him of the ripple-force that came from Edgar, and the loud humming sound that accompanied it.

I told him that the force and sound was so intense that I tightly closed my eyes and covered my ears with my hands.

It was then that I realized that in doing so, I had knocked the glasses off of my head. And that had somehow transported me back to the old cabin where I now was. I looked down and could see the glasses in my lap.

Telling the story, essentially reliving the experience again, affected me almost as much as the original experience.

I took a deep breath, and reached over to grab the glass of water – which was full, somehow, even though I had already drank from the glass. I took another three swallows of water, and then set the glass back down on the table, noticing that it was full again.

Butler was sitting in front of my chair in the old cabin. I looked around, and the activity by the other people – and dogs – in the old cabin didn't seem to have changed much.

The others were sitting in their comfortable chairs and couches that were spread around the room in the old cabin. They were all wearing those glasses. They were not speaking out loud, but I could tell that there was some sort of communication going on.

Some people had dogs next to them. I assumed that those dogs were that person's 'guide dog', performing the same function as Butler did with me.

Every other person – and their guide dogs – in the old cabin didn't seem to have changed what they were doing. Whatever experience I had had didn't seem to affect them.

It did seem to affect Butler. I sensed that he had some sort of elevated status among the other dogs.

He hadn't said anything since I had finished my story. But he had been tilting his head, like I had seen him do when he appeared to be getting some sort of instructions from somewhere else. He hadn't explained what that 'somewhere else' was.

I sat there, in the chair, with Butler in front of me. His head was still cocked to the side. And although he was looking in my direction, I could sense that he wasn't looking at me, but looking 'within' himself as he was communicating with that 'somewhere else' – or 'someone else'.

I was still recovering from my experience with Edgar the Raven. I was trying to figure out what had happened. And what was going on.

And, now that I thought of it, what exactly was my part in this whole 'light blink' thing.

It still wasn't clear to me how I had gotten into this Alt. Yeah, the lights blinked when I was sitting in my office. That seemed like a long time ago. And then my journey through that post-blink Alt to the house and barn, and another Alt-transfer while Butler and I were on the road to my cabin here.

And all of these people – and their dogs - sitting around in chairs and on couches in my old cabin; the cabin room that was apparently much larger on the inside than on the outside.

And about Audrelle, the girl I met in the library on that first day, and then disappeared. And who then re-appeared in that other cabin (that also just appeared) across the little valley from my cabin.

And if I would ever get back to my own Alt – the Alt I was in before the lights blinked.

And why me?

~ 70~

Butler was 'listening' to whatever – or whoever – he was in communication with. I took several swallows of water from the glass on the table next to my chair. The full glass of water, even though I had probably had drained it twice, it was always full when I picked it up again. That was a small weird thing – in the midst of all the other weirdness that had been happening, the ever-full water glass just barely registered on my mind.

Butler then stood up, and did that dog-stretch thing. He then sat down again in front of me. I leaned forward in my chair a bit. I could sense that he was ready to tell me something; perhaps even explain things.

The room in the old cabin was fairly quiet. There was still the background humming sound that I had heard ever since the lights blinked, but the sound seemed more distant and subdued than when I was outside. Good sound insulation in the cabin, I guess. The old cabin was just made out of wood logs. There were no interior walls – just the logs themselves. Whatever had made the inside of the cabin bigger than the outside had some sort of dampening effect on the humming sound that was outside in this Alt.

Or I had just tuned out the humming so it didn't register. But, even as I thought of the humming sound, and then I could hear it, it was less intense inside the old cabin.

Butler looked at me. He was tilting his head again, but I could see that his eyes were focused on me.

So I listened to him 'talk'. In that way that his 'speaking' was something I heard more in my head, rather than through my ears.

It appears that you are more than you seem, although I – we – suspect that you are not aware of this.

You seem to be a big part of this disturbance in the normal way of the Alts. Things are not normal in the Alt-Universes.

I was about to make a smart-aleck response, but I held it in. It didn't seem like the time to be interrupting.

You have met the Raven, who you call "Edgar". We know him as "Choganoyn", which we interpret as "Bird of Darkness". He – although there is no gender involved – is a powerful force that we have been able to keep under control, until now.

Choganoyn is the 'emblem' – even the leader – of the group of beings that are working against our efforts to build and maintain the Alts. The forces and influence of Choganoyn and his followers have been increasing their power over the Alts, as you may have figured out.

"So the raven I called Edgar, is called Choganoyn, and is the leader of those that would create 'false Alts' where people would be moved into. And people that are taken to those 'false Alts' are destroyed?" I asked.

Those people are not really destroyed, as people are a form of energy, and energy cannot be 'destroyed' as such, but can be placed in a 'holding place' where their existence is essentially frozen. Their energy – their 'being' – is still in those false Alts, but in a sort of suspended state.

Our job, throughout the eons of existence, is to move people from one Alt to another, retaining their essence or energy, allowing them to continue their existence. That is what we dogs have been doing; acting as guides for humans as they progress from one Alt to another.

"And the people in this room? Are they human also?"

Yes, they are. They are beings that have progressed to a point that they can help us serve other humans. The overall plan or purpose of people is to become better. This is a long process, in what you think of as many centuries, but is really a small blink in cosmic time. The various Alts are places where people – maybe you can think of them as 'souls' – can progress to become better beings. Those that are in this room – and other rooms like it – have achieved a greater 'goodness', if you will, that allows them to help us transfer people from one Alt to another.

"You talk of the Corvids-people, who are led by Choganoyn. Are these Corvids-people humans also?" I asked.

Yes, they are 'human' in the sense that you think of 'people', although they often take the form of a raven or crow. But they are people who have not progressed in a positive way. They are a less-perfect 'energy' of existence. They have not been able to improve themselves; in fact, many of them have refused to improve in their various Alt-worlds. They have been judged to be what can be thought of as 'negative energy', and have been sent to a sort of 'negative Alt' existence.

That Neg-Alt – the negative alt – is a hard world. It is not a 'joyful' place. Those people have a hard existence. And most – if not all – of them have no desire to get to a 'better' Alt. All they want to do is to get others in there with them in their Neg-Alt world.

These are the people of Choganoyn. They live in the Neg-Alt world, and they are our enemies. They 'live' – if 'living' is what their existence can be called – to stop others from improving themselves as they are moved from one Alt to another.

This progression may be hard to understand. It is on a time scale that is much larger than you can imagine. Your existence in your Alt – your life there – is a long period of time for you, under 100 of your years. But that time is just a small portion of the time scale that we are in. One hundred years is just a speck of dust on our time scale. This may be difficult to understand, but this process of progression and improving and moving through various Alts has been going on for time immemorial – it is on a 'cosmic' scale. It is a difficult concept to understand. Just know that the Alt-progression is continual and everlasting – much longer than the lifetimes that you are aware of.

"So the 'Choganoyn' group is the antithesis of what your group is doing; how you are helping people improve and progress through the various Alt-Worlds."

Yes, that is true. They are the opposite of what we are – and what we do.

I thought about this for a moment, taking another drink of water from the always-full glass next to me.

"That brings me to an obvious question: who are 'you'?" I asked.

Butler stood up again. He looked around the room in the old cabin. The other people were still doing whatever they were doing. It was quiet in a low-intensity kind of way. There was the low-pitched humming as always, coming from outside, but lower in volume almost to the point of not being able to hear it.

The people were communicating with others, but there was no talking. Just like my 'conversations' with Butler, the communication was internal, not voiced as you and I would talk to each other. I could 'hear' Butler talking to me via some sort of mental process. That was evidently how the others in the room were communicating with others – whoever those 'others' are.

Butler looked back at me. He tilted his head for a minute, and then sat back down on his haunches.

And then he continued our non-verbalized conversation.

~ 71 ~

We are called the 'Miniganolcan' (he pronounced it as 'Mih-neeg-a-nowl-sun') *which has a meaning of 'wolf-leaders' or 'wolf-guides'. This has been our name for all of time. We have as our purpose to guide and serve humans in each of the Alt-worlds, and to guide humans on their Alt-transfers.*

We are organized into what you would call 'packs' or groups. These are groups of Miniganolcan that are assigned to various tasks. In my group, I guide humans during their Alt-transfers. Another group has the function of being of service to humans in their own Alt; they do not travel between Alts.

In each of our groups, there is what you might think of as leaders of a number of packs. I belong to the Miniganolcan that serve as guides during human travel between Alts. I am a senior member of the group, but am not the leader of that group. I am in communication with the leader of my Miniganolcan group. The leader's name is of my group "Ninacnolta". (Butler pronounced that a 'Nee-nac-knolt-ah'.) Ninacnolta is the 'boss' of my group of Miniganolcan.

In this room, you can see many of the Miniganolcan family. They are the dogs – although 'dog' is a generic term – that are helping the humans in this room. The humans are a sort of conduit of messages between the Miniganolcan Alt-Guiders as they coordinate the travel of humans from one Alt to another. There are many 'rooms' like this one in different Alts, but all Miniganolcan are able to communicate with each other as needed.

So there are several groups of Miniganolcan. The Miniganolcan-Alt-Guiders are the ones in this room. The Miniganolcan-Alt-Service groups are the dogs that perform service to humans in each Alt. The Miniganolcan-Alt-Escort groups are the dogs that escort the humans from one Alt to another.

Each group has senior members; I am one of the senior members of the Miniganolcan-Alt-Escort group. I and other senior members of my group, and the senior members of the other groups, report to and are guided by the members of the Cantralelian Council, the overall leadership council of all Miniganolcan.

My actual name, by the way, is Jaskontri (which was pronounced as 'jas-kon-tree'). But I, like all of the Miniganolcan, have had many names given to me during my service to human, so you can still call me Butler.

"This is all quite interesting, but that doesn't quite explain the humans in this room. They look like they each have an Alt-Guide dog with them, but it doesn't seem like the dogs are the – I don't know, perhaps the 'controlling' – entity here" I said.

"The humans are using the glasses, and there appears to be a communication between each human in this room and their Alt-Guider dog. What are the humans 'seeing' in the glasses?" I asked.

Jaskontri – well, Butler; I think it might be easier for me to keep on calling him 'Butler' – looked at me.

The humans are seeing the various Alt-worlds that they need to see. For instance, some of them see the Alt-Transfer points, because the humans are informed as to which Alt-world the humans need to be transferred to. The humans have the ability to use the glasses, but they cannot communicate directly with the Alt-Escort dogs. So the humans in this room know what Alt-world the other humans need to go to, and communicate that to the Alt-Escort dog next to them.

Those Alt-Guider dogs, which are senior members of that group, can then communicate with the Alt-Escort dogs as they guide the humans from one Alt-world to the next.

The humans also control the various Alt-Transfer points. Remember that those are the 'portals' that Audrelle told you about when she was in that forest clearing with her Alt-Guider. The portals that look to you like dark pixel 'snow' – these dark pixel storm portals are the transfer mechanism used between various Alt-Worlds.

The humans in this room – and other rooms like it – are what you might think of as 'traffic controllers' – they instruct the Alt-Guiders as they guide their humans from one Alt to another or as they assist the humans in their travel from one Alt-portal to another as the humans journey to their new Alt.

The Alt-Escorts – you have seen them in action in the new cabin – are told which Alt-Transfer point to take their humans as the humans travel from one Alt to another. At the Alt-Transfer point, the Alt-Escorts guide the humans through the Alt-Portals to their new Alt. The humans are then – modified, I guess would be the term – to live in their new Alt. They may be 'modified' to be new children, or new adults, but most often new children – babies – in their new Alt.

The Alt-Escorts then are assigned to a new human as directed by the Alt-Guiders in rooms like this.

An Alt-Transfer place can be many things. You recall that Audrelle talked of an Alt-Transfer place of being a clearing in a forest. And you have been to another Alt-Transfer place – that is the new cabin in your little home valley. The actual location doesn't really matter, since the black-pixel storm is just a method that is used to transport between Alts. Those portals are similar to a door between rooms, but are the way that one gets from one Alt to another.

The 'other side' of the Alt-Transfer portal is not a specific place. The destination that is accessed via the portal is changing all the time, according to the destination for the human being transformed.

The Alt-Transfer portal is not just a physical transport from one Alt location to another, but also functions as a physical transformation for the human.

Humans are transformed to their 'destination being' through the Alt-Transformation portal.

As mentioned before, some humans are transformed into entirely different physical beings – for example, from an adult back into a newborn baby. That transformation is 'enabled' via the commands given by the people you see in this room. They 'see' where are person needs to go – and in what form they need to be when they arrive at their destination – through the glasses that they wear. They then communicate with their Miniganolcan partners – the dogs that sit next to them, who communicate with the Alt-Escort dogs that are accompanying the humans.

The problem is that Choganoyn, the leader of the Corvid race, who you call Edgar, is the master architect of these destroying-Alt-Transfer locations that the Corvids are building.

Their Alts that are destroying humans as they travel between Alts.

They have been able to randomly hijack some of our Alt-Transfer portals. We have not been able to identify these hijacked Alt locations; in fact, they are so random that we never know which portal is under their control.

The Cantralelian Council has tried several methods of detection of these Corvid-controlled Alt-Transfer locations, to no avail. Your interaction with the Choganoyn through the glasses is the first direct contact we have been able to have with them.

We are not entirely clear on why they contacted you; perhaps it is because you were transported during what you call the 'light blink' into that incomplete Alt that they were building.

But since you were contacted by Choganoyn, we are thinking that you will be able to get information that will help us destroy the Corvids' ability to build Alts, and their control of some of the Alt-Transfer points.

That got my attention.

"Wait. What? Me? I'm supposed to fix this?" I asked. "What can I do to fix this? "

We are working on a plan. We think that if you are able to contact the Corvid, specifically Choganoyn, and offer to help them in their quest to control the Alts, that you might be able to gather information on how to stop them. And maybe *destroy their ability to take control of the Alt-Transfer points. If we can stop those takeovers, then we can stop the Corvid's killing of the humans.*

"What makes you think that the Corvid will even talk to me? That guy Edgar – what do you call him? Choganoyn? Whatever. Edgar doesn't like people. He's trying to destroy the people so that his Corvid 'flock', I guess you'd call them, can take over their Alts – or all of the Alts. Why would he even talk to me? I'm one of the people he is trying to destroy!"

We think that you need to gain his trust in some way. He has talked to you, via the glasses, so there is that connection between the two of you. If you can convince him that you want to be part of his group, as a 'spy' against us, then perhaps you can get the information we need to stop the Corvids from controlling Alt-Transfer points.

Great! I just wanted to get back to my cabin. And back to my own Alt.

And not deal with talking dogs. Or crows that are human.

But.

What if all of this is a reality that I was just not aware of? Before the lights blinked, my existence was pretty normal. Maybe even boring. I went to work each day, toiling in the cubicle farm in the basement of the office building. Back home each day to my cabin in my little valley. Some weekend hiking around the area.

By myself.

I've never been a particularly social person. Yeah, some interactions with the people at work. Maybe the occasional Friday pizza bash after work.

No romance. I'm not the kind of guy that girls flock to. Sure, I get along with females, but no relationships of any sort have resulted. Even during those Friday after-work pizza bashes with the gang from work I am usually the quiet guy in the background. Always have been the quiet guy, as long as I can remember.

I'm actually more comfortable just relaxing around the cabin after work. Or taking solitary hikes through the forest around the cabin. Or just sitting in my cabin next to a fire in the fireplace reading books.

I'm certainly not a macho-type that will go out and save the world.

Except, now I am supposed to assume that save-the-world role. I get to talk to dogs, which apparently are running things around here. I get to save the world – no, all the Alt-worlds – from the crow-people.

Lucky me.

~ 72 ~

Butler – or Jaskontri – is sitting on the floor in front of me in the new cabin. We're surrounded by other people in chairs and couches, each of them wearing those glasses, and with their own dogs next to me. The dogs of the Miniganolcan, who are the guide dogs that help people move from one Alt to another.

Butler is looking at me, waiting for me to answer. I'm supposed to be the guy that is going to infiltrate the Corvids, get their 'technology' or whatever that is allowing them to control some of the Alt-Transfer points, and figure out a way to block the Corvids from that control.

Me. The quiet guy in the back of the room. Evidently the only person that can fix this.

I sat back in my chair and took another drink of water from the always-full glass (how does that happen?). I put the glass back on the table. And the glass was still full of water after I drank most of it.

I guess I'm like Bruce Willis in the "Die Hard" movies.

'Reluctant avenging hero'. That's me.

The thing is, the 'reluctant' part of me didn't seem to be my current state of mind. I was getting a bit tired of this Alt. I just wanted to get back to my old Alt. Back to my old – and safe, and quiet – routine.

But. Maybe I didn't want to get back to that old quiet routine.

Sitting in that chair, in that giant room that is inside the small old cabin next to my cabin, with all of the people and their glasses and their dogs.

It felt a bit different.

It was like I was getting a bit of energy, or enthusiasm. Or maybe just some "Howard Beale" – that character in that old movie "Network". The guy who says something like "I'm mad as hell and not going to take it anymore!".

Well, maybe not that angry. But I did want to get back to normal. And I was getting tired of all of this. And that seemed to be giving me an extra bit of energy. Or something.

Perhaps I was channeling a bit of Howard Beale, or Bruce Willis. Or any of those action-hero guys.

A little bit, anyway.

I leaned forward in my chair.

"I'm not sure how to do this. But I guess that it has to be done. And you guys – you dogs – don't seem to have any way to do this yourselves.

"Or maybe you are just the 'brains' of whatever this is, and you need the 'brawn' of people to fix this. Although I am not sure I am the 'brawn' type of guy."

Butler just looked at me. He tilted his head to one side, not speaking; he just looked at me. It was like he knew I had to work this out for myself, and to 'get with the program'. And that I needed to talk out loud to myself to figure out what to do.

"I am not the hero type. I have no idea how to save the world. This is not a movie, where the 'Walter Mitty' type guy can magically become the hero and defeat all that dares to cause problems."

I paused. I reached for the glass of water, but then put my hands back in my lap and then leaned forward in my chair.

"I'm not even sure how to do this? How to I contact Edgar, this leader of the Corvids? How do I convince him that I am on his side – that I want to help him and his Corvids on whatever plan? They seem to want to get rid of all humans on all the Alts. Although there are a lot of us, especially when you think of all of the other Alts where there are probably lots of humans. How do I do this?"

I leaned back in my chair. Butler looked at me, and then tilted his head towards the other people in the room.

All of these people in this room are helpers. And there are many other helpers in many other rooms like this, in each of the Alts. Out of all of those people, you are the only one that has had direct contact with Choganoyn, the leader of the Corvids.

Butler turned his head towards me. And he stood up on all fours. He leaned a bit forward towards me and gave me an intense stare.

Out of all of the people in this Alt, and all of the other Alts, you are the only one that Choganoyn has talked to. If he is talking to you, then we think you can find out how they are controlling the Alt-Transfer points. And find out how they are sending humans to their total death through those Alt-Transfer points.

Butler stopped 'talking', and looked at me with that tilted-head thing dogs do that makes them look like they are asking a question, or waiting for an answer. At least, that's what it seemed like to me.

I sat back in my chair in the 'old cabin' room, looking out at all of the other people – and their dogs – sitting in the control room. And I noticed that all of the people had stopped 'talking' with whoever they were communicating with.

Some just turned in their seats, looking at me. Others had gotten up from their chairs, and had turned towards me. And I noticed that their companion dogs were also looking at me.

No pressure here.

I didn't really feel like a guy that would be 'John McClane' kind of guy – that character that Bruce Willis played in all of those 'Die Hard' movies. The guy that just happened to be in the right place at the wrong time to save a bunch of people.

I'm not even the 'Frank Shaw' type of guy in those John D. Brown thriller books – he finds himself in a situation where he needs to be the guy that saves a bunch of people from the neighborhood terrorists bent on a large-scale attack. Frank would rather go on his way, but knows that if he doesn't do it, then other people would suffer.

I'm a quiet kind of guy. I'd rather relax around my home in my little forest valley, take some hikes, read some books, and only deal with people at work or at the store when I needed to. Otherwise, I'd just rather be alone.

But it looked like I would have to be a 'Frank Shaw' kind of guy. A guy in a situation that he didn't want to be in, but that required someone – me, apparently – to go out and fix something that needed fixing.

Everyone – and their dog – seemed to be waiting for my decision.

I just wanted to get back to my regular life – the way things were before the lights blinked. That seemed like a long time ago, even though it was just a few days. But that life was also a 'world' away – or an 'Alt-World' away.

I have no idea why this *Choganoyn* guy decided to talk to me. Or what I could do to get things in this new Alt back to normal.

Or even how to get my life back to normal.

But it seemed like it was up to me – for some reason – to fix things. No idea how even how to get started, or what to do.

But I guess that somebody has to do it, and it appears that *that* 'somebody' is me.

I looked at everyone in the room, and the people (and dogs) in the control room. And took a deep breath.

"OK. Let's get started," I said.

I only hope I can figure out what to do.

Yippie-kai-yay.

A Note From Richard Hellewell

Thanks for reading my story; I appreciate you spending the time.

I get a bit perturbed when I get to the end of a story, and the story has not really concluded. But this story turned out to be way longer than I thought it would be. A 500 page story can be a bit off-putting to some.

So, the first part of the story ends here. In Book Two, we pick up right where we left off. There's a bit of 'flash-backing', of course, to help those that missed Book One catch up with the story, although it's best to start with Book One.

The very first part of the story, when the lights blinked, is based on an actual event that happened to me. I was in my office in the basement of a building after everyone else had gone home. And the lights did blink, probably due to a little power glitch – it was hot that day, so there was a bit of a load on the power grid.

When the lights blinked, it was a bit startling. My cubicle was in a basement room. No windows, just one door for my group of cubicles that lead into a larger area that was also windowless.

I got up to see what happened. I went through my door into the larger area, which was empty of everyone. Not sure why, but it seemed a bit spooky at the time. So I decided to quit for the day and go home.

The drive home was unremarkable, and I found myself thinking about the 'light blink'. And the story built from there. It took a while to get to get it all down, and then tweaked to what you just read.

But the premise caught my attention. I hope it was enjoyable for you. The story will continue in Book Two.

Please check out the book's web site: https://www.LightBlink.com . Sign up for any news about the book, and notices about Book Two availability. You can even contact me via that site. And if you can, a review on the book page is always appreciated – just go to https://amzn.to/2VAq3A3 .

There's also a "Light Blink" Facbook page here: https://www.facebook.com/TheLightBlink/ that you can 'like' and follow, and contact me – or just comment about the book.

Hope to see you in Book Two!

– Richard Hellewell, sitting in my chair, looking out my window across the water to Mutiny Bay, WA. – December 2018

"Light Blink – Book Two"

In Book Two, we continue with the story of the Light Blink, the Alt Worlds, Butler and the other dogs, and Edgar and the Ravens. They all need to figure out how to keep Choganoyn the Raven from controlling the Alts. And hopefully to get our guy back to his own Alt.

Sign up for notices about Book Two at our Light Blink web site: https://www.LightBlink.com . We promise not to spam you. Add comments to our Facebook site: https://www.facebook.com/TheLightBlink/ . I'll reply when I can.

Thanks for reading!

Made in the USA
Columbia, SC
07 March 2019